The Island
VILLA

D0049903

ALSO BY LILY GRAHAM

The Island
VILLA

Lily Graham

Bookouture

Published by Bookouture in 2018

An imprint of StoryFire Ltd.

Carmelite House
50 Victoria Embankment
London EC4Y 0DZ

www.bookouture.com

Copyright © Lily Graham, 2018

Lily Graham has asserted her right to be identified
as the author of this work.

All rights reserved. No part of this publication may be reproduced,
stored in any retrieval system, or transmitted, in any form or by
any means, electronic, mechanical, photocopying, recording or
otherwise, without the prior written permission of the publishers.

ISBN: 978-1-78681-568-2
eBook ISBN: 978-1-78681-567-5

This book is a work of fiction. Names, characters, businesses,
organizations, places and events other than those clearly in the
public domain, are either the product of the author's imagination
or are used fictitiously. Any resemblance to actual persons, living or
dead, events or locales is entirely coincidental.

For Barbara Marie Little, Kathy Schaffer and all the readers and bloggers who have kept me going, thank you.

ONE

Formentera, present day

I'll never forget the day I saw the villa for the first time, sparkling like a clean sheet in the sleepy Spanish sun. The shutters were the colour of pale lichen, and dusky bougainvillea trailed over the whitewashed stone.

It was a simple place, in a sparse cubic design, that was centuries old, as old as this oft-forgotten slip of an island itself. The house, dominated by views of the sea: a paint swirl of turquoise that met darkest navy across the horizon, vast and unknowable and full of promise.

The air seemed somehow to whisper with it, and I had this feeling, there in the warm, citrus-flavoured sunshine, the scent coming from the orange and lemon trees that had grown wild and abandoned in the forgotten garden, of something inside me stirring. Like some bone tapestry had threaded beneath the ground and called out to my flesh to bring me home.

The feeling was powerful, yet fleeting, over in the length of a sigh, but for the first time in months I felt something shift and, for a moment, as if just maybe I'd be all right.

The villa was a chapter from a familial past of long before my birth. It belonged to a sepia-coloured photograph of an almost-forgotten corner of my family history. People whose names had been all but washed away by the changing tides.

Yet here I was. Like a message in a bottle washed ashore from the wide arms of the ocean, like flotsam. Not by chance, though. But by love. By my husband, James.

Because one of the last things he did before he died was buy this house.

He always did have a flair for the dramatic. I found out about the villa on the day of his funeral. Like we were in some epic film, the drama of which he would have loved. I can almost imagine him planning it. The way he would have pictured it in his head, arranging all the players and waiting for the last possible moment to make his announcement – to have the final word, even in death. I found out after the guests had left.

Sage, my teenage daughter, was in bed, cried out and exhausted, and the house was quiet. Too quiet. The sort of stillness that demands a scream. I was sitting in the living room with the curtains closed, the twin doors pulled shut, a tumbler of whisky on the side table, wearing the black silk dress we'd picked out together, when we could almost convince ourselves that it wasn't really for *this* occasion. He'd chosen it because he'd liked that it showed off my legs.

But that was then; it hung off me like a sack now as I sat, my head between my knees, while I tried and failed to contemplate the future without him.

Charlotte Woolf: forty-five, mother, mystery-novelist-has-been, *widow*. I'd made peace with my advancing age and my flagging career, but I wanted no part in the last. *None at all.*

There was a faint knock on the door and Allan, my brother, came in. He was wearing that smile, excavated from somewhere deep and broken. The smile, the living reserve for those left behind.

He took a seat and put the letter down on the side table, propping it up against my whisky glass.

'It's from James, his last wishes and all that, Twig,' he said.

My brother has called me Twig for most of my life, even when I'd long since stopped resembling a stick insect with twig-like limbs, even when the nickname seemed more ludicrous still when I put on a load of baby weight that never quite went away for a decade. He appeared a little nervous as he crossed and uncrossed his slim legs, hands brushing his wool trousers.

Allan always appeared a little anxious, though, as if a loud noise would make him bolt, but he was made from stronger stuff than he appeared. I knew this only too well, considering how much I'd been relying upon him these last few weeks – this whole year, in fact.

I blinked. 'He left me a letter?' I repeated, dumbly.

When had James had the time to write me a letter? And why would he have when we'd been together every day since he was diagnosed? It made me sad to think of it. Him writing me some last wrist-slashing note in those last days in the hospital, as his body shut down after its long fight against the cancer that had spread through every inch of the six-foot frame I'd loved so much.

Stage four melanoma.

In the end his death had been quick, and not as drawn-out as it might have been. That's what all of his doctors said. There were five, so I suppose they knew best. I was meant to take comfort in that. The short answer was: *I did not.*

I didn't want him to have suffered, of course not, but I couldn't help wishing that there could have been some middle ground. A few more months or even weeks, when he wasn't in pain. Horribly selfish, I know. But how could he have died at the age of forty-six? It's not what we'd signed up for. Not by a long shot. I wanted the midlife crisis complete with the too-flashy car that had never quite arrived. The grey hair and age spots. Him walking Sage down the aisle. The day he would hold his grandchild for the first time.

Not *this*.

I closed my eyes and leant my head against the sofa, where the tears coursed up onto the brushed linen of the sofa, melting into the pale blue fabric. You'd think I'd have used up all my tears by now, but they just kept coming, as if that's all my body knew to do – like a wound that seeped regret.

Allan clutched my hand, the one that had James's wedding ring on the thumb, where I'd worn it since he'd told me that there was no point in him being cremated with it on. Allan squeezed my hand, then got up and poured himself a whisky too, his eyes clouded with unshed tears.

'What does it say?' I asked.

He sighed. 'I don't know, Twig. He told me that it was something he thought might help. You know James.'

Present tense, I noted. Like James was still here. Like he was just in another room.

God, how I wished *that* were true.

I wiped my eyes, took a gulp of whisky and reached for the letter.

Allan looked as if he was going to leave, perhaps to give me some privacy, but I shook my head. 'No, stay, please.'

He nodded, and then sat down next to me again. I unfolded the letter from the envelope, my vision a blur of tears. A loose photograph fell onto my lap. I frowned. There was only a one-line sentence from James, written in his messy scrawl.

I bought you a house. Don't be cross.

I blinked, then made a sound between a snort and a laugh. I kept staring at the note. Trying to make sense of it. What the hell?

'What?' asked Allan. 'What is it?'

I looked at him, realising that I must have spoken aloud.

'He bought me *a house.*'

'What?' Allan said, blinking his grey-green eyes. Clearly James hadn't told him of his plans either. I handed him the letter and he looked at it just as blankly as I had.

'That's it – no explanation or anything?' He turned the letter over to check, in case the words had somehow scuttled onto the next page, as if all the things James had left unsaid were somehow gathering up their courage overleaf.

They weren't.

I picked up the photograph that had fallen onto my lap, and felt a little jolt of recognition. The small sepia-coloured image fitted into the palm of my hand in a perfect square. The corners had serrated edges, and the picture looked oddly familiar, like something I'd seen in the distance years before but couldn't quite remember where.

The image was of a small white stone villa, surrounded by trees, looking out to a vast, foamy sea. The picture was faded, and much worn, by time and, perhaps, the longing touch of fingers. I turned it over and sucked in my breath.

'Marisal,' I breathed, reading the name written in a beloved, familiar hand.

Allan's eyes widened. We both knew that name – we'd heard about it from our grandmother often enough as children. It had been a promise as kids, when we begged her to tell us stories about her old family home and she'd told us only enough to tantalise our imaginations, never more. Allan and I used to promise each other that one day we'd go there, that we'd uncover the secrets we knew were somehow still there, secrets we could never prise out of her lips. A promise I'd forgotten about during the whole business of growing up and starting a family of my own.

Till now.

*

I took a deep breath and lifted my gaze to the golden sky, making the sun penetrate my retinas. I didn't want my first time seeing the villa to be through a veil of tears, and neither would James.

It was that thought that pushed me forward more than anything else. Towards Marisal.

I opened the small, low garden gate, where I could see the name, almost faded into the carved stone.

I was here at last.

TWO

A month before

'So, let me get this straight,' said Sage, my daughter, who was nineteen going on thirty-five. She was packing her bag and I was pretending that it wasn't breaking my heart that she was going back to university.

It was a week after the funeral and we were trying to be normal, and failing miserably.

There were two lists on the bed next to her open suitcase, written in her neat, capable hand.

One for her, the other for me. Hers a checklist, mine a survival guide, with emergency numbers, useful information and reminders. Like I was the child, and she the grown-up.

Her way, I supposed, of coping, knowing she was leaving me in our family house, alone. The house James and I had slowly turned into a home over the years. It had taken me a few days to tell her about what her father had done. I hadn't known where to start really, till I'd run out of time and ended up blurting it out just before she was about to leave.

She looked at me, incredulously. 'Dad bought you a villa, in Spain? Do you think that he'd lost it a little in the end?' She was part serious, part not. She paused her packing to stare at me with her solemn ebony eyes, her dark blonde hair scraped up into its customary ponytail, and for a moment I was reminded of the little girl whose laugh reminded me of soap bubbles and hundreds and thousands sprinkles, the little girl who lives for ever inside my heart, alongside this heartbreakingly grown-up version.

I took a seat on the edge of her bed, picked up Scruffy, the old stuffed grey rabbit she used to carry around with her everywhere, and touched his worn ears. I held back a laugh as I looked at the list, which said things like: 'Go for a walk every day. Eat three square meals (chocolate is not a meal, Mum).' This was underlined, twice, so it was obviously very important. 'Maybe phone your editor, ask for an extension for your novel, again? Stay *away* from Grandma.'

The last made me snort, then grow sad again. My mother and I had a somewhat strained relationship at the moment. It had been that way for a while, since James was diagnosed; her way of 'helping' had been to try bringing all sorts of baffling New Age remedies for him to try. I had known, even as we fought, that she was just trying to be kind, just trying to help, really, but it drove me insane. It was hard enough trying to accept the impossible – that the love of my life was about to die – without having her keep trying to get my hopes up with some wild goose chase. One that only ended in disappointment, and made us constantly keep causing each other pain.

Sage stared hard at me, her eyes welling up. Then she shook her head fast and started unpacking. 'I'll defer or something. Start again next year. This is ridiculous. I can't just leave you alone and go back to uni as if nothing happened. *I won't.*'

'Yes, *you will,*' I said, putting on my little-used stern voice. 'You're going into your second year of med school, it's your dream – that's where your life is now, all your friends. You don't need to worry about me, all right?'

Sage had been born an old soul. Wise, competent, hard-working, sometimes too hard on herself. James had always had to tell her it was okay to have fun, to just let go, to not have everything add up the way it 'should'. To wear the pricy, yet fashionable clothes that fell apart in the wash, instead of sensible Marks & Spencer jumpers and shoes. There'd be time enough for old and sensible later. It was okay to just be nineteen without a plan for everything, and to not feel responsible for everyone. Those talks would be up to me now. I put her clothes back inside the bag.

'Staying won't solve anything, for either of us. I'll just have something else to worry about if you do that.'

I suppose Sage feared that I might live off sugary cereal and never get out of my pyjamas with her gone. I was forty-five, and a *widow*, with a job that meant I never had to leave the house (or the job I would have if I ever finished the new manuscript I'd promised my editor a year ago). Working in my pyjamas and eating rubbish was *my right*.

'And no – I don't think that Dad had lost it. I think, actually he was a lot like you. He was worried about what was going to happen to me – to us, really – and he thought this was a good way to move forward.'

This was guesswork. Mostly.

She looked at me incredulously. 'With a house in Spain?'

'Technically it's on a little Spanish island, right next to Ibiza.'

Her dark eyes popped in surprise, and she snorted. 'Oh my God, *Ibiza?* Dad wanted you to go partying?'

I laughed. I could well understand her shock and confusion. 'No. It's different on the little island. Much quieter, far away from the crowds and noise, thank God.'

According to Google, the tiny island of Formentera is inhabited by a few thousand people. It's long and narrow and covered in grassy farmland, pine forest and miles of untouched, sandy beaches. It's only eighty-three kilometres in size and on each of its rocky headlands there is a solitary lighthouse.

Since I'd found out about the house, I'd spent some time looking at pictures of the island, trying to imagine going there and when I'd ever feel up to it. The colour of the sea arrests the eye, a dazzling sweep of turquoise that glitters as it mixes into the dark swirling blue of the vast ocean that surrounds it.

The real problem is that the only way to get there is by flying to Ibiza first, then getting the ferry to the smaller, sister island. It seemed incongruous, to say the least; me heading off to the world's most famous party isle, filled with loud, drug-fuelled nightclubs, ageing hippies and hedonists after my husband had died. Perhaps he *had* lost it, a little.

But I knew the truth, of course.

'It was your great-grandmother's house. That's why he bought it – he wanted us to get to know it, I think, and for it to be back in the family, where I'm sure he felt it belonged.'

Though he hadn't explained it as such in his note, I knew that was the reason. We'd spoken about Marisal over the years, and the promise Allan and I had made to each other as children to go to the island and find it. James had always been supportive of it, but somehow, I just never got around to doing it and Allan's interest had waned the older he'd got. Mine hadn't, but somehow, I'd just never found the time. Perhaps buying the house, making the decision to do it, was James's way of ensuring that I did. I handed my daughter the photograph, then held her shoulder.

She looked at it and frowned. 'This was your grandmother's?' she said, taking a seat and holding the photograph in both hands as she stared at the grainy, sepia-toned image of an old white house surrounded by a wild sea. Her dark eyes were solemn.

I nodded. Sage hadn't met my grandmother; she'd died not long after my daughter was born. 'A long time ago. She escaped in the Spanish Civil War in the thirties, I think, and not long afterwards she met my grandfather and they came to live in his home country. The house – Marisal – was lost somehow. I'm not sure of the details, she never really told us much, but I know that it hurt her that it wasn't in the family any more.'

'Didn't she ever tell you what happened?' asked Sage, turning to look at me with a frown.

I shook my head, gave a small sigh. 'No – she didn't like to talk about the past. Especially the tough times. But she loved it there.' I knew that much at least. 'And she would have been pleased at the thought that it ended back with us somehow, particularly through Dad.'

I couldn't help thinking of what it would have meant to her.

Sage smiled. 'She liked him?'

I shook my head. 'She *adored* him. It was embarrassing. He was always trying to speak to her in his terrible Spanish, and she loved him for it.'

'That sounds like Dad.' We shared teary grins, and dashed away the moisture from our eyes.

'So when are you going to go? To Formentera… to Marisal?'

Not an if, I noted. I suppose we both knew there wasn't much choice in it. Though the thought of jetting off there now seemed impossible. Too bright, too beautiful… too much, really.

'In a couple of weeks, or months, maybe,' I hedged. Perhaps when the urge to ask them to cremate my body, too, passed. I didn't *say* that, of course. 'Maybe you could come out when you have your next break, see it for yourself? I don't know what sort of state it's in so we'll just have to see. The lawyer, you know, Steve Linberg?'

She nodded.

'Well, he didn't mention if it was habitable or not when I checked in with him but I got the sense that it's a bit neglected. He said that no one has lived there for a few years.'

Sage snorted. 'When you blasted him to find out what the hell Dad was thinking, you mean?'

I grinned. She knew me very well.

'Pretty much. Anyway, who knows, maybe we'll have somewhere to spend Christmas this year. Margaritas on the beach?'

Her eyes widened. 'That could be good.'

It could. I hadn't done much thinking about the future, apart from just trying to keep breathing and getting from one day to the next, but Christmas away from the memories of our family home seemed like a good plan, I thought.

I'd got hold of some of the details behind James's decision to buy the house from Steve. Including the name of the estate agent he'd used when I'd tried to follow up James's short, mysterious note.

I'd found out that Steve had been the one who'd taken care of everything for James when he'd told him what he wanted to do. His plan for buying Marisal.

I'd told Steve that perhaps he should have consulted me, but he assured me that James had been of sound mind when he'd instructed him to look into buying the house several months ago, when he'd discovered that it had gone to auction.

Financially, it had been a good deal. The money had come from James's own private fund, from when he sold off his design business, so he had been within his right to buy it. It hadn't caused any financial strain to us, which was a relief. I just wished he'd told me what he was doing, or what he'd been thinking. It didn't feel right leaving our home to fly to a Spanish island right now. Especially when all I felt like doing was going to bed for the next year. At least when I dreamt, James was still there. Perhaps that's what he'd been afraid of.

The thing that no one says about death is what a toll it takes on your liver. I just didn't really know how to face it sober.

It was so much worse when Sage left. I hadn't quite realised just how much I'd been keeping it together for her until she wasn't there.

The other thing no one tells you about is what happens after the funeral. When the casseroles stop coming and the phone stops ringing. That's when it hits you. In the silence. When you wish everything would just *stop*, but it doesn't. The sun keeps rising. The tides keep turning. The birds keep singing. And the mail just keeps on coming.

I jumped as the mail came through the letter box, landing on the pile I hadn't had the will to clear the day before. Fliers. Advertiser editions of weekly papers. Catalogues.

It took everything I could not to open the door and shout at the postie to have some respect. That I didn't fucking need a half-price window-cleaning special right now; I needed more vodka and perhaps he could add that to his rounds tomorrow?

But I didn't. Instead, I just sat on the stairs staring at the brown envelopes, the ones addressed to James, and cried.

Even though we'd changed everything to my name, and cancelled everything else, it was like no one had listened, because they still kept coming, addressed to someone who was no longer here.

It's those little indignities that drive you mad.

When the phone did ring in those first few weeks it was usually my mother or Allan, checking in. As if I was in a coma, my body trapped inside this silent house, and they were just making sure that I was still breathing.

I was. *Just.*

'What have you been doing?' asked my mum.

I paused, looking at James's urn in my hands; I'd got into the habit of taking it with me to every room I visited. He'd told me, 'You'll know when to scatter my ashes when the time is right.'

He'd want to be somewhere close to us, somewhere with a view, I knew. Right now, though, I was just keeping him close. I didn't know if the time would ever be right to let him go.

I didn't think my mum would approve if she knew. She'd probably want to do some weird ceremony, with crystals or something.

'Darling, perhaps I should come over again? Perhaps we should get out?'

Despite Sage's warnings, you couldn't stop my mum. She kept coming around, even if we just sat on the sofa not saying much and trying not to get into an argument. Whenever she came over I took James's urn to another room, though; if I couldn't be spared, there was no reason he had to be subjected to it, too. I figured he had enough on his plate, being dead and everything.

The only place worse than home, though, was 'out'.

Out was magnified; the world rushed past and people laughed and spoke and slammed into you and no one noticed or cared or realised that the very worst thing in the world had happened to you. That you had seen what hell looked like and were still standing. Except there was no telltale wreckage or explosion that others could point to, to know or to understand, just the broken shell of you, left behind.

Going out wasn't good for others either. It wasn't great for the people who had the misfortune of being in my path. I'd lost that switch, you know? The one that prevents you from telling people what you *really* think.

So home was best, really. When I was at home, I could lie. I'd become rather brilliant at lying, at the pretence that I was doing 'just fine'. In fact, my life was busy, and quite full. It was devastating, of course, but I'd been preparing. I was surviving. I was going to be all right. Which was wishful thinking, of course.

I figured people like to hear about progress. When it doesn't happen, it makes them uncomfortable. As an ingrained people-pleaser, lying seemed to me the best, and the simplest way forward.

So, I told my friend Terry that I *was* going to look into that Zumba class that helped his mate Steph when she lost her husband at the age of seventy-three, when really I was just planning on drinking some more vodka that night. I told my mum that I would get in touch with that counsellor – the one she left the number of on the fridge – when instead I did a practice round with James's ashes, with James playing the role of the therapist.

'You're depressed because I'm dead? How *strange*.'

'I know, it's a shocker. It's almost a month. I should have won the charity bake sale by now if this were a novel, you know?'

'Yes, but you don't bake, remember?'

'True.'

'Maybe you *should* try therapy?'

'Maybe… *or* I could just have some more wine?'

'Sure, that'll work, too…'

The worst, though, was how I lied to Sage about how well I was coping, while I worried about how she was doing, hoping that she wasn't falling apart like me. But she seemed to be coping in her own way, getting stuck into her studies, spending time with her friends. So I didn't let her know that some days the only responsibly adult thing I'd done was to check in with her to see if she was okay. Then I'd hang up, and cry and get back in bed with James's urn.

To chase away the shadows, I watched a lot of bad TV, though I'm not sure I took much of anything in. Perhaps because I drank my way through a lot of it, with Allan popping in every so often, as well as my best friend, Hannah. I didn't mind them coming over. Hannah came over every couple of days whether I wanted her to or not, like a carer making sure I wasn't getting any bedsores. She was that kind, you know? She didn't take offence if I opened the door with hair that hadn't been washed in a week, wearing James's bathrobe, a drink in my hand as I sighed, 'Oh, it's you,' when she interrupted an episode of *Doctor Who*.

She'd just nod. Then steer me towards the shower.

Hannah was my oldest, no-bullshit-between-us friend. You know the kind?

She was the one who could tell me just about anything, the one who saw things in me that I didn't even know about myself. The one who saw through everything I said.

She was tough. Straight-talking. A powerhouse. Kind to those she cared about. To the rest of the world, she was pretty terrifying.

Hannah was the one who told me to go to Marisal.

Just when I'd thought that I'd got great at lying.

'You're not bloody fine,' she said, looking at me, a month after I'd found out about the house.

'Yes. I am.'

Her dark eyes remained unconvinced. 'Charl, you look like a ghost, you've got scary thin, frail thin, like you're fading away. He wouldn't want this, you hiding away in here like Miss Havisham or something.'

I gritted my teeth. 'What did you expect, Han? That by now I'd be joining in the local bingo and bake-off? My husband has *died* – I'm sorry if I can't just pull myself together by snapping my fucking fingers.'

'You know that's not what I mean.'

I huffed and looked out of the window as she continued. 'No one expects you to be *okay*, but you don't have to go through this on your own. Besides, I think you should go and see the house he bought. It might do you some good to get away. James—'

'Wasn't thinking,' I said, crossing my arms. 'I can't just fly off to some bloody Spanish island and start making merry with a villa – this isn't some bloody romcom, it's real life.' I took a shuddery breath. 'I never wanted any of this, Han – not without him.'

Which was when the sobs came. I was angry. Angry at James. Angry at the rogue cell that had mutated in his traitorous body, which had decided to check out before me. It wasn't meant to be that way. How did I go on without him?

Hannah put her arms round me. 'Oh God, Charl, I'm sorry I made you cry. You always were a tough nut to crack.'

I half sobbed, half laughed. 'Not any more.'

She smiled, smoothed back my hair, then fetched my bag, where I was keeping the cigarettes I hadn't told her about. 'Shall we go have a fag in the garden?'

How had she known?

I laughed. It reminded me of when we were thirteen, the first time we'd done just that with her mother's fags, how we used to sneak out and puff away on them.

'I'm going to take these with me when I go though,' she said sternly, after she handed me a lit cigarette. I nodded. She was right, as usual. Some things a person didn't want when their husband had died from cancer: picking up a habit that could give it to you too and make your only child an orphan. Bloody Hannah. Like I said, death is absolute hell on the liver.

In the end, I bought the ticket at 2 a.m. after I'd finished the last of the whisky, wrapped up in James's old bathrobe, which I pretended still smelt a little like his aftershave. I had been busy contemplating throwing myself off the nearest bridge with his urn in my hands so we'd go together. Going to Formentera instead seemed the saner option.

Allan drove me to the airport a few days later, mumbling all sorts of things as we sped along the motorway.

'You've got your passport, Twig? And the motion sickness tablets for the ferry? What about towels, I doubt there will be anything like that there, did you remember to pack some? Maybe you should have just booked a hotel instead? What if there's no electricity or running water and you're stuck? Maybe I should come with you? I can't just let you run off by yourself.'

He said all this rather fast and I stared back at him, panic beginning to creep in. His anxiety was catching.

I'd packed a bag for a week, though I hadn't booked a return flight. My reasoning was that I didn't want to be too committed, despite the fact that I'd promised Allan that I'd give the place a chance before returning home to my bathrobe, whisky and illegal fags. At least with a no-return trip, I could get the next flight out if I wished.

THREE

The air smelt like the ocean, wild rosemary and that first whisper of summer.

There was a warmth to the air that was a surprise after the cold of London, making me sling my jacket over my arm, and my skin itch from sweat; making me realise that I hadn't packed properly for the weather. It had been hard to imagine sunshine after such a long, hard winter.

I'd docked at the port of La Savina, which teemed with bars and with tourists renting mopeds and bicycles, all with thoughts of a holiday in mind. I was eager to get away from the sunshine-dwellers, away from the easy smiles and puzzled looks of people who saw something in me, something perhaps that announced I didn't belong.

I didn't have much to go on, just the name of the house and that it was located in an area known as Can Morraig, one of the more remote parts of Formentera. I'd managed to get a taxi and it had stopped on the street where the driver thought my villa was meant to be. I waved him off telling him I'd walk the rest of the way and only realised my mistake once I had to walk up a long, barren road that stretched for half a mile, surrounded by low stone walls and farmland.

My suitcase was small and wheeled. I traipsed up the hot tarmac, dragging it behind me, wiping the sweat from my eyes.

I was grateful for the lack of people though. At last I could breathe, and stop forcing my pained smile. Ibiza had been an overload for my strained senses, and the ferry had been much the same. Too many partygoers, excited teenagers and people whose happiness only seemed to highlight my own deep sorrow, as if they were in colour while I had faded to black and white. It was a relief to be away from it all. To let my face sink into its comfortable, though all-too-familiar, sorrowful folds.

As I walked, I passed by whitewashed houses, some modern, some neglected and old. Here in this older section it felt a little as if this were a place that time had forgotten, and here I felt a little more of a sense of release.

As I made my way up a slight incline next to a low wall, I saw it. Just the lip of the house at first – and then there it was: a small white villa, with pale pink bougainvillea trailing along the old stone.

Marisal.

Nature had had its way with the small front garden; there were hedges and weeds that obscured the path, and a large orange tree stood next to the front door, heavy with fruit, the scent offering a taste of the summer still to come.

I bent down beside the tree to find the fat blue flowerpot, which held the key to the villa, as I'd been instructed.

In his letter, the estate agent had explained little about the house's present condition, and I saw now why; perhaps he'd been afraid that I would change my mind. Although considering that buying it and coming here was the last wish of my husband, he can't have thought that was likely.

Besides, it didn't matter what state it was in. This house had been a part of my family once, and a part of me couldn't help feeling like I was looking at more than just four stone walls.

I opened the weather-beaten door, which was sticky with age. The air inside was musty, that scent of years of oceanside dwelling, reminding me of childhood summers spent by the coast. I made my way to the small front window and opened one of the shutters, then jumped back as it fell apart, crumbling onto the flagstone but offering a chink of warm, lemon-coloured sunshine that brought the shadows to life. Most of the furniture was covered in thick, cloying bands of dust, which coated everything, making me sneeze. I'd been told that the house had been sold in an auction, after whoever had lived here left or died. I guessed that was why there was still furniture here. My eyes trailed around the room, noting the fireplace in the corner, the small window that overlooked the ocean, the thick stone walls and the coolness of the interior. There were discarded newspapers stacked in the corner, and on the windowsill several old wine bottles remained.

Still, there was something beneath the dust, that kind of warmth that some houses have, welcoming you in.

I stepped through the house, perhaps less reverently than I would have imagined earlier, certain that I would be stepping in the shadows of ghosts; but though I looked in cupboards, and in corners, I found no trace of them here.

In the centre of the small farm-style kitchen with its wood-fired stove, there was a small, cheap Formica table, the kind that reminded me of school gyms and hostels. On top of it was a new kettle, a few mugs, plates and a bottle of washing-up liquid – some things I'd asked the estate agent to get when he'd kindly offered.

In the corner of the room were several large bottles of water. The tap water was likely to be salty – at least that's what the guidebooks had said. I tested the mains and found electricity, which was a relief. I'd text Allan later and let him know.

In the small main bedroom there was an old iron bed frame and a bare mattress that had seen better days. It was sunken slightly in the middle, and faded to the colour of old, milky tea.

The other two rooms didn't seem much better; both contained piles of discarded furniture from floor to ceiling. It would take days to clear it.

For a moment, I contemplated booking myself into one of the hotels Allan had suggested. Where there'd be fresh sheets, a television and, perhaps more importantly, vodka. I'd passed a resort on my way here, but a wave of weariness decided me against it. The truth was that I wasn't up to the hassle of people, not now, not after being surrounded by all those partygoers heading to Ibiza on the plane.

I'd spied a small shop down the street on the taxi drive here that looked as if it sold basic essentials. I could walk there later and get a few supplies. I went back into the bedroom, wheeled in my small case and opened it. Then I took out James's urn and placed it on the bedside table. 'Well, we're here now,' I said, touching it. Then I shook my head.

'I hope you're happy.'

FOUR

It felt strange to wake up in a house I'd only ever heard about.

As a child, it had been fun on days when the rain lashed the windows and the grey sky looked like an old bruise to imagine a lost, far-flung, sun-drenched family home.

But the stories were few and far between, prised from my grandmother's oyster-like lips on rare occasions and only after much pleading.

Perhaps it was harder for her on those dark, grey days, too; perhaps on days like that she was trying *not* to remember.

If I closed my eyes I could picture her saying the name, almost reluctantly. *Marisal*. Smell the ocean, and the wild oranges from the garden, picture the old white villa. See how her eyes would grow sad and dark when we brought out the album with the crimson velvet lining from the old wooden chest, where she kept all her other memories too, and ask her to tell us about it. The brown, parchment-like skin of her fingers would trail the dark leather cover as she reluctantly told Allan and me about our Catalan roots. Each word fell from her mouth like it hurt, like it cost her money.

Even by the time she'd died, we still only knew the bare essentials. We knew that our family had lived on the island for as long as she could remember, that they'd originally come from Majorca and that some of her relatives lived in Ibiza too. The family spoke Eivissenc, a dialect of Catalan – forbidden by many of the country's rulers throughout the centuries in favour of the common language of Spain.

We knew that the Alvarez family, from whom Allan and I were descended, had red hair and beards, which is where my own auburn hair came from, or so my grandmother said.

Green eyes were also a common trait. Most of the family had had that colouring, except for a great-great-grandmother who had been dark and beautiful, with an ebony waterfall for hair, and eyes like India ink. My gran had stopped speaking suddenly when I pressed her for more about this woman, then pursed her lips as if she'd said too much. You had to be gentle, and go slow in case she clammed up, which happened all too often.

When I'd complained about my gran's reluctance to speak about the past, my mother had told me that they were all like that, not just my grandmother but most people who had lived through the war. 'None of them like to talk about their old lives – they all just want to leave it in the past, and she left one war only to come here and enter another…'

It couldn't have been easy, I knew, to leave your country in the midst of a terrible civil war, to flee, only to find yourself in the midst of one of the worst in history, the Second World War, just a few short years later. It wasn't fair. And it was hardly surprising she hadn't wanted to speak about it, considering how much pain and heartache she experienced, how much she had witnessed. But it was a pity, too, that she wouldn't let us know about it because when she was gone, that was it – a lid closed for ever on that part of our family's history.

As I looked around, I realised that there was so much I didn't know about this place. Who had been the people who once called it home?

Who was the mysterious dark-haired female relative my grandmother hadn't wanted to speak about?

The house itself offered no real clues.

I got up, still wearing James's old bathrobe, which I'd put on partly as a barrier against the bare mattress, partly because I liked to think it still smelt like him, although that was now unlikely as I'd worn it too often since he'd passed and if it smelt like anything now, it was me. The sun had moved high into the sky and the light had entered the room, making the air warm and drowsy. I poured myself some water and got started on airing out the house and getting rid of some of the thick bands of dust, leaving James's urn in the bedroom.

I got changed into a pair of tracksuit bottoms that used to be slightly snug and now hung off me, catching sight of myself in the mirror on the wall with a grimace. I looked haunted, deflated, even to my own eyes. I looked away, then put the collar of my shirt over my mouth as I began tackling the dust. I was still making little progress some time later that morning when there was a knock on the door.

I opened the door, shading my eyes against the glare, when a short man came into view, wearing a dark grey wool suit, despite the heat of the day.

His hair was like steel wool and he had kindly, crinkly eyes. His was the sort of face where you could only guess at his age; he could be anywhere from early sixties to eighty.

'Charlotte?' he asked, his voice lilting and musical and as warm as the sunshine that was trickling inside the cool interior of the house.

I nodded.

'I am Escobar de Riba.'

'Hola, Señor,' I said, recognising the name of the estate agent.

'I come to check everything is okay. You find the *finca* all right?'

'*Finca?*' I asked.

'The farmhouse?' he said with a quirk of his eyebrow.

'Ah,' I said with a grin.

His English was pretty good, I realised, grateful. 'Fine, thanks – and thank you for everything else,' I said, indicating the supplies he'd bought – including my new kettle and mugs.

'It's no trouble.' He hesitated, frowned, then cleared his throat, staring at me rather nervously.

'I…' he paused, then shook his head and gave me a polite smile as he stepped back.

'What?' I asked, puzzled.

'It's just I couldn't help to wonder about you. Well, after everything.'

I frowned. 'You wondered about me?'

His face reddened slightly. 'Yes – I'm sorry. I wondered about you after I spoke to your husband…'

'You spoke to James,' I repeated dumbly.

'Many times.' His eyes grew sad. 'Such a good man, I thought. I was sorry to hear that he'd passed.'

My eyes smarted. I could only nod, looking up at the sky, trying, desperately, not to cry in front of this well-meaning stranger.

'It's why I'm here today, really,' he said, then gave me that smile – the one that everyone had been giving me since he'd passed, full of regret. 'To give you this.'

It was another letter.

FIVE

My fingers shook as I pulled the paper out the envelope.

My love,

Okay. So, you're furious with me. I know. I'm sorry.

I wanted to explain everything straight away – you know how I am with secrets. Impossible. But I knew you had to get here by yourself first.

To the island, I mean. And if you're reading this, that's where you are, which is kind of amazing.

It couldn't be me telling you to go – even though, I'm sure, 'Honey, I bought you a house' probably felt a bit like that. I hope you didn't feel pressured – that's not what this was about.

Okay, that's a lie, it's a little bit what this is about – I did want to pressure you, but subtly though. And dare I say, with a dash of mystery too? Cue Sean Connery's voice… Anyway, I wanted to do it without the monumental list of reasons you would have given me against going.

Clever me, no?

But seriously, I'm sure you've guessed by now that I just didn't want you at home, lost and wasting away. I think it's that thought that kills me most.

Yeah, I know. Bad joke.

So anyway, this is what I want you to do, all right? I want you to think about living, really living, and well, an island just off Spain seems pretty great from where I'm sitting. Though I know you, you'll resist, but don't, okay?

I hope it's fun, or something like fun, at least. This past year has been hell, period. I'll be happy knowing you're doing something positive, something that brings a little joy, I hope.

With that in mind, I did some digging while I've been stuck here – with Steve's help. Apparently, the house has been lived in by some hippies who abandoned it some time ago so there's not much in it that belongs to your family, more's the pity, so it's not much to go on.

But, Steve hired a detective. I know, sounds so sleuthy – and you know how much I love that. All those detective novels I read in the bath…

Anyway, he traced back your grandmother's ancestry and well, he found out something interesting. It turns out that her sister is still living on the island. Her name is Maria de Palma. Did you know she even had a sister?! I'm sure you never mentioned it to me. Here's her address. Apparently, she knows a lot more than she would let on to the detective. I'm told that the locals are a bit like your dear gran when it comes to sharing their history – very closed up.

Still, you'll have some family to get to know – which is a good start. I wish that I was there to help – maybe this is how.

I love you.

J.

I didn't know what I felt afterwards. No, that wasn't true. I felt almost, for just a moment, like James was back here with me. The letter was so *him*. He used to light up a room, make you laugh so hard you snorted things from out of your nose. It was like hearing his voice again after all this silence, and all I could do was sob. Which was when I got angry. I couldn't help it.

For James, this had been like some sort of play, but for me it was real. A really big, aching part of me really did just want to go to bed for a year and not get up until the pain of losing him had become something manageable. Wasn't that my right? I didn't want to be here on this bright, beautiful, hippie-overtaken island trying to find some link to my family's past. Not yet, anyway.

So, I took his urn and put it in the wardrobe, and closed the door. I couldn't face him right now.

Then I went for a walk, in search of mobile reception. I found it about half a mile from the house. I texted Allan and Sage telling them that I'd arrived safe and sound, sending them a few photographs that I snapped while I was standing there. One of the house, and the surrounding countryside and turquoise ocean, my brain not even taking in the beauty of it. I didn't tell them about James's letter, not then anyway.

Later I went to the small shop around the corner. It had dusty shelves crammed full of tinned produce and toiletries. An old man, whose face was like a crumpled towel of lines, wearing a faded black hat at an angle, sat outside the shop on a little stool, watching the world go by, though occasionally breaking his watch to play a round of dominoes with a small boy with laughing brown eyes. The old man introduced himself as Francisco, and the boy as his grandson, Andreas.

I got a few things from the shelves – tea, a packet of lemon biscuits that were coated in a thin layer of dust, some cleaning materials, a basket and what turned out to be Francisco's home-made wine. 'This cures everything,' he said with a knowing sort of look. 'Take it just up to here,' he warned, with a thick finger noting the amount on the bottle, as if he were a pharmacist. He stared into my eyes as I was paying, and I looked away, wondering when the pain in them would not be so obvious.

*

At three in the morning, after I'd had more than Francisco's recommended dosage and was feeling better, I went and fetched James.

'Look. I'm sorry I was angry,' I said, and put his ashes on the bedside table with a relieved sigh. I couldn't sleep knowing I'd stuck him inside the wardrobe. He didn't deserve it, not when all he was trying to do was look out for me. 'I know you meant well, but love, this seems crazy to me, even just being here.'

I'd given up thinking about how madly *I* was behaving with his ashes, grateful that at least no one was around to witness it. Just me and him, really, and well, even when he was alive, James had been well used to my peculiarities, so I was fairly sure it came as no surprise to him that they had got worse now that he was dead. The way I had to light a candle before I started writing. Or how I couldn't fall asleep unless the bedcover was straight. Now I couldn't function without taking his ashes along to every room I visited.

It was after he was back where he belonged, next to me, that I thought about what he'd said in his letter – about my grandmother having a sister. A sister she'd never spoken about. Despite everything, I was curious. Had this relative lived here on the island this whole time? And if so, why hadn't my grandmother got in touch with her – or returned here after the war? Maybe she had, though? Perhaps she'd just never told me. But why not? And why had she never mentioned her to us at all?

'It's a mystery all right,' I told him.

SIX

In the morning the lemon-coloured sunlight arrived early, casting dust-mote rainbows from behind the closed shutters. The air was scented with olives, wild rosemary and salt, and it stirred my senses as I slept, making me think of long-ago summers and sun-kissed memories with James.

Everywhere here smelt like the sea, and it was all you could hear at night.

I blinked at the warmth behind my eyelids, sighing as I remembered where I was. Sometimes, I could swear I heard James's voice while I slept, like he was just here, waiting for me to wake up. It usually made me sad when I did awake to discover the painful trick my brain was playing on me, especially when my eyes fell upon his ashes.

I got out of bed, touching them. My grandmother always used to say, 'When you can't do anything else for the day, make your bed.'

It was good advice. It was just a pity it had taken me nearly forty years to understand what she meant. I made some coffee, taking James with me to the kitchen, and decided that my first order of business was to find something to put on the bed besides James's bathrobe and then to carry on with the clean-up of the house. At least then when Hannah, Allan or Sage phoned me, I could tell them that I was doing something productive with my time, instead of talking to my dead husband's ashes, and slowly waiting out the week I'd promised Allan I'd give the place before crawling back into my own bed back home in the Surrey countryside.

When I popped round to the little shop for some advice and some paracetamol, Francisco told me where I could venture out for some bedding, noting my slightly hungover state with a shake of his head. 'It's strong stuff, I did warn you,' he said, pouring me a glass of water right there so that I could take two of the pills he held out in his palm. I took them gratefully and left, with a sheepish grin and a promise to take it more slowly next time.

The sun was warm on my shoulders as I walked to the port at La Savina that afternoon, my headache finally beginning to abate. I decided that I'd have to either hire a bicycle for the rest of the week or risk blisters from walking in my sandals in the baking sun. Still, the walk was pleasant, the air mild with a cooling breeze, and I was feeling a lift to my spirits as a result.

I took in the scent of paella, farm-fresh salad and just-roasted coffee from the bars and cafes. The more I saw of the town, which according to the guidebooks was a centre for million-pound yachts, sailing and regattas, the more I could see that it still retained some of the flavour of the bygone hippie era. On its seafront stalls there were artisanal one-of-a-kind items for sale mixed in with the cheap and cheerful. The people were friendly and laid-back too, and I felt myself enjoying the day more and more as I browsed.

As I walked I saw cars, scooters and bike rental places and the buzz of people arriving from the ferry, which created a masala mix that seemed like a summer festival, a snapshot of paradise, and for a moment I felt a part of it, glad to be where I was.

My mother had told me when my father had passed away that death was something you managed, not something you ever truly got over, and that some days were easier than others. I was grateful that today was one of those rare easier ones.

I'd rented a bicycle, and purchased a particularly pleasing bed set in a soft blush pink with grey accents, and was continuing to browse the stalls, when I met Isla. A thirty-something singer and artist from Alabama, who seemed to fit in with the old hippie culture as if she was born in their generation, rather than being about forty years too young for it. She had dark eyes fringed by thick lashes, a blue gem stud in her nose and shoulder-length brown hair that fell in waves across her tanned shoulders. She moved with a dancer's grace as she showed me her artworks.

They were beautiful seascapes, dreamy and impressionistic, and I bent to look at them more closely. One in particular, of a lonely lighthouse, charmed me so much that I bought it then and there, hoping it would fit into the little basket of the bicycle I'd rented. Marisal could do with some life, and colour. The price was ridiculously low and I felt a bit bad offering so little for such lovely work.

'It's of the lighthouse at Cap de Barbaria, have you been?' Isla asked, waving a casual hand to silence my offer to pay more.

Her voice was soft and soothing. The kind of voice that accompanied the lilt of spa music and healing crystals.

I shook my head. 'No, I've heard it's a bit of a trek.'

She nodded. 'Worth it though. Take some water, that's my advice if you do go,' she added, noting my bicycle, laughing at her memory. 'I got caught out. I was stranded, literally in the middle of nowhere, dying of thirst, and I almost barrelled into the first people I saw, these two romantic hikers, who were having a little moment until I fell upon them, gasping for their water bottle.'

I couldn't help laughing at the image. 'That's just the kind of thing that would happen to me. Thanks, that's a great tip.'

She grinned. She had small, very even teeth. 'You here for a while, or just a day-tripper?'

There were a lot of day-trippers from Ibiza, I guessed, probably escaping the noise and getting a bit of calm.

I shook my head. 'I'm not sure really.'

She cocked her head to the side, and her hair bounced in a shiny wave. 'How's that work?'

I laughed. 'Well, I'm here for longer than a day, I suppose, but I'm not sure for how much more.' I explained a little more about booking a one-way ticket and the family house, but didn't go into any more detail. Somehow, I couldn't help fearing that blurting out that my husband had just died and bought me a house that had once belonged to my family might not come across as terribly sane or appropriate conversation for someone I'd just met.

'That's so spontaneous, I love it. My kind of gal, for sure,' she said appreciatively. 'Well, if you are going to be here a little longer, you should come to the Blues Bar. It's just 'round the corner there.' She pointed to a little street away from the stalls. 'I sing there with my band.'

'You're in a band?'

'Yeah, it's just me and Big Jim, and his wife, Sue. Jim plays bass, and Sue plays keyboard. I play guitar and tambourine.'

I grinned. Of course, she did.

'Just folksy, indie stuff, you know?'

'I like that. My daughter is into that sort of thing too.'

Her eyes widened. 'You have a daughter? Cool, how old?'

'Nineteen,' I said, my heart doing a little lurch for my girl. Isla looked surprised. 'Wow, you don't look like you're old enough to have a nineteen-year-old daughter!'

I shrugged. 'I'm forty-five, so it's not that strange.'

Perhaps that sounded old to Isla, because she said, 'That's some good genes.'

I shrugged, deciding to take the compliment. Particularly as lately I felt nothing but old.

'Thanks.'

That night, I debated going to the Blues Bar. It was at the moment that I'd shrugged back into James's bathrobe with a glass of Francisco's wine for company that I felt a stab of guilt for doing exactly what James didn't want me to do. It's not like I could even pretend any differently after reading his letter. I shrugged off the robe and went in search of jeans and a blouse.

I figured they had alcohol there and that perhaps something besides home-made wine would at least offer some variety for my liver – and perhaps my head in the morning.

The bar was little more than a beach shack, with a tin roof, a sandy floor and shabby-chic painted wooden benches. There were string lights and plenty of people swaying to the music supplied by Isla's three-man band.

Big Jim, or the person I assumed to be Big Jim, was indeed pretty huge, with a long grey ponytail and a massive tie-dyed shirt straining against his impressive belly as he played the bass guitar. Sue looked a bit like she might run the bake sale in our local village, complete with gran-curls and jumper, except that she played the keyboard with a transformed expression on her round face. I liked them immediately.

I ordered a beer, then took a seat. Isla stopped mid-song to welcome me. It was that sort of place, and I couldn't help but grin as a few people waved at me.

Isla had a lovely tone to her voice. Like expensive cigars, mixed with fine brandy. It was smoky and sweet and silky-smooth, and the songs she sang were haunting, yet somehow a little quirky and funny too.

There was one about a man who sat in the belly of a bear for the winter to escape his nine-to-five. Another about a girl who lived beneath the sea in a city made of sea glass. Isla was a storyteller I realised, and I was enjoying myself much more than I had imagined when I'd had to convince myself to come.

After their first set, the band took a break and Isla, followed by Big Jim and Sue, came to join me. I bought them a round of drinks.

'You're all incredible,' I said, meaning it. 'Your voice, Isla – wow.'

She smiled at me. 'Thanks. It's just some fun, you know?'

'But you don't want to take it professional? You've definitely got the talent.'

She shrugged, took a sip of her beer. 'Yeah, thanks, but not really…' she hedged.

Big Jim shook his head at me. 'You don't recognise her?'

Isla looked at him imploringly. 'Big Jim, don't…'

'What?' I asked.

Big Jim looked at me with his round blue eyes. 'She already did.'

'What?'

She sighed. 'It was a long time ago. A lifetime ago now, actually. In fact, I was trying my best to forget it…' she said with a pointed look at Big Jim.

He rolled his eyes, ignored her protests and not-so-subtle hint to keep quiet. 'Kids. They think a decade is a lifetime. And why should you forget it? You should be *proud*. Hell, I'm proud just knowing you!'

At my blank look, he explained further. 'Have you heard of the Riddles?'

I paused. They did sound familiar.

'They had a hit song, "The Muse".' He hummed a few bars and I turned to Isla in shock, my mouth falling open slightly as I exclaimed, 'That was you?'

I thought I had recognised that voice! That song had been a pretty big deal a few years ago. You couldn't listen to the radio without hearing it. They'd played it non-stop for months.

'Yeah, well. It was me and my best friend Jules, and my boyfriend, Sebastian. We went from playing low-key gigs, mostly practising in my parents' garage, to touring most days of the year. Then, I dunno – we were all just burnt out, I guess. And our lives centred on everything but the music. The recording studio wanted a certain kind of song, and then they wanted us to go the more commercial, more pop route, and I just couldn't do it any more. I just liked writing music and singing, you know? I didn't want the other stuff.'

'But couldn't you do a bit of both?' I asked, thinking it was a shame if no one else got to hear her but the customers at the Blues Bar.

'Yeah, I'm not sure, maybe one day. I'm happy for the first time in years. I don't mind not having it figured out for a while.'

I looked at her and nodded. 'Yeah,' I said. 'I still need to work on that. I'm at the "trying to be okay with not having everything figured out" stage,' I admitted.

Actually, I was very firmly at the 'trying really hard not to completely fall apart' stage but I kept that to myself.

Big Jim looked at me, and for a moment I could have sworn that those big blue eyes saw straight into my heart, because he touched my shoulder and said, 'Well, that's a road worth driving, hon. Mind you pay attention to the signs, it'll get you there.'

I half laughed, half swallowed back the tears. I was getting life advice from a real ageing hippie. James would have *loved* that.

I listened to their next set, and tried a cocktail called Pineapple Lady, and another called Ring a Rosé, knowing I'd probably regret it in the morning. It was after 2 a.m. when I got home, driven by Big Jim in a beat-up Nissan Micra, my rental bicycle in the boot. He gave my arm a punch and said, 'You're gonna be just fine, kiddo,' before I stumbled out into the night.

When I got into bed, though, I thought of what Big Jim had said, about not ignoring the signs on the road.

I sighed, and picked up James's letter again. It wasn't just a sign, it was a roadmap. 'I'll go and try to find her tomorrow,' I told the urn. 'And I'm working on the other part too, okay? Tonight *was* fun.'

Just in case he was listening.

SEVEN

I twisted James's ring on my thumb as I walked. My fingers grazed the interlocking pattern of shiny and smooth zigzags that I'd designed with a tiny diamond in the centre, over twenty years ago now. I had got into the habit of twisting it whenever I was feeling particularly nervous.

For all my promises to James last night, it was midday before I went in search of my grandmother Alba's sister, Maria de Palma.

I'd got a map book from Francisco at the shop, and had decided to see where Maria lived. What was the harm in introducing myself? She would either welcome me or she wouldn't. I could deal with that. What else did I have to do besides clean and think of James?

I rode my rental bicycle for forty minutes, pausing often to sip water as I passed through untouched countryside dotted here and there with small white houses alongside sandy roads, basking in the warm Spanish sun. The scent of wild rosemary was strong in the air, along with the briny scent of the ocean, today a calm clear turquoise that was dazzling against the ribbons of soft, white beaches as I pedalled, a cool breeze for company.

It took me the better part of an hour to find where she lived.

It was a villa with faded blue shutters, much like my own, surrounded by dry farmland. The house was in the familiar cubic design of many of the houses here, one that allowed for the dwelling to spread out over the years as the family grew. In front of the old house, a wooden pergola was strung with vines. The grapes, a rich plum colour, glinted in the sun. I could see beneath their purple haze that the house was cool and dark. Houses like these were designed for the heat and the wind, and I knew that, just as with Marisal, this one's thick stone would keep the house cool even on a hot day like this.

A boy with dark tousled hair, nut-brown eyes and an impish grin was playing in the front garden. He was chasing toy cars in the red-brown sand, making a 'vroom' noise that made me grin. When he saw me he started speaking in rapid Catalan, and when I responded in a muttered mix of broken, beginner's Spanish and English that I didn't understand, he only shrugged and carried on playing.

A noise made me look up. I saw an old, wizened wisp of a woman, with dark, amber-like skin and greying brown hair, wearing a dress that looked like a faded black tent. Her bent hands were knotty with arthritis, and they hugged her arms beneath her shelf-like bosom.

She stared at me for some time, her head to the side, waiting for me to speak.

I stood next to my bike and smoothed my hair nervously, clearing my throat, not knowing how to introduce myself now that I was here. I'd brought no proof, and it seemed somewhat presumptuous of me to have just turned up on her door, now that I thought about it properly. Perhaps I should have tried calling first? All of this ran through my head in a matter of seconds while I stood there, my mouth slightly open, no words coming out, my hands twisting and turning James's wedding ring.

A group of children ran past, about six or seven years old, and called out to the boy, who chased after them. They laughed and screamed and created a tangle of tanned limbs, leaving behind a cloud of reddish dust in their wake.

When the dust began to settle I moved nearer to the woman, and she uncrossed her arms and frowned, saying something in Catalan.

I apologised. 'I'm sorry, I don't speak the language,' I said, wincing.

She nodded, her eyes dark and appraising. Few could speak the local dialect here, and most of the locals were used to the tourists.

I hesitated. 'Are you Maria? Maria de Palma?'

She nodded, and then frowned, her eyes wary. 'I am.' Though it sounded more like '*I yam*'. Then she gave me an expectant look that caught me a little off guard.

'I'm Charlotte, Charlotte Woolf, though, um, my maiden name was Alvarez.'

She stared at me for some time, then she snorted and looked up at the sky, then back at me, as if she was berating God for playing some bad joke on her. Her eyes though warmed considerably. 'You're Alba's child?'

I shook my head, no. 'Her granddaughter.'

She hit her forehead, nodding her grey head. 'Too young, of course, to be the child.' Her dark eyes were appraising me. Noting perhaps my red-brown Alvarez hair, my dark green eyes. 'I was wondering when you'd come.'

Then she turned round and walked back inside. I stood, rooted to the spot. Did she want me to follow? Or had I been, somehow, summarily dismissed? Was she perhaps enacting some grievance upon me that she'd harboured for my grandmother? Had I come all this way only to have the door slammed in my face?

'Uh, Maria?' I called after her, hoping that the latter wasn't the case.

She turned back, pausing in the doorway.

'You coming in? Or do you want to stand there all day in the hot sun trying to decide?'

EIGHT

I made my way inside the cool interior, where the scents of furniture polish, lemon and the tart tang of tomatoes meeting a buttered pan greeted me. I was inside a large old-fashioned, farm-style kitchen. There were heavy wooden shelves where cups and plates sat in a colourful helter-skelter of a display. Herbs were drying on the windowsill and there was a rotund grey cat asleep on the flagstone floor, in a hazy ribbon of sunshine.

'Take a seat,' said Maria, pulling out a slim-backed wooden chair and giving it a pat with her brown paw.

Her English was impeccable. Somehow, looking at her I wouldn't have expected that. She seemed so traditional. I supposed that looks could be deceptive.

I hesitated, but then she smiled. It was the kind of smile that did wonders, transforming lines that had settled around the eyes and the mouth, till you saw the person underneath. I couldn't help feeling a little relieved.

She shook her head as she looked at me in wonder. 'You look a little like her, you know that?'

I nodded. People had been telling me that I looked like my grandmother all my life. Same hair, same eyes. Same freckles across the nose and, despite my Catalan roots, same pale, prone-to-burning skin.

'You thought that I'd come?'

She nodded. 'After that man came round, I suspected.'

I frowned. 'A man?'

'Snooping… asking questions about me, the family. Soon after he came I heard that the old house had been bought and, well, I wondered… I suppose I hoped, really.' She shook her head, and muttered, '*Ai carai*, after all these years. You can't kill hope, eh?'

I smiled. 'No, you can't.'

Maria took a seat next to me. In front of her was a bowl of potatoes, and she pulled it towards her and started peeling them.

'You stay for lunch.'

It wasn't a question, but I nodded anyway, hiding a grin. My grandmother had been the same.

'Good. That's good.'

I watched her as she peeled the potatoes, noting the black streaks threading through her grey hair, remembering what my grandmother had said – that there *had* been an Alvarez woman with dark hair – but she'd made out like this was many years ago… was her sister the woman she'd been referring to?

There was something in the way she held herself, though, an expression in her eyes, the tilt of her head and the shape of her mouth, that reminded me of my grandmother. It was at once strange, sweet and sad, this connection I had never known existed.

Maria looked at me now, and seemed to steel herself. 'She's dead, yes?'

I swallowed and nodded. She bit her lip and I saw her eyes fill. She took the corner of her apron and dabbed her eyes. Her shoulders shook, and she drew in a deep, shuddering breath. Then she looked up at the ceiling.

I didn't know what to say.

'I'm sorry.'

She nodded, a tear slipping fast down her old, worn cheek. I felt terrible to have been the cause.

'I thought maybe… but yes, when I stopped hearing from her, I suppose I *knew*.'

I blinked. 'She kept in contact with you?'

She nodded. 'Yes, though not as often as I would have liked… but yes, sometimes over the years. After she arrived in England and met your grandfather, she sent a few letters.'

'She – well, she didn't say much about her life here,' I said, hesitating, not wanting to tell this woman that she'd never mentioned the existence of a sister to me at all. Had my father known? He'd died when I was in my late teens, so it wasn't like I could ask him. Perhaps he'd told my mother. I'd have to ask her – phone her. Though I didn't relish the idea. I hadn't told her where I was going – just that I was going away to Spain for a break, somewhere in the sun. I'd simply texted her, not wanting the third degree. She'd loved her mother-in-law deeply, so I wasn't sure if she'd approve of me digging up her old ghosts. Still, didn't we have a right to know our own family? Know where we'd come from?

Maria sighed, putting down her knife temporarily. 'I didn't think so. I think after what happened, well, she just wanted to forget about everything.'

'You mean after the war?'

She nodded. 'Yes, but not just that – she made a choice when she left, to leave it all behind. Something she said once makes me think of that now.'

'What do you mean?'

'It was about faith. A lot of the others gave up their faith, too, on the island, it wasn't just her – many of the other families did, too, you know? It's ironic, because we kept it secret for so long – some of the children today don't even know… some people, when you ask them why they are doing a certain thing, like why they pray the way they do, why they sweep the floor away from the house, or why they always light candles on a Friday night, they just say, "Well, it's what my family always did", they don't *know*, which is to me the saddest part because in the end, when you forget, when you give up on being who you are – well, that's when they win, you see.'

I stared at her. Something inside seemed to halt at her words. But I didn't understand any of it. 'Give up what?'

Her eyes widened, and she shook her head in disbelief as if, somehow, my words confirmed her worst thoughts. 'Did she never tell you about it – about us?'

I frowned. 'Well, she told us a bit. Always reluctantly though. She told me that she used to live here – that all the family had, for many years – even back before the Spanish Civil War, she said, the Alvarez family lived on this island for several generations, but that can't really be true, can it? I mean, well...'

She gave me a slow nod.

I nodded. 'Exactly – I mean, even in the guidebooks they say that the island was uninhabited for a long time, that it was prone to piracy and the shores were dangerous and it was poor, so no one lived here at one time.'

'Well. They're half wrong. There was a period of abandonment, yes – but it wasn't for as long as people think.'

'How could the guidebooks be wrong?'

What was she telling me? I couldn't help fearing that perhaps I'd made a mistake. Maybe she was some mad conspiracy theorist. Perhaps there had been some other reason my grandmother had chosen to disown her sister. Perhaps this was it.

'Because not everyone knew the truth, you see, especially the government. There was a time, during the early eighteenth century, when it wasn't actually abandoned, when a few families came over from Majorca to live here in secret. Including ours. Nowadays it is like people have erased it from history, from existence – many people helped to do it. But you can't bury everything, oh no, especially not memories, and sometimes if you're lucky memory can get a little help, too.'

She got up and went to a chest of drawers across from the table, coming back with a big black album. In it was a scroll, written in a different alphabet. I stared at it in puzzlement.

'You know what this is?' she asked.

I shook my head.

'It's a Hebrew scroll, rare and precious, and at one point dangerous to own. It alone would have been proof that could have been used against our family during the Inquisition, if they'd known about it. The family used to keep this one in the cellar in an old stove,' she said, with a small sad laugh as she remembered. 'There were others too then, but this is one of the last that survived. Back then, during the Inquisition, if someone had found this – well, it would have been enough, you know.'

'Enough?'

She looked at me. 'To prove who we really were.'

I frowned.

'Who you really were?'

'*Chuetas. Marranos. Conversos,*' she said. She raised her eyebrows at my blank stare, then she whispered, even now, after all these years, 'We were Jews… secret Jews.'

NINE

'Secret Jews. Here on Formentera? I don't understand. They…
we're *Jewish?*' I blinked in surprise. 'How is that possible? How
could I not have known about this?'

It was no small matter – an entire faith, culture and identity.
How could my grandmother never have mentioned it? I shook
my head. It wasn't possible. I remembered her attending mass,
the rosary beads she always kept. How she would often besiege
the saints when Allan and I pushed her to the limit.

'But my grandmother was Catholic,' I said, shaking my head.

She laughed, '*Ai carai*. Aren't we all?'

At my shocked look she continued. 'After the Inquisition,
thousands of people were forced to convert to Christianity, to
Catholicism. Eventually they were given a choice: convert or
leave. Many left, those who couldn't stayed. What they didn't
tell you is that those who stayed were punished for it, and were
never treated the same. The history books will tell you that in
the Balearics, the history of the Jews was all the same. Genocide.
Torture. Ridicule. It relied mainly on the events of Majorca,
which is where our family originated. There, it's true, there was
untold suffering and persecution – but that wasn't the case on
the islands of Ibiza and Formentera.'

'They came here, you mean – our family, Jews?'

She nodded. 'They left during a particularly bad uprising in
Majorca in the late seventeenth century. There were a few other

families who came here, too, to resettle. They had heard that the islanders here were more tolerant, and not so ready to pry. Formentera was mainly deserted, and so they came secretly and resettled the area.

'It was a good choice for them. Of course, they had to be careful. In fact, I'd say the only time they were truly in danger of being found out – which would have meant torture, imprisonment or death – was in the early eighteenth century.'

I tried to take this in. My family came from a line of secret Jews who'd made their home on the island, and who to this day very few people knew about? How was that even possible?

'No one knows that Jews were living here – even now?'

'Oh, some *know*, of course, it's just not advertised. I suppose because a lot of the families left after Franco's horrible war, and then the salt trade mostly collapsed and people left after that – it was look for work elsewhere or starve. But they say that many of the local inhabitants of Ibiza and Formentera can trace their roots back to a Jewish heritage. The islands were given a choice during the Inquisition – they could give up the names of the Jews living here, they could even do so anonymously… but they never did.'

I gaped at her, trying to imagine that. Not a single soul betraying them?

'It's true. They protected them. Here you were an islander no matter what your faith. You were one of them.

'I can you tell you about it if you like – about what life was like then. I think in a way that's where we should start if you'd like to understand why Alba never told you about her life here – so you can understand who we were first. Would you like that?'

I nodded. 'Very much.'

Her dark eyes softened. 'It's important to tell the young about the past, before it's forgotten.'

I couldn't help but agree. It had pained me that much of my family history was lost after my grandmother's death, and this was a chance now for me to understand – and perhaps to understand my grandmother more, something I'd been trying to do ever since I was a young girl, when all I encountered were heavy silences and a wooden chest filled with memories she wouldn't share.

Maria got up to turn the heat down low, adding in fish and carrots and red and green peppers to the buttery tomato mix, tucking a strand of black and grey hair behind an ear.

'I heard the stories from my own mother and hers before her. I think they stayed with me so much because I looked so much like the woman they said had risked it all.'

I frowned, remembering something my grandmother had said. 'Someone with dark hair? My grandmother said that she brought shame on the family… though she wouldn't go any further no matter how much I pressed.'

Maria nodded. 'Yes. Well I suppose that was because to her it was a repeat of what happened between us.'

I stared at Maria, blinking, and she shook her head. 'I'll tell you about that later. Maybe.'

I hoped she would. I couldn't come this far and not know why my grandmother had left it all behind, why she'd never mentioned that she had a sister at all.

It felt strange and oddly full circle to be sitting here in my grand-mother's sister's kitchen with the scent of her seafood stew bubbling, and outside the sounds of children playing, hearing, at last, the sorts of things I'd tried so hard to discover from my grandmother as a child.

'She told you that all Alvarez people had red hair and green eyes, and skin that was pale?'

I nodded, then smiled. 'Except for one, who was dark and very beautiful. She was a bit of a black sheep, or at least that's what I'd thought… the way that she spoke of her.'

'Well, it was because of her – and the man she fell in love with, Benito Nuñez – that we were almost discovered. It threatened to expose the community that had lived here peacefully for over a hundred years, without the authorities being any the wiser. At the heart of that story were two sisters.

'My mother used to say that in some ways we were like them, Alba and I. As different as night from day. From our colouring to our temperaments. But the truth is, like with our own brother, who cost us the family home when he gambled it away – which is a story I will tell you too, another day perhaps – it was their brother who put them in the predicament that was to shape the rest of our lives. I think that is where we should begin.'

TEN

Formentera, 1718

There were rumours of a stranger on the island.

The young woman's dark eyes darted behind her, scanning the coastline as she ran silently over flat scrubland to the old church where her mother was waiting. Her feet in their soft leather shoes barely made a sound. She'd learned to be silent very young, and very fast.

Strangers meant one thing on this small, often forgotten Spanish island.

Caution.

She could see it in the eyes of everyone she'd passed that morning. The subtle shifts that only an islander would know.

The carefully visible addition of rosary beads peeking out of a pocket, and the sudden appearance of simple crosses tacked to the doors of the small white houses that dotted the landscape like sugar cubes.

'Remember,' whispered an old man wearing the traditional garb that most men reserved for special occasions, white trousers with a wide belt sporting a knife, a red hat and a black jerkin. He didn't look up as she passed, just sat outside his home, carving a small wooden flute. He put it to his lips to test the sound, and she heard the haunting melody as she ran. She hadn't responded to him. It wasn't as if anyone could ever forget.

Her mother was waiting by the church door, her mouth pressed into a firm, anxious line, her hand making a peak over her eyes as she peered into the early-morning sun to better see her. Her eyes showed relief when she did. Once she was safely inside, the girl helped her bolt the door.

'Did anyone see you?' she asked, bringing the kerchief she wore on her head lower down her forehead. Her hair, like that of many of the women on the island, was worn in a long plait down her back.

The young woman shook her head. She didn't mention the old man – that wasn't who her mother meant. She saw the addition of the cross to the *gonella* her mother wore, the gold necklace that ran in over eighteen ropes from shoulder to shoulder, but said nothing about the addition. Her mother's dark eyes softened. 'Good. Come. They are waiting for us inside – it might not be what we fear.'

Despite her words, the young woman could see how her mother's mouth tightened.

As the young woman hurried after her, her gaze took in the rows of empty pews as they rushed towards another door in the wall ahead, almost concealed by the panelled wood. Her fingers found the secret groove, and she lifted the panel to reveal stairs to the basement and the small room where the others were gathered. At the entrance was a box full of discarded rosary beads. Her mother laid hers on top, ready for her to pick up when she left, like a mask.

Together they went and sat on a bench next to the other women. The men were seated to the right.

Where the young woman sat there was a crude carving of a pointed star lightly scarring the old wood. A Magen David, she knew. One of the few words she'd collected over time, words that were forbidden and could only ever be whispered down here where it was safe, where no one could hear. She wondered at who had dared to draw it. Her fingers traced the raised edges as a short man up at the front smiled his welcome. A handkerchief was placed over the back of his head, and as he turned back to the rest of the community his face resumed its worried expression.

There was no admonishment of their lateness, not from him or any of the others. They understood. Caution trumped everything here.

Because here in this room, where above their heads sat the empty church with its rows of wooden pews for some phantom congregation that never would materialise, lay the truth, the secret at the heart of the building – it wasn't a church at all. It was a synagogue.

ELEVEN

The Mediterranean Sea, 1718

The island pirates hid themselves not in coves or in tempests, but in plain sight. The capture of the Moorish sloop vessel was over before they had a chance to load their guns. They hadn't seen the pirates coming in the summer haze until it was too late. It was an old island trick, one they played very well.

They raided the sloop in minutes, carrying their bounty on board to the gleeful shouts of the bloodthirsty crew. A human bounty that consisted of two prisoners from Majorca, who'd long been on the run and smelt of sick and defeat, the kind of defeat that crumpled men, and conquered souls.

The prisoners were traitors to the crown, their country and the religion they'd sworn their allegiance to.

They were *chuetas*.

A word that on the Spanish mainland caused many to gasp and make the sign of the cross. It was a word for swine, a word for a faith-breaker. A word for a secret Jew.

The prisoners were the reason the pirates had decided to change course and go after the Moorish ship in the first place. The reason they decided to risk discovery with the *Invictus*, one of the Mediterranean salt route's most recognisable ships, and to raise their secret pirate flag, one that could have them put to death if discovered. But the risk was worth it, everyone agreed.

The *chuetas'* ransom would fetch a heavy price, one the Holy Office would gladly pay for such wanted criminals.

But there wasn't a single man aboard who would consider taking the money or handing them over.

Because *chueta* meant only one thing aboard this ship. It meant *brother*.

Antoni had become captain of the *Invictus* in the spring. And, in a moment that was true to form for the young, handsome sailor whose impetuous nature had been a source of both delight and worry to those who loved him best, his first voyage began with him risking the lives of every member of his crew.

They'd traded their cargo of red salt and were due to set sail for Genoa with the rest when he'd heard about the Moorish sloop and its cargo of Majorcan *chuetas* and decided to change course to go after them.

Antoni had learned how to be a sailor from his father. 'Out here, on the high seas, a man can be free,' he always used to say, his dark eyes solemn, his face weather-beaten, and proud. Freedom was something every Ibicenco – the name given to people who came from the islands of Ibiza and Formentera – valued more than gold.

Freedom was why Antoni's father had become a sailor in the first place. He hadn't had an easy life and, unlike some of the crew, who were the sons and uncles of some of Ibiza's most distinguished leaders, important officials of the salt trade, Antoni's father had started out poor. His first job had been mining the salt pans. Under the harsh sun for months on end, he'd work the white gold that had shaped the island in back-breaking shifts, twelve hours a day. There were no days off, and his father said that he never got used to the painful red eyes and the salt-dried skin that burned with every step. His back would never recover either, and he suffered especially on cold days. As soon as he'd heard that a local ship needed a crew and were willing to take untrained swabs, he volunteered, making a mad stab at freedom. He'd work all day and all night on the deck of the ship, scrubbing, if it meant that he didn't have to work the salt pans any more.

It was the best decision he ever made. He'd worked his way up through the ranks to rigger, and fast. It wasn't long after this that he climbed his way to first mate and, finally, captain, shortly before he died in the Spanish War of Succession, which put the present King, Philip V, on the throne. Antoni was glad in some ways his father never saw this occur – it meant that the salt trade was now no longer under the islanders' control.

Antoni liked to think that, had his father heard that there were Majorcan Jews on board, he would have gone after the Moorish ship, too. After all, they had been Majorcan Jews themselves, once, many years before.

Now, three weeks later, Antoni was making a promise to a dying man. A promise that wouldn't just affect his crew but his family as well, as it was them who would have to pay the price.

That's the trouble with freedom, it always comes with a cost.

'Promise me,' said Paulo, his feverish eyes locking on to Antoni's own. Antoni nodded. The two men had struck up a friendship soon after the prisoners realised their good fortune in being rescued by the Ibicenco traders masquerading as pirates. But now, despite the crew's best efforts, Paulo was about to die, and if Antoni didn't help, Paulo's brother might die as well. Antoni had to get him off the boat to the only person he knew could save his life. His sister, Cesca, who'd trained as a nurse with the island doctor. The trouble was that if he took the prisoner to her, he'd be risking her life in the process – and all of his family's.

But he'd given his word to Paulo, as the man lay dying, that he'd keep his brother safe no matter what it cost. So Antoni made the promise, because he believed, the way his father had before him, that freedom was something worth dying for.

TWELVE

Formentera, 1718

The cold wind skipped over the flat rocks, where it picked up the scent of rosemary and salt and spread its slithery fingers down the small patch of skin that exposed her neck, making her shiver as she walked close to her mother's side.

Cesca crooked her arm inside her mother's and they leant against each other for warmth, the sea thundering in their ears. As they neared the house, Cesca saw the light beneath the door and paused. Her mother turned to her, her body stiffening, her dark eyes mirroring the fear in Cesca's own.

The house was cold, and there was a rank smell that hit her nostrils as she stepped inside, like death, and misery. A man sat in the shadows of the kitchen, slumped forward in a chair. A lantern was burning low on the table before him.

He startled when he heard the door, raising tired, wary eyes. Cesca sighed in relief as recognition bloomed. It was Antoni, her brother.

She closed the door behind her, and their mother rushed forward to embrace him. He closed his eyes as they hugged, taking a moment of comfort in what had been a long and dangerous voyage. He'd had to load the feverish passenger into the rowing boat from Ibiza by himself, and he'd paddled for most of the night to reach Formentera, travelling by darkness to ensure that no one saw him. It had cost him his last bit of strength to get to their house unseen.

'I've done something... something perhaps foolish. Forgive me.' He looked exhausted, but his face was anxious and it made her nervous.

Cesca frowned. It was only then that she saw the other man lying on a pallet on the floor. This was where the rank smell was coming from, she realised. The man's body was starved, his clothes filthy and worn, his long hair bedraggled and matted with dried blood. His eyes were glazed, and he mumbled feverishly.

'My God, what happened?' she breathed, stepping forward to see the stranger better. She closed her mind to the stench and listened to his heart and lungs, the way Señor Garcia had shown her all those years before when she'd first become the doctor's apprentice at the age of eleven, when his wife had died and her father had volunteered her for the role of his assistant, much to everyone's surprise. She put her head to his chest, listening to his ragged breathing.

Her mother seemed to have grasped the danger they were in better than Cesca though, understood what bringing a stranger here to this island meant. What it could end up costing them.

'Antoni,' she breathed. Her hand gripped his shoulder and she looked unsteady on her feet. 'What have you done?'

Her brother's eyes closed in stark acknowledgement of all that he was asking of them.

'Did anyone see you?'

'See you?' asked Cesca, failing to understand her mother's concerns as she felt the man's pulse. Antoni had brought injured animals and friends home for her to care for many times in the past, so why was this such a concern to them both now? She assumed he was simply one of his brother's crew, someone they hadn't met from the big island. She didn't stop to wonder why he hadn't called for a doctor there. Her first interest was her patient.

She could ask those questions later, but for now they were wasting valuable time. 'I think we'd better fetch Señor Garcia. This man's sunk into a fever and the doctor might have something stronger to help lift it – my supplies are a bit low. *Mare*, will you go?' she asked her mother, casting an eye around the small farm kitchen to where a new collection of herbs was drying, towards a small shelf that held small ceramic jars full of the tinctures and cures she used most frequently. Over the years, she'd built up a small medicine chest that had been bolstered through Antoni's travels across the seas – each voyage he returned with new things she'd asked for on a list. But the severity of this man's starved and feverish state called for a more experienced hand.

Antoni shook his head. 'Francesca, we can't call him, not yet – not until you understand. I must explain.'

Cesca looked up, away from the sick man, with a frown and pushed back a thread of auburn hair that had fallen across her forehead into her kerchief.

'Explain what?'

'The Inquisitors were going to kill him if they got hold of him. There was nothing else I could do.'

Cesca still looked puzzled, so her mother made an impatient sound. 'He's a runaway, Cesca,' she said, explaining. 'A *marrano*, correct?' she said, looking for confirmation at her son, who simply nodded. *Marrano* was another name for secret Jew, like them.

Cesca gasped. 'From where?'

'Majorca, though his brother was born in Bayonne, I gather. They were fleeing investigation.'

Investigation often meant prison or torture or, worse, death, they knew.

'His brother?'

Antoni explained about the capture, about what his crew and he had done to save them. The promise he'd made to a dying man. 'I have to go back tomorrow, to avoid having anyone come looking here, but I had to bring him here, to you – I think you could save him, Cesca. You're the only one I can trust with this. Could you help him?'

She swallowed, grasped her brother's hand. 'I'll try.'

Their mother hadn't said a word. Antoni looked at her again. He flexed his jaw, didn't drop his gaze. 'I didn't have a choice.'

Cesca nodded. 'No,' she said. 'You didn't.'

'But…' said their mother, her eyes large, and dark with fear.

She knew the stories about the people from the Holy Office, the ones who came in the dead of the night, sniffing out the truth – the Inquisitors. How people said that they had rubber wheels fitted to their carriages so they could come silently in the dead of the night. How they took away the girls. Always the girls… And how they tortured them, how they got them to speak. She feared for her daughters.

Cesca shared those fears, but she touched her mother's arm. 'We can do this, we can protect him, like the islanders protected us.' She meant the islanders who had taken in the bands of Majorcan refugees who'd escaped to this island, like her grandfather and grandmother some fifty years before. She raised her chin as a thought occurred to her. 'He's our cousin. *That's* what we'll say if anyone asks.'

Brother and sister obviously shared the same thought.

'Rafael,' concurred Antoni. 'I'll speak to *Tio* Alfonso when I return to Ibiza, before we set sail.'

Their cousin Rafael, from Ibiza, had just passed away. No one knew about it yet – perhaps no one ever would, if this man took his place.

'I don't like it,' said Esperanza, her younger sister, when she came home later that morning. Her dark eyes were full of mistrust.

The trouble was, she'd said it three times already and it was wearing Cesca's already frayed nerves. She took a breath, and explained. Again.

'He was a prisoner who was about to be handed over to the Inquisitors. They might have killed him otherwise. Is that what you want?'

Esperanza's dark eyes were unchangeable. 'I understand that, I'm not some monster, Cesca. But should we go to prison for him? For some strange *chueta*?'

'Esperanza,' admonished Cesca, darting a look at the man they'd moved closer to the fire.

Chueta was a dirty word. It meant swine. 'He's one of *us*.'

They were *chueta* too, only no one called them that here, because here, on the island of Formentera, they were free, because their family had escaped. They'd made a pact with some of their best friends from Majorca in the dead of night, many years before, to flee here. He was just like them, apart from the passage of time.

Esperanza scoffed. 'No, he's not. He's a peasant runaway. That was years ago now and we brought something to the island – workers, people willing to work the salt pans. We brought food, clothes, money – he's here with nothing and putting us in danger, threatening to expose us all. He should have just converted to Christianity properly. I would have if I lived there.'

Cesca looked at her sister in bemusement.

'Why? Why should you be forced to give up your faith and your culture just because of someone else's beliefs?'

'We did, didn't we – or else why would the whole island be sporting new crucifixes and telling each other to play the part simply because some stranger from mainland Spain has come here?'

News that a stranger from Barcelona had come to the island had set everyone's nerves on edge. No one knew what he was really doing here and very few bought the story that he was here to study the flora and fauna, which is what the stranger had told some of the elders.

Most thought he had been sent as an emissary from the Holy Office to check that there were no people practising the laws of Moses here. The Holy Office seemed to do that every so often, usually about once a decade, when they remembered – it was good to be seen to do your job, which was to excise any last remaining Jews. The Inquisitors had come before, and they'd left without finding any evidence. The islanders had made sure of it.

Cesca stared at her sister now in disbelief. 'That's different. We have to play the part when we are asked. It's part of our protection.'

'Protection or imprisonment?'

'*Protection*. You're a fool,' Spranza. Here we get to be ourselves, because the other islanders have been tolerant – the only difference between the prisoner in our care and us is that he wasn't lucky enough to live here from the start.'

Esperanza's dark eyes widened with disbelief. 'Lucky? To live here?'

'*Yes.*'

'A poor island in the middle of nowhere that most people are surprised isn't completely abandoned, where no one comes to visit except for barbarian pirates? Where hardly anything grows except salt and a few straggly herbs?'

Cesca shook her head. Her sister just didn't get it. It was tough here, and poor, it was true, but they did better than most. Their *finca* had figs, olives, oranges, lemons, hens and a goat, and with their brother as captain of a ship belonging to the Rimbauds, key officials of the main island, Ibiza, they were doing better than most.

'We're free here, and that's what counts.'

Esperanza scoffed. 'You think so when we can't ever leave. And we can't ever truly be who we really are. That's not freedom, Cesca. That's *prison*.'

*

Antoni left the next day at dawn, taking the small boat back to Ibiza, to his uncle's house. Cesca watched him leave. She'd got up before dawn and followed him down to the beach. It was important that he went back, that he played the part. People were going to start looking for the man in their kitchen soon, and Antoni couldn't give them any reason to look on this island. Especially now that someone from mainland Spain was here, snooping around. It worried him that this was happening now. He hadn't known about the stranger when he'd thought of bringing Paulo's brother here to his sister's care, but it was too late now. They couldn't move him; they'd just have to hope that the stranger from Barcelona left as soon as possible, and that he never heard about the man they were hiding in their home.

He pushed the boat into the water, giving Cesca a last kiss on the cheek. They'd said everything they needed to say. It would be up to them now to keep it secret.

THIRTEEN

Formentera, present day

Maria's story was interrupted by the elfin-faced boy who'd been playing outside. He tore inside now with a gurgling laugh before launching into rapid Catalan while he tugged at her skirts. He was followed closely on his sandy heels by an army of six- or seven-year-olds, who, it appeared, were all demanding lunch.

Maria laughed even as she waved a finger at him for interrupting her tale. She introduced us and I found out that the imp's name was Ben, short for Benito.

I helped her to dish up the stew, marvelling at how different children were here compared to back home as they began attacking their bowls of seafood stew with gusto, blobs of fresh tomato sauce dribbling down their waggling chins. Most of the children I knew had a diet that ranged from fish fingers to sausages and chips. I still remembered the meltdowns Sage would have at that age when I ventured anything as exotic as un-crumbed chicken.

We didn't get a chance to discuss further what Maria had told me about my long-lost relatives, the names of whom swam in my mind: Cesca, Esperanza, Antoni… I didn't even know if the man they'd taken in, who they decided to pretend was their cousin, had survived. I had so many questions, but with a house full of interrupting children, I knew they would have to wait.

I was at once a stranger, yet family too, and I was treated as such. I found myself enjoying Maria's company, and my welcome into her lively home.

After lunch, I left, promising on Maria's request to come back the following afternoon. She promised me that she would tell me more.

As I cycled alongside the dry scrubland, the scent of wild rosemary, mixed with the briny scent of the ocean, filled my senses, perfuming my thoughts of the past.

My head swam with all that I had heard, as I tried to reconcile the stories Maria had told me with the knowledge that these people were part of my family, and that I had come from them.

I thought of the sea captain Antoni, and his brave sister Cesca. A nurse who had somehow learned everything from a local doctor? I couldn't help but admire her gumption. That couldn't have been easy in those times.

I would like to think that had I been in their place I would have reacted like them, taken in someone who needed me, but would I have? Or would I have reacted like the other sister, Esperanza?

'She was young, and she had a lot to learn, and you know those are the people who learn the hardest,' Maria had said when I'd interrupted her story to question how Esperanza couldn't have seen how fortunate she was during the Inquisition to have lived here. But I couldn't blame her exactly for not wanting that man in her home initially. Not really. Not if I were honest, and his being there could have meant that my family were put at risk. I couldn't be sure that I wouldn't have behaved just as she had. Would I have risked everything like Antoni and Cesca had, for a stranger?

I arrived home with a head full of questions and got stuck into cleaning the kitchen, all the while filling James's ashes in on what had happened.

'So, of course you know that you were right – there was a story there. I'm sure you're feeling very proud of yourself right about now.'

I looked at the urn and rolled my eyes as I went to the sink to wash out a rag covered in inky black dust. He was proud of himself, I could tell.

'It's incredible to think that it all happened here, in this house.'

I couldn't help wondering how different the villa was now than in the past, when Cesca and Esperanza were alive. I pictured the shelf full of herbs and tinctures. The family seated round a table. Not this one of course. I was quite sure nothing as hideous as this old, wonky Formica table had been around back then.

I made myself a cup of tea and decided to phone Sage. She'd want to hear about Maria, I knew.

I found reception at the bottom of the garden, and my daughter's incredulous voice came through strong on the crackling line.

We spent the first ten minutes chatting about her studies, and how she had thrown herself into her work, which I was glad about. Then I told her about the last couple of days, including meeting Maria.

She gasped. 'You're kidding, Mum?' said Sage as I relayed to her what Maria had told me about our family. Though it was difficult to convert it into a telephone conversation over a somewhat faulty mobile line. 'They were secret Jews?'

'Yeah,' I said, still trying hard to believe it myself. 'Well, that's what she says, anyway. She's been telling me a bit about it – about our past. It's pretty incredible actually.'

'Wow, that's really cool, I wish I was there with you! I thought it was great and everything about the house— well, no, I thought it was bonkers of Dad actually,' she said, with a laugh that I couldn't help echoing.

'But to find out that there's family still living on the island! That's insane. I can't believe he left you a letter like that and had done some digging into the past while he was stuck in hospital.'

There was a pause, and I could hear the catch in her voice. 'It's— God, it's so *Dad*. He really loved you.'

I sniffed, my fingers twisting the wedding band on my thumb, tracing over the small gem. 'Don't start, or I'll lose it, too.'

She made a funny little half sob, half laugh that tore at my heart, and then she sucked in a deep breath and said, 'Okay, you're right. So, what's she like? Does she look like us?'

'Actually, yes. She looks a bit like Gran, but she's got dark eyes, like you.'

'Wow. It's incredible to think that there's been this link here to that side of the family all this time, people living there with the same eyes, similar faces and chins… incredible. Sad too in a way.'

I knew what she meant – if James hadn't bought this house, hadn't set me on this path, I'd never have met her. I would never have even known that she existed. The secret would have just died with my grandmother.

'So, what does that mean for you now that you've found her? You can't just come home in a few days like you planned, can you? I mean she's old, isn't she?'

I blinked, taking her words in. I stared back at the house, almost looking at it differently as a result. I hadn't considered that far really.

'Must be well into her nineties, but she seems incredibly healthy and spry,' I said.

'But still…' she pushed.

I closed my eyes. Sage had a point. A woman in her nineties couldn't be around for ever. I wouldn't get this time back – I had to make the most of the time she had left. I understood that now more than anyone. I hadn't been planning on extending my trip longer than the week. 'You're right, I can't just leave now, can I?'

'Yeah, exactly, you can't,' echoed my daughter. 'Anyway this will be good, Mum. At least I'll know you're getting out and stuff. I have my studies, so you don't need to worry about me, and Uncle Allan can check in on things at home, and Gran, I'm sure.'

They'd been round to the house to water plants and that sort of thing while I was away, and it was true, they wouldn't mind carrying on for a while, till I came back. But how long would that be?

'So, you really think I should stay on a bit longer?' I asked, my eye falling on the villa, with a frown. *Could* I stay here longer?

'I do, Mum. I think this will be good for you. Tell you what, get my room ready, maybe I can come over for a long weekend at some point soon. Well, not *soon* soon, because I am the idiot who decided to study medicine, instead of what all the cool kids are doing, so I'm pretty much going to be studying for ever, but when I get a gap, you're *it*.'

I grinned. 'Okay, you've got a deal. And you know, love, I think you're cool.'

'You're my mum, you have to think that.'

'I'd think that even if I wasn't.'

'You have to say that too.'

I laughed. 'Well. Anyway, I'm proud of you, you're working so hard.'

'Thanks Mum, and you know, Dad's right, don't resist this.'

I sighed. I was getting it from both ends now.

I walked back inside the house and put on the kettle again. By the time I'd made myself another cup of tea, I had made my decision.

'Okay,' I told James. 'I'll stay for a bit longer, all right?'

I'd use this time to recover, to find out about my family and perhaps to start writing the novel I'd promised my editor a year ago. If Sage could find the will to work so hard at her studies, I could do this, too. They say the old have a lot to teach the young, but it's often the other way round as well. I felt something ease inside of me at the decision to stay a bit longer, to find out more about my family and get to know Maria. I hadn't realised just how much I'd been in limbo till I made up my mind to stay.

It was early evening when I heard a knock on the door. I'd been using the back of a napkin from a nearby pizzeria to sketch out some ideas for a story, and chatting aloud to James's ashes about it.

I hadn't brought my laptop with me, as I hadn't really thought that after a decade of not writing I would decide to write now, and was making a mental note to go and buy a notebook as soon as I could when the knocking interrupted me.

I paused in the hallway, wondering if the estate agent had come back. My heart started beating at the thought of another letter from James.

I opened the door with a degree of trepidation, only to stare in surprise when I found Big Jim standing outside, with his long grey ponytail hanging over a shoulder. He was wearing round, sixties-style glasses, faded denim blue jeans and another tie-dyed shirt that strained across his ample belly.

'B— er Jim, hi,' I said, opening the door, hesitating to call him Big Jim. While I'd enjoyed meeting him and spending time with Sue and Isla the other night at the Blues Bar, I wasn't sure if I'd earned the privilege of the moniker just yet.

'Good evening, Miss Charlotte,' he said, taking off his glasses and bowing like an old-fashioned gentleman. There was a twinkle in his cornflower-blue eyes.

I laughed.

'I've come bearing gifts,' he said.

'Oh?' I said in surprise.

'Yep,' he replied, then went to his beaten-up Nissan and took out a bicycle from the boot. 'I know you're fond of your rental – the one I sort of dented when I crammed it in the back of my boot the other night, sorry! But' – he gave me a somewhat bashful, though boyish, grin for his sixty-plus face – 'I had this lying around my garage taking up space and I thought maybe you could put it to good use, save you those rental fees at any rate. What do you say? Why not see it as part of that new road you're on?'

'Jim! That's so kind, thank you,' I gasped, staring at the bicycle in shock. 'It's kind of strange, perfect timing really – I've just decided to stay on the island a bit longer than I originally intended.'

'Ah,' he said tapping his nose. 'Something told me that might be the case.'

'Really?'

'Nah, had no idea! Had no idea you were originally intending it to be a short stay, not when you mentioned that you'd recently bought a house here.'

I laughed. That made sense.

It was an old mountain bike, with thick tyres and a navy frame, and an impressive set of gears that I knew would make getting around a lot easier than the heavy rental bike I had been using. 'But why give me the bike? I mean, not to sound ungrateful or anything, it's just you hardly know me.'

He rocked on his heels, swinging his ponytail over his shoulder. 'That's what we do here – look out for each other. Also, you know, it's sort of nice just to be called Jim for once…'

I frowned. 'What do you mean?' I asked, genuinely perplexed.

'You've never called me "Big Jim". It's not that I mind the nickname, but you know sometimes I'd like for people not to greet me by first sizing me up. I'm kinda more than just "a big guy", ya know?'

My eyes widened, and I nodded, feeling oddly touched. He was a bit of a gentle giant really.

'I know what you mean – my brother's called me Twig for most of my life. I mean, I don't mind it now, but it used to drive me bonkers…'

'Twig? You?'

I laughed, especially when he spluttered, his face reddening. 'Not that you're not thin… or nothing, I mean you are very, er, I'll stop now.'

'Don't worry.' I laughed again. 'I used to look a bit like a stick insect as a kid.'

I was thin now, I knew, but hardly twig-like, not with my hips, alas. Something childbearing had given and never taken back.

He grinned. 'Sibling love, can't beat it.'

'Yeah – though he's great, Allan. You'd like him.'

It was probably true, even if they were about as alike as oil and water.

'Would you like a coffee?' I offered.

He shrugged. 'Won't say no,' he said and followed me inside to the kitchen, where I put the kettle on and fetched two of the four mugs I currently owned, quickly taking James's urn and putting it into a cupboard, whispering a quick sorry under my breath that I had to put him away. Though it wasn't as if Jim would know that the urn held my husband's ashes, I thought. Still I didn't want to have to explain *that*.

Jim brought the bike inside and leant it up against the wall in the hallway.

'Thanks so much for the bike. I could pay you for it?' I offered.

He shook his head. 'Like I said, we weren't using it. Actually it was Sue's idea – it was her bike, but she's got a scooter now.'

I grinned. 'I like Sue.'

'Feeling's mutual. You know she's read all your books.'

I blushed. 'Really?'

'Yeah, she went online and bought them when she heard you were *that* Charlotte Woolf. Thinks you're pretty great.'

I looked down, blushing. The truth was that I hadn't been *that* Charlotte Woolf for a long time. I hadn't written anything for years. I'd written a few novels that had done okay in the nineties, but my last book had been rather poorly received, and as a result I'd decided to take a break. *For ten years.*

For most of the last decade I'd been a writer more in theory than anything else. What I had been really was a housewife. A role that had pretty much become defunct when Sage left home and James passed away. Was there such a thing as a housewidow? It was a depressing thought.

'I didn't know they were still in print,' I said, pouring the coffee from the cafetière that Escobar, the estate agent, had bought for me before I'd arrived.

'Yeah, she got them second-hand,' he admitted.

I laughed.

Before I could change my mind, I found myself asking, 'Jim – would you and Sue, and Isla, if she's free, like to come for dinner tomorrow night – if you don't have plans?'

'Plans? The last time I had plans they were still talking about knocking down the Berlin Wall. Sounds great. What can we bring? Sue will ask.'

'Just yourselves.'

'Okay, great. Sounds good to me. We can bring the wine though – got a friend who makes the best *costa* wine. That means coast. It looks a bit iffy – it's brown – but it tastes pretty good.'

'Really?'

'No, plonk really,' he said, laughing. 'But you gotta try it, man. It'll put hair on your chest.'

I giggled. 'Um, I don't really want that…'

'Yeah, okay, good point. But try it anyway.'

I grinned. 'Okay.'

Then I told him about my local shop owner, Francisco, and the wine he made. It turned out that wine-making was a bit of an institution here, just like olive oil production. There was something about the idea that appealed to me, even though for a housewife I wasn't all that domestic. More an undomestic goddess than anything else.

Jim looked around and said, 'So, this house – Isla told me it used to be in your family but you bought it again?'

I nodded, and then decided to just tell the truth. 'My husband bought it actually – as a surprise present – before he passed away.'

His eyes were huge. 'That's some surprise.'

'You're telling me. I'm still not sure what I think about it.'

'How did he go?'

I bit my lip. 'Cancer.'

One word that explained so much.

'I'm sorry, kiddo.'

I sucked in a deep breath, looked away. 'Thanks.'

'But the house used to belong to your family? How's that work? And how did he get it back?'

There was something likeable about Jim, something non-threatening, warm and a little endearing, and before I knew it I was telling him the whole sorry mess of it all.

I was halfway through the part about the first letter from James when he put up a hand and said. 'We need wine for this, girl, where's that bottle from your shop-friend?'

I grinned, tears in my eyes, and got up to fetch it, pouring it out into my last two coffee mugs, making a mental note to get some glasses tomorrow for my guests.

As Big Jim sipped on his mug of wine, he stared at me and shook his head. 'Well, I think it's pretty amazing. I knew there was a story there – sorry for saying so, but I saw it the other night. There was something in your eyes... man, it was a bit like some of the guys I grew up with, when they came back from 'Nam, their eyes looked like that – like they'd seen too much.'

He was talking about the Vietnam War and it felt odd to be compared to those poor souls, yet in a way I could understand why; I'd been through my own private war as well, though I hadn't realised that you could see it just by looking at me. I didn't love that thought, to be honest.

He squeezed my shoulder and poured us both some more wine. 'But you're going to get through this. I know you will.'

'Thanks, Jim,' I said, meaning it.

I liked his calm assurance. After he'd left, I took James's urn out of the cupboard and placed him back on the table. Then I looked at the bicycle Big Jim had left behind, thought of the fact that I'd promised to make Jim, Sue and Isla dinner the following night and almost laughed.

'Did I really I tell him I'd cook?' I asked the ashes in disbelief.

I wasn't a great cook. It was kind of a family joke. But I'd watched Maria make that stew this afternoon, and I figured maybe I'd give it a try for dinner tomorrow.

The meals I'd made in the past generally included macaroni cheese, spaghetti Bolognese, vegetable soup and reheated pizza... the things I made when James wasn't home or was ill, really. They were 'James's Day Off' meals. The home-style equivalent of going through a drive-through, just a bit healthier. They were perfectly edible, but compared to James's cooking they were not the sort of meals you'd like to have that often. They were the sort of meals no one ever asked for unless they were past starving and there wasn't a drive-through open.

You would have thought that, having a gran like mine, and with my Catalan roots, I would have learned from her, or that it was in my blood, but I hadn't and I'm not sure it really was. We hadn't lived that close to my grandparents growing up, as they were about forty-five minutes away in the Kent countryside, close to where my grandfather, Sam, had grown up. He was English, but he'd met Gran during the Spanish Civil War and whisked her away to England. When I was growing up they used to come over often for weekends, and we went down there too, but Allan and I were always far too interested in the garden or trawling through their old sea chest for old photos and other treasures to spend that much time in the kitchen. I regretted that now. You never know it's too late until it is. Before Gran died I used to fetch her for little outings, like trips to the seaside, museums and teashops. Maybe I should have spent more time with her at home; maybe then there would have been more chance for us to talk. Or perhaps I'd be a better cook. The only real cooking reference I'd had was my English mother, and her culinary expertise was about as broad as my own. Which is to say: not broad at all. Toast with jam mainly. With cheese if she was feeling wild. Dad had inherited Gran's passion for cooking, but after he died Allan and I were subjected to Mum's lack of passion in the kitchen.

I wondered if I could ask Maria for some tips tomorrow… it would be rather lovely to learn some family recipes from her. Things that had perhaps been passed down through the genera-tions? Things I could share with my own daughter. I smiled at myself. It was a first – looking forward to something. I hadn't felt this way in a very long time, but I was looking forward to getting to know Maria more. To finding out more about my family's past, and their present for that matter. I looked at James's ashes, and shook my head. 'I hope you're happy.'

FOURTEEN

Formentera, present day

Maria's house was filled once again with the sound of children's laughter and the scent of cooking. There were fresh-picked lemons from the trees in her garden sitting in a bowl, herbs that she'd picked just that morning chopped and waiting on a wooden board for the large *dorado* fish that she was going to cook in lemon butter for lunch.

I learned that afternoon that children and cooking were two of the greatest passions of her life.

Maria had welcomed me back with open arms, giving me the customary kiss on both cheeks. We were strangers no more, I realised, and was glad. The first thing she did was put me to work. Giving me my own apron. She was pleased when I told her that I'd like to try making the stew she'd made for lunch the day before.

She turned to me in surprise. 'You never learned at home?' she asked, dicing a tomato for a bread and fish salad she was making, one of the island's classic dishes, so she told me.

I told her about my mother's cooking – or lack thereof – and how I hadn't really learned from my gran, and she shook her head. '*Ai carai*, Alba,' she lamented of her sister, looking up and beseeching the heavens. Then she frowned, seemed to consider something, and gave a little shrug. 'Well, she wasn't really much of a cook herself. So maybe not so surprising.'

I protested. 'But she was a *great* cook.'

The old woman laughed. Her big, dark eyes widened considerably as she stared at me, perhaps considering if Alba had improved as her life went on. Then she waved a hand. 'Ah, but you're English,' she said, nodding as if that explained everything.

'What does that mean?' I asked.

She had a wicked gleam in her eye. 'You don't know any better.'

I laughed. 'We have got a bit better, you know.'

She made a sound, a bit of a snort. 'If you say so.'

I argued about the great chefs we had, the fabulous cheese we made, our world-class sausages… This only seemed to make things worse. She didn't seem convinced. She raised an eyebrow. 'English food always seems to come in a set. Why is that? Pie *and* gravy. Sausage *and* mash. Bacon *and* egg. To me, the only things that should come in pairs is socks, not food.'

I shrugged, hid a grin. I liked all of it, but I could see her point.

She took down a pan, then gave me an appraising look, sizing me up. 'You're still young, maybe there's still time.'

I found myself laughing at that.

As I helped her, I learned that she had been married for sixty years, her husband, Pedro, had died two years ago and her sons and daughter all lived a few houses away. She had two children, and little Benito was one of four great-grandchildren. I also learned that she was trying her best not to show favouritism, and that her granddaughter, Louisa, Benito's mother, kept calling her out on it.

'You shouldn't have favourites,' she acknowledged. 'But Benito makes it hard,' she added indulgently. I found out that she looked after him while his parents were at work.

I told her about Sage, how it was easy to have a favourite if you only had the one, and she agreed that this would make things easier. 'You never wanted more?' she asked.

I shook my head. 'We thought about it – it would have been nice, but somehow it just didn't work out that way.'

I didn't mention how often we'd tried. The failed IVF treatments, and how in the end we'd just decided to shower as much love as we could on the one we did have. There'd been a time when I'd got so focused on trying for another I'd lost sight of how lucky I was to have Sage.

Maria was interested in hearing more about Sage – or perhaps she was just being polite and perhaps I went on a bit too much, telling her about how she was studying to become a doctor, how she was always looking after everyone else.

'She sounds a little like my great-grandmother's mother's sister, Cesca.'

I looked at her, and considered. 'Maybe it's in the blood, studying medicine.'

As I diced tomatoes that Maria had grown in her garden, mixing them into a salad with breadcrumbs, cheese and fish, she returned to the story she'd begun the day before in which I'd met the two sisters, Cesca and Esperanza.

As I cooked, I listened, and before I knew it, I felt myself borne along, like a boat at sea, swept back in time.

FIFTEEN

Formentera, 1718

When Cesca got back to the house after seeing Antoni off, the sun was casting a hazy ribbon across the horizon and her mother had started on breakfast. There were anxious worry lines around her almond-shaped green eyes, but she smiled when Cesca entered the cool interior of the dark kitchen, where the small window offered a glimpse of the turquoise sea. Nearby a seagull was making its strange cry.

It was going to be a fine morning. The storm had passed and she could feel summer on the way.

Esperanza was still lying in bed, as usual. Her eighteen-year-old little sister was one of life's late risers, and could only be coaxed out of bed with the threat of losing her breakfast to Grunon the goat.

Reading her mind, her mother tied a kerchief round her head and threw her long red and grey plait over her shoulder as she stirred the pot.

'I'm giving her another five minutes before Grunon gets it.'

Cesca chuckled, then got started on a herbal remedy for fever. The night before, she'd given a tisane made of cloves and cinnamon to the man her brother had brought for them to care for; she'd spooned it into his lips. She'd make another today and hopefully it would go some way towards his recovery. He'd been sleeping fitfully, crying out softly in his sleep, but that had stopped now, thankfully.

He was young, perhaps in his late twenties, thin and battered. One eye was swollen almost completely shut from the blows of his captor's fists. It was difficult to tell the colour of his hair, she thought – due to the matted dirt and dried blood that had collected in it. His features, beyond the bruises, were even, handsome, she thought. Or perhaps they would be if he hadn't been so bruised. She'd found herself staring at him, perhaps more than she ordinarily would. Strangers were rare on the island. But she didn't allow herself any other thoughts besides trying to get him well; she had been promised to the doctor, Señor Garcia, since she was a young girl. Arranged marriages were common on the island, particularly in their secret Jewish community.

Her mother shook her head. Didn't share her own thoughts and worries, which mainly centred on what they'd do if the man died – what would they do with his body?

Cesca's main worry right then, though, was mostly about kicking her lazy sister out of her bed so that she could help with the morning's chores. The fact that only ten months in age existed between them was a surprise to most people, who thought that Cesca, with her quiet authority, was many years her sister's senior.

She made her way into her sister's room and pulled back the covers.

Esperanza groaned, then looked at her with groggy slits for eyes. Her dark hair was a messy waterfall on her pillow. 'I'm tired, leave me be.'

Cesca sighed and shook her arm. 'Come on.'

'Another five minutes, I was having a good dream.'

Cesca sighed. Shook her again. 'It's your turn to collect the eggs and clean the goat pen. Why do I always have to drag your lazy behind out of bed?'

Esperanza groaned and turned over. 'Ugh. I hate that goat.'
Cesca hid a grin.

Esperanza put her hair up in a kerchief, then stomped her way
outside. The kitchen still smelt like the man her brother had
brought for them to care for. It smelt like death, and it made her
feel uncomfortable, and a little frightened despite her brave talk the
day before. She didn't want to be like him, forced to flee her home.

The wind was howling, and the ground was cold, and she faced
the day with a scowl. She'd been dreaming that her brother and
sister hadn't in fact brought a wanted man to live with them – one
they would now have to pretend was Rafael, her *cousin*. If he
lived, that is. From the smell alone, she wasn't sure of that, and
she gritted her teeth at the thought of having to help her sister
and mother dig a grave.

She put Antoni's old boots on – the ones with the hole by the
big toe where the damp crept in. She'd have to stuff some more
paper in it later. She sighed again. She was tired of everything
always falling apart, everything always being second-hand and
half broken already. Most of her clothing was hand-me-downs
from her sister.

Flea came to meet her, his tail seeming to wag him. He was
a springy, feather duster of a dog with muddy brown matted fur
and only one eye. Cesca had given him the name because she
said that he was just a bag for fleas. He was. He was also the love
of Esperanza's life. She patted him and kissed the spot where his
other eye used to be, and he followed devotedly after her as she
trudged into the hen coop.

Collecting the eggs was the only chore she enjoyed, so she
did it first. She liked the hens. Their soft, warm, cuddly bodies.
Her mother told her not to get too close, but she never learned.

'Hello, girls,' she said, greeting the matriarch, Gertrudis, and running a hand over her soft downy feathers. Soon Dolores came over for a cuddle, too.

Afterwards, with her shoulders squared, she went to find Grunon, the goat.

Cesca had brought the demon goat home from the market two months ago, amazed at the deal she'd got. Esperanza wasn't that amazed. Grunon gave new meaning to the word stubborn.

She wouldn't come when Esperanza called, refused to budge, and whenever she tried to milk her she kicked her legs and the milk pail went flying across the pen. Most days they were lucky if they got even half the milk they should have. It hardly seemed worth the hassle. Esperanza had said time and again that they should trade the goat for something else. But Cesca was sure Grunon just needed time to settle into her new home. Besides, they wanted to make their own cheese and butter, not to trade for it – that was the plan anyway. 'But if you keep this up,' she said, whispering into the grumpy goat's white, straggly-haired ear, 'maybe they'll just put you on a spit on the next saint's day. Maybe I'll *help*.'

Grunon knew a threat when she heard it, and lashed out, kicking over the bucket and ensuring that the precious milk spilled all over the floor.

'Gah! You horrible creature,' Esperanza moaned, picking up the pail and trying to drag the goat back into her stall. Forty-five minutes later she came inside the kitchen with her milk-slopped dress, hair a tangled dark mess and her face red and shiny with sweat. And the man who had been fast asleep in the kitchen cried out for water.

Esperanza set the pail down in the corner with a thud, and came forward despite her annoyance.

The man was covered in bruises, one eye purple and swollen. His hair, a filthy, matted mess. He smelt of sickness, and sweat, and he was muttering in a mix of Spanish and French. They heard the word water again a few times. Cesca rushed forward with a glass and Esperanza stopped.

Her mother looked at her, then Cesca, shook her head and pointed at the stranger lying in the corner. 'What was your brother thinking? What if he can't speak our dialect – how are we going to pass him off as your cousin then?'

'I'm sure he can speak Eivissenc,' said Cesca.

She was trying to allay her mother's fears, though she had been worrying about the same thing. How was this man meant to pass for one of them? Especially if he didn't sound like a local? Besides, he didn't look like Rafael, their real cousin, either. Rafael had been pale and thin, with fair hair. This man was dark and muscular. Though, she thought, maybe not many people on the island would remember what the real Rafael looked like. It had been years since she'd seen her cousin last, and he'd been young then – people changed.

Rafael had died of fever. It had happened suddenly and with no real warning. It had been a shock to find out. It seemed odd, prophetic in a way, that this man here now, who was meant to be passing as Rafael, was suffering from a similar illness.

Cesca spooned small dribbles of water into his dry, parched lips, slowly, so as to make sure that he swallowed and didn't choke, and soon he drifted off back into a deep, soundless sleep.

But there was something else that couldn't be avoided.

She heated water in a pot over the fire. 'I think it's time that he had a wash,' she said, squaring her shoulders, ignoring her mother's look of horror.

Esperanza nodded. 'I agree.' Then she got some dried lavender and fetched the bar of home-made rosemary-scented soap and handed it to Cesca. Afterwards she announced that she was going out for the rest of the day.

Cesca sighed. She supposed that was about as much help from Esperanza as she could hope for.

Cesca worked up a lather with the bar of herbal soap and scrubbed the man's face and neck, as gently but firmly as she dared. Then she pulled up his filthy shirt, which looked like it had dried with a mixture of dirt and blood, asking for her mother's help to support his weight while she pulled it off him. She could see dark bruises around his ribs and she felt them for damage. 'Broken,' she said with a wince.

Her mother helped her, muttering the whole time, 'It's not right, not appropriate for you to be doing this…'

Cesca sighed. 'What does that matter, *Mare*? Must we leave him to suffer in this filth because I am unmarried, promised to the doctor? Or would you like to try washing him by yourself?'

Her mother shot her a look of reprimand, and Cesca felt a stab of regret at her sharp tone. She knew that her mother felt bad enough that her daughter was in this situation.

She looked at her kindly and joked, 'I'll close my eyes before I see anything I shouldn't.'

Her mother's lips twitched. 'You'd have to look to know.'

She grinned, then carried on scrubbing the man's arms. She washed his hair in a mixture of lavender and rosemary, both gathered from the plants that grew wild on the island. They would help with the lacerations on his head, and would clear the matted tendrils of any dirt and debris.

She'd learned about natural remedies from Señor Garcia. He was the only doctor who lived on the island and, after his wife passed away, Cesca had become his assistant. It was because of him that she and Esperanza had learned how to read – he liked to read medical studies, and he thought it would be a good idea if she knew how to read them as well, so that he could share his findings with her and have someone to talk to about it. He'd taught her (and Esperanza, because she refused to be left out when he offered) how to read and their father hadn't objected.

In fact, it was something her father had taken pride in, when Señor Garcia had asked for his permission to teach the girls. 'Imagine having two daughters smarter than most of the men on this island,' he used to boast. Most people couldn't read or write beyond their first name here, some not even that.

'*Pare!*' Cesca had reprimanded when she was a child. The men here would not take too kindly to that idea and, after all, she would most likely have to marry one of them.

He'd simply shrugged. 'Don't lower your standards for others, child, always make sure that the people around you raise theirs.'

Her father had often said things like that. Before he died, he'd spoken to the doctor about taking on Cesca as a wife. It was a good match, though he was much older than her. Most marriages on the island were arranged by parents long before their children reached adulthood. Esperanza had also been betrothed to a cousin, since the age of six. It was just how things were done. For Cesca, the fact that her future husband had so much to teach made her proud. Señor Garcia was a trusted friend, and she looked forward to learning more from him. Esperanza, of course, had often threatened to run away before she could be married off, but she was the exception – most young women on the island just accepted it as their fate.

It was Esperanza's turn to make the bread and she preferred to do it without her sister's sighs. She was forever telling her how to do things right. Her way, she meant. Unfortunately, when it came to Esperanza, Cesca often had a point. She had an unfortunate tendency to burn things because she liked to gossip too much with her friend, Riba, or she got distracted by her dog, Flea.

Who, despite his small stature, was a champion walker, and cove explorer, and swimmer, keeping up with her long strides and never taking his one eye off her.

Flea wasn't allowed indoors, to Esperanza's deep, abiding regret. It was Cesca and her mother's hard and fast rule. Which is why she often spent as much time as she could out of the house.

They didn't mind the dog that much at the communal bread oven, which served a few of the neighbours. Esperanza went there every few days to make bread with the other women, but mostly she liked to catch up on all the news with Riba, her best friend, and get out of the rest of the chores for the afternoon.

Riba used to live, many years ago, on the main island, Ibiza, and Esperanza liked hearing her stories about it. The wealthy traders, and merchants, the officials, some of the bigger estates. She longed to live there herself one day, and would have, as the cousin she'd been engaged to had made his home there. It was the only thing about her marriage that she had looked forward to – the idea of getting off this tiny slip of an island and having a big house and a servant! It would be bliss to have someone else worry about the goat for once. When she used to speak like that to her mother or her sister, they would just shake their heads. 'It doesn't do to fill your head with dreams, 'Spranza. It only makes life harder.'

Which, Esperanza knew, was probably true, but the trouble was, the dreams felt so good when she was imagining them. Wanting more than a life here was unfathomable to Cesca and her mother. Esperanza sometimes cursed her own overactive imagination, and Riba's glamorous tales about the parties, the dresses, the jewellery and the well-heeled men…

It was a world away, she knew, and now it was all gone anyway. Things had changed, almost overnight. The man she'd been promised to was dead, which meant leaving this island was probably never going to happen now anyway, and all that she'd done was get her hopes up about a life that was never going to be hers. She'd be stuck here with that goat for ever.

Still, maybe she had more say in her future now, after all. Perhaps with her brother away and her father gone, she could choose a husband for herself. She liked that thought, although she had no idea where to start. Most of the boys she'd grown up with felt more like brothers than potential suitors and if she swapped her house for one of theirs it would still just be more of the same in the end. Perhaps just a different goat, she thought with a humourless chuckle.

As she kneaded the dough and shaped it into a loaf, waiting her turn to put it into the big fiery oven, she heard one of the other women mention again the stranger from mainland Spain, and all thoughts of her future were dashed out of her mind. This new stranger from Barcelona who had recently arrived on the island had all the residents worried. The rumour went that he'd said he was doing a study of the surrounding flora and fauna, but few believed that tale. Most people assumed he was some kind of an official, that he was checking in on them somehow. Perhaps he even had ties to the Holy Office, or was an Inquisitor. That was the big fear, of course. With their secret community, they had learned to always err on the side of caution; it was what kept them safe, and alive.

The fear the presence of this man, this Barcelona stranger, had caused had ensured that there were now crosses nailed to every door and no one went near the secret synagogue except under cover of darkness.

It made Esperanza even more nervous as she considered their own stranger, hiding in their kitchen. What would happen to them all if the man from Barcelona found out about him?

'I saw him,' said Riba now, and Esperanza started. It was as if the woman had been reading her thoughts. She looked up, her dark eyes wide.

There were five women in the small room they used to make their bread, and they all turned now to Riba, who nodded her own dark head.

'You did?' said Esperanza, swallowing nervously, pushing the strands of hair that had fallen out of her plait away from her face.

Riba nodded. 'Yes. He's staying in one of the governor's houses.'

Esperanza let out a small, relieved sigh. Riba was talking about the stranger from Barcelona. The governor had a few houses on the island, which were mainly used by people in the salt trade, but they were people like them, long connected with the area.

There were more than a few nervous stammers from the women.

'What's he really doing here, do you know?' asked a woman with pale, reddish-brown hair and wide cornflower-blue eyes.

Riba stoked the fire in the oven and turned back to look at the woman who'd asked. Seeing the fear in her eyes, she shook her head. 'I don't know. I'm just hoping that it's not what we fear – that he's working for the Holy Office. He's been asking a lot of questions about the salt trade, so he might be connected with that. But he didn't say.'

They shared anxious looks. 'But it's not like he would admit that he was from the Holy Office – not if he were here trying to detect any secret practices,' said one of the older women.

They all nodded.

None of them would dare to call them *Jewish* practices here, not aloud. It just wasn't done, not in public, and hardly ever in private either. You never knew who could be listening. Even now.

SIXTEEN

Formentera, present day

The air stirred with the gentle lap of the ocean, the tantalising aroma of sun-ripened tomatoes, butter, saffron and the sound of laughter and music.

My first impromptu dinner party was on one of those languid evenings that make for the perfect summer's night.

I'd made *paella de mariscos*, using a recipe that Maria taught me that afternoon when I'd asked. She'd taken me to a local market that smelt of fish and hard work. It was crammed with shouting men and women, all intent on getting the best deal of the day, and with Maria as my guide, I walked away with a good deal from a local fisherman for two bulging bags full of freshly caught lobster and prawns. The dish Maria taught me how to make was the Ibiza version; the paella was a golden colour from the saffron, with a crunchy base. It was rich, and deliciously spicy, with diced squid, mussels, prawns, rice and lobster.

Isla, who'd arrived to my amazed delight with one of her beautiful seascapes as a housewarming gift, was dressed in a flowing purple dress and leather sandals with little charms that jingled when she walked. After we'd eaten she said that it was one of the most authentic paellas she'd tasted. 'Maybe it *is* in your blood,' she'd said, as she took a bite and closed her eyes in delight.

I'd decided on taking the party outdoors. I'd found an old blanket in a cupboard and put it under the orange trees in the garden, with a few well-placed candles to create some ambience, and though I only had four mismatched plates and more forks than I had knives, my guests didn't seem to mind.

'Shabby chic,' said Sue, and raised a toast, with a glass of sangria from the jug that she'd made. Her plump cheeks were rosy, and her short blonde curls shimmered in the fading light.

We'd given up on Jim's friend's *costa* wine after a couple of glasses. It was the sort of thing that could strip paint and cause brain haemorrhages, but I decided I'd worry about that in the morning, when I'd no doubt be feeling the effects.

Big Jim dunked large pieces of sourdough into the remaining stew and sopped it up, declaring it a 'triumph,' and I felt something inside me shift, something lighten for the first time in ages.

As the sun went down, the sky a paint swirl of magenta and salmon against the backdrop of turquoise ocean in the distance, Isla played guitar and sang a song about the long road home, and I got that feeling I'd had the first time I'd seen the villa, as if maybe this place could offer me something I was missing – a small feeling of home. It was that feeling that had vanished from my life now that James was gone and Sage was at uni. It was like a tiny green shoot of joy, the kind of thing I didn't want to hold too close to the light in case it withered away – but I had found some of it these past few days, meeting Maria and now sitting beneath the sunset sky, in the company of my new friends. As I sat and listened to Isla sing, and looked from Big Jim to Sue, I realised it was people who turned a house into a home.

The other thing that turned a house into a home was a funereal, dark-eyed man by the name of Emmanuel Sloviz, who arrived on my doorstep shortly after dawn one morning when the air smelt of olives and sea salt.

He'd been given my name by Big Jim, after I'd told him that I was in need of some assistance with the house. He was thin, with short, curly hair and the patched-together look of someone who had recently been down on his luck.

'Big Jim mentioned that you might need some work done around the house,' he said, eyeing Marisal's outside walls. Walls that were in desperate need of a fresh coat of whitewash.

His jeans were covered in paint, and he looked like he could do with a good meal inside him.

'I do,' I said, hoping I wouldn't regret the decision. Big Jim was a kind-hearted soul, the sort who'd give his money away to strangers. He was also enormous, and anyone who took advantage would no doubt soon regret it if his massive arms were anything to go by.

Still. You just had to trust sometimes.

A week later, while Emmanuel was finishing up painting the outside walls, which he'd primed and damp-proofed, I had to admit that he was an excellent worker. And with a few more nutritious meals in him, he might even lose his lost, haunted look.

In the afternoons, when I came home after seeing Maria, we'd speak. At first it was halting, mostly monosyllabic, but later he opened up more.

'So, you're a writer?' he asked one afternoon, seeing me in the garden, my notebook in hand. He'd helped me to lug an old, weather-worn table from out of the spare bedroom into the garden, and I'd placed it under the orange trees.

'Yeah, though it's more in theory than anything else these days. I wrote a few books a decade ago – then life just seemed to get in the way.'

'Yeah, I know how that can work,' he said. Though he didn't elaborate, and I couldn't seem to find the words to pry. We seemed to have come to an amiable solution, him working on the house and me out in the garden, and I didn't want to make things awkward by getting too personal.

'Anything I might have read?'

I laughed. 'Doubtful. Mysteries mainly, mostly airport sort of reads.'

'No airport here,' he said, his mouth almost curling into a smile before it stopped itself.

'Yeah.' I snorted. 'Maybe, that's why I'm here.'

'So that's why you're still there?' came Allan's incredulous voice down the line that evening. I was standing at the bottom of the garden, next to an old tyre that was once part of a swing. It seemed to be the only place where I could get mobile reception.

I'd filled my brother in on meeting Maria and some of the things she'd told me over the past week, and told him that I was thinking of staying for a while.

'So that you can hear all this stuff about Gran's past?'

'Well, not her past exactly – but our past, about what life was like back then.'

Allan had been just as shocked as I had to find out about our secret Jewish roots. 'I still can't believe she kept this from us for all these years. Do you think Dad knew?'

'I don't know. Maybe. I want to ask Mum, but you know her…'

He groaned in sympathy, and did an impersonation. 'What do you mean James bought you a house on an island in Spain? You can't move to an island! Why don't you come home, love, and I'll make you an appointment with my lovely naturopath, there are fantastic herbal treatments for insanity nowadays. I'm sure he can mix you up one.'

I laughed, though it was a bit too close to home. My mother and I had had a fallout based on her beliefs about natural healing methods when James was first diagnosed and it was still a sore point. Still, I knew deep down that she *had* meant well and I did love her. I knew I should just phone her and explain things properly. For now, I'd resorted to just telling her that I'd extended my holiday by turning it into a writing retreat. Apparently, the words were simply flowing and I couldn't stop them. If only.

It had made me feel a little guilty, how pleased she was about that: 'Darling, you're writing again? How lovely. That's my girl, never let the critics keep you down. I'm so proud.' Which of course had made me feel even worse.

How could I tell her that I spent my nights speaking to James's ashes and my days thinking about the ghosts from my father's side of the family? It hardly seemed sane.

Though there were positives too, ones she'd approve of. Like the fact that I was now actually getting out of the house, and not simply lying about it like I used to – although 'out' mainly consisted of going to Maria's house, and the Blues Bar occasionally to hear Isla's band sing – but it was a start. I was enjoying going to Maria's every day, the long cycle through the countryside and past the beautiful sweep of turquoise sea, the scent of wild rosemary and salt in the air and the feel of summer on my skin.

For now, this was like a secret reprieve, a space where for a moment I could hit pause on my old life, and I was enjoying that, along with the new people I'd met. People who, apart from Big Jim, didn't really know about what I'd been through in the past year. Hadn't been there to witness it like my other friends and my family. For the first time in ages there were gaps in my day where I didn't have to think of all that I had lost, and that was helping more than I could have realised.

Part of this was keeping busy. It was a cliché, sure, but it was one that worked. It was one of the best things I could do for myself right now, and the villa provided enough to keep me occupied when I wasn't visiting Maria or attempting to write. Attempting being the operative word.

Despite the plot I'd written on the back of a napkin the other evening, the furthest I'd got was two lines in the cheap notebook I'd got from Francisco's corner shop, with blue lines and a dusty cover, along with a black Bic pen from the same shelf. You didn't need much more, I had thought to myself a bit smugly at the time. But you do need a story – and for now that was eluding me.

'Just show up, that's all you need to do,' used to be my motto when I was stuck with a scene I hadn't a hope of finishing. Enough time in the chair plus a deadline was the cure for any block – or so I used to think. Before I got it, I thought writer's block was nothing more than myth meeting lack of discipline. Until I got it and found that I couldn't write anything. *For ten bloody years.* That showed me, didn't it?

'The good news is that no one is expecting anything, so the pressure's off, so why not try something just for practice? Maybe try writing something else for a change,' said James's voice inside my head while I sat trying to write.

I heard his voice sometimes, just before I was about to fall asleep, or just before I woke up, like he was right there talking to me. Like maybe he was just in another room.

Some days I looked for him without realising that's what I was doing.

I'd find myself getting up and going to find him, only to pause en route when I realised that it had all been in my head.

When Emmanuel was around, I found that I couldn't bring myself to take James's ashes everywhere I went. Unless I put him in a beach bag to hide the urn — but even I knew I had to stop myself from going that far. Perhaps now I was substituting having him with me by conjuring up his voice in my head.

Was it mad to listen to voices in your head? Maybe not. It seemed like a good idea, to try something different. Just to get the words flowing, perhaps. So, I turned the page and wrote about the leaves on the orange tree, and the way the sun filtered through them, and how beyond that tree lay a turquoise ocean, and before I knew it I had developed sunburn and written the start of the first chapter. It wasn't the story I'd been meaning to write, the one I'd started plotting on a napkin the other night; it was something new and different, set on an island in the middle of nowhere, about a family who'd had to live in secret for all their lives.

And though it took a while, what I said to my mother soon became true – the words did indeed, at long last, begin to flow.

SEVENTEEN

Formentera, 1718

Cesca was alone when the man in the cellar finally woke up. They'd moved him there because he had been tossing fitfully, muttering in a babble of Spanish and French, and they worried about who might hear if they walked past the house.

She tried to soothe the babble, now, by dribbling water into his parched lips. He swallowed, slowly, painfully. Then his eyes opened, fevered and glazed with sickness, but bright blue, like the sky, and blinking up at her in clear confusion.

'Paulo?' he asked.

'Shh,' she said, 'you're fine now,' her hand on his arm, and he relaxed. Before she could say any more he had fallen back asleep.

Antoni had mentioned that the man was travelling with a brother. Was that who he'd been asking after? Was that Paulo?

She left him to sleep and got started on a soothing herbal blend that could be made into a tea to help ease the pain of a young girl who had just begun her menses and was suffering from cramping. It was cases like these that had decided the local doctor on training Cesca in the first place, when she'd showed an interest in medicine. He knew that most women and young girls would feel more comfortable being examined by a female nurse when it came to such matters. Cesca had been a model student, throwing herself into learning all that he could teach, so that now, still only nineteen years old, she could almost have passed for a doctor herself.

When she came back in to check on the man some time later, she startled. He was sitting up, wide awake. He stared at her in equal surprise.

She blinked. He was thin, and half naked, but with his hair clean and the bruises fading from his face, she saw he had high cheekbones and full lips. He was more handsome than she had imagined, and she coloured, realising that he had been watching her this whole time.

He spoke something that sounded a little like the word for angel in French and she laughed a little, responding in Spanish, as her French was limited at best. 'I fear you may have just knocked your head, Señor, you aren't with the angels – but you are with us. My mother, my sister and me.'

He tried to sit up, then winced, feeling his ribs.

She winced with him. 'You have two broken ribs, I'm sorry.'

He frowned, then nodded, looking back at her. 'Where am I?'

'Formentera.'

He gazed at her, not understanding. 'The little island off Ibiza? But how? Why?'

'My brother, Antoni, brought you here, don't you remember?' She'd responded in the dialect of the island, and then repeated it in Spanish when she realised what she'd done.

He shook his head, and the action caused him to grunt and hold a hand to his head like it was causing him pain. Almost naturally he slipped into Catalan, perhaps for her benefit, and she felt a part of herself sag with relief. It would make it much easier if he could speak like a local.

'No, I remember that we were running… then there was a ship, a pirate ship,' he said, frowning.

'Then—' suddenly his eyes widened and he looked around. 'Paulo, is he here, too? What have they done with him?' He made to stand, but she rushed over. 'No, you must rest.'

He nodded as a wave of nausea hit him and he doubled over, coughing and wincing, holding his side. Cesca felt helpless. It must be so painful with his broken ribs.

'Where is Paulo?' he repeated eventually.

She stared at him, biting her lip. Her green eyes full of remorse. 'I- I'm so sorry.'

He closed his eyes, his face a mask of pain, and leant his head back against the wall. 'It's my fault.'

'No, you mustn't say that. He was ill, he'd caught a fever – you both had, there was nothing you could have done,' she said, rushing over to his side.

Antoni had told her about how his brother had died while they were at sea, how the sickness had caught him and taken hold of his malnourished body and never let go. It was a miracle that the same thing hadn't happened to the man here now in her cellar.

He opened his eyes and stared into her own, wanting, needing someone to understand. 'We wouldn't have needed to run if it hadn't been for me.'

She shook her head. 'Don't speak like that, it won't help you now.'

He clenched his jaw, nodding.

He looked around the dark cellar with its small solitary window high above their heads.

'How did I get here?'

'My brother, Antoni. He brought you from the ship to hide here, with us.'

He frowned, trying to understand.

'Why?'

'Because we are like you.'

He blinked, then his eyes widened in understanding. 'You are *marranos? Jews?*' he whispered.

The word made her wince, but she nodded. No one ever said it aloud. Or even whispered it.

'But how?'

She explained about the island, about the people like her, the families that had come from Majorca all those years ago to come and live here and in Ibiza, and the secret community that had lived on the island ever since.

'I can't believe it. Most of the people here, they are Jewish?'

She nodded. 'On this island, yes. With the coast so often attacked by pirates, not everyone thinks to look here or wants to come and investigate. Most people still think it is abandoned.'

'They are only rumours, then, about the pirates? Made to deter strangers?' he guessed.

She shrugged. 'Now, yes. Though pirates have come here before.'

She left him lying in the cellar and went to make him something to eat, something that wouldn't be too rich on his empty, starved stomach. She returned with a thin porridge from a pot she had placed on the fire. She handed him a wooden bowl with a spoon and advised him to eat it slowly. It was wasted advice; the starving man fell upon it fast, shovelling it into his mouth. She snatched it out of his hands. 'No, you'll make yourself sick!'

Unfortunately, they knew too well about starvation here on the island, and Cesca had learned from an early age that a starved man could only eat the smallest amount of the plainest food or risk getting sick. She had to take the bowl away, even though he protested. 'I will give you more soon. Just give your stomach a chance to take that in first.'

She was right. Within seconds his face turned green and he started to gag. He broke out into a cold sweat and choked out the little bit of porridge he'd had on to the cold, hard cellar floor.

'I'm sorry,' he gasped, wheezing and holding his broken ribs in pain.

'Don't apologise,' she said, getting a cloth and wiping his face, not looking into his bright blue eyes that seemed to bore so fiercely into her own. She got up, away from his gaze, and swept up the mess.

'You must go slow, trust me.'

When his colour had returned to normal and he'd tried some more of the porridge, giving his body a chance to adjust, he introduced himself.

'My name is Benito Nuñez.'

That name was being spoken on the island already. The Nuñez brothers and their escape by pirates.

'I am pleased to meet you. But we must call you something else. People will have heard of your escape.'

He blinked. 'Then I should leave. I will be putting you all in danger,' he said, sitting up, trying to stand. 'It's only a matter of time before they come here.'

She shook her head and helped him sit back down. 'They wouldn't think to come here, not at first, anyway. My brother took you in a rowing boat at night from his ship, the *Invictus*, which was docked in Ibiza. It will take some time – they'll be searching the main island before they think to look here, if at all.'

Though she said the words to help ease his fears, she wasn't sure how much she believed them. It would have been easier to have hidden the man on the bigger island. It was easier to hide in a crowd.

'We have a plan though,' she assured him, trying to make her voice sound confident to allay his fears. She knew well enough that worry was the foe of any recovery.

'To risk your lives for me – a stranger?'

She shrugged. 'Would you prefer that we turn you in? It's not our way.'

He looked ready to protest again, but Cesca saw that he was tired, so she shook her head. 'Sleep. When you wake up you can meet my sister and mother. Hear about our plan.'

'And your father? What does he have to say about it?'

A shadow passed over Cesca's eyes. 'He's gone.'

'I'm sorry.'

'Don't be. He would have approved,' she assured him.

Her father had always been the big risk-taker in the family. The one who believed in the importance of doing what was right, no matter the cost.

But Benito didn't smile at her, or seem to feel relieved. He looked as though a worrying thought had occurred to him. 'So, it's just women here? You mentioned a sister, a mother? Is there no one else, no husband, or brother?'

'No, I'm sorry. My father passed away some time ago and my brother Antoni had to return to the ship, so I'm afraid, you're stuck with us.'

He blinked. It was clearly worse than he had imagined. 'I can't do that – I can't put a house of women at such risk.'

Cesca shook her head. 'Yes you can, and you will.'

'You want me to pretend to be your cousin?' Benito said the next morning, dumbfounded, when Cesca brought him another bowl of the thin porridge he'd spat up the day before.

He'd learned his lesson. He sat up and took a small spoonful, despite his roiling belly crying out for more. Everything ached – his head, his ribs, his very skin and heart. He couldn't believe the trouble they were willing to put themselves through for him – a stranger – he didn't want to be the cause of it, didn't feel that he deserved it either. Not after what he'd done, how his actions had caused the death of his older brother.

How much more was he willing to risk to save his own life? It hardly seemed just.

There were two other women in the room now alongside the woman who'd been tending him, the one he'd confused with an angel, with her fine red hair and sea-green eyes, and gentle touch. Cesca. The older woman looked like an ageing version of her. She was tall, probably in her late forties. Her hair a faded rust-like red. The third woman was dark, with skin like honeyed silk and a dark waterfall of hair. She had deep, dark eyes with thick lashes. Beautiful. She was the little sister, called Esperanza, he had learned.

She was staring at him, a frown on her face. Her arms were crossed, and she didn't look at all happy about their situation.

Benito looked away. 'I don't mean to cause you trouble but I can see I have. As soon as I am able, I will get passage out of here.'

Esperanza looked relieved, but Cesca shook her head. 'You are not causing trouble.'

Esperanza snorted, and Cesca hissed, ''Spranza, stop it.'

'As far we are concerned you are our cousin, Rafael. Your mother sent you here to be cared for by me and Señor Garcia. No one will question that here.'

'I can't ask you to lie for me.'

Cesca shook her head. 'It's not a lie, well, not really. Our cousin, Rafael, died last week – no one knows this here, word hasn't spread from Ibiza. Antoni has already spoken to my uncle. You will take his place.'

'In everything?' asked Esperanza, looking at her sister with wide, shocked eyes.

For a moment they stared at one another in silence, their eyes saying more than words. 'Perhaps not in *everything*,' said the older woman, with a sniff.

EIGHTEEN

Formentera, present day

Every day like clockwork, Emmanuel Sloviz arrived at sunrise. He took the coffee I made him outside, in one of the four mugs that were still all I owned, and got to work on painting the rest of the house.

He was a quiet man, with methodical ways. He often left the sandwiches I made him or the cereal I left out for him when he was absorbed in whatever task he was busy with, which might have explained his waif-like appearance. I could see that he would need reminding to eat. Perhaps he often forgot to eat, so consumed was he in the work that he was doing. There was something to be admired about that.

He hummed softly when he worked, and I found the sound soothing as I puttered around the house, trying to make a dent on the spare room so that Sage or Allan would be able to come and visit soon. I found that Emmanuel's presence chased away the shadows, and brought a sense of routine to the day. There was something about knowing that he was around that made the mornings a little less lonely, even if we hardly spoke to one another.

I had got into the habit of working when he did. Starting with the spare rooms, I had decided upon which furniture would stay and what would need to go. Unfortunately, a lot of it was unsalvageable, flimsy MDF that had seen better days, but there were a few pieces that could be used. Like a bed frame for one of the spare bedrooms, and an old wardrobe that Emmanuel helped me to move into the main bedroom, replacing the flimsy one that had been put there. It was one of those old-fashioned ones with claws for feet, and once it had been cleared of dust and debris – old newspapers and blankets, mainly – it added a sense of charm to the room. Emmanuel offered to help me paint it, but it seemed a shame to go over the old cherry wood with anything but some polish.

It wasn't until he'd been working at Marisal for more than a week that Emmanuel began opening up, ever so slowly, to me. I'd found that the only way to guarantee that he would, in fact, eat the food I made him was to stand around and ensure that he did. It was a good way to make sure that he took a break as well. He worked like a man possessed, a man who used work to chase away the devils inside his head. I couldn't help wondering about what drove him to work that way. At first I'd admired it, his doggedness, his reliability, but after a while I began to see something else in his eyes as he worked, something I recognised from my own – the need to keep going, the fear of what would happen if you stopped.

Despite my hesitations about crossing any boundaries, the truth was that I found him fascinating.

This stranger who had come into my home, with his dark good looks and half-starved frame. I was curious to find out more, but I knew that his was a story that would probably take many months to prise out. There was something about his manner that reminded me a little of my gran, the way her eyes would grow dark, and how she too would clam up whenever questions were asked.

Even the simplest ones I asked Emmanuel were evaded. 'Where are you from?' I asked as I handed him a baguette filled with tuna salad, one afternoon when the sun had gone from tangerine to blood orange, and the sound of the ocean was a lazy sigh in the wind.

'Oh, not far from here,' he responded.

Healthy protein, a source of good fat. I was a mother whose only child was away, so perhaps it wasn't that surprising that I couldn't help the need to nurture those who I perceived to be in my care, unintended or not.

'But where?' I persisted, holding out the plate to him. He looked at me, his dark eyes showing something like a flash of amusement, then he put down his paintbrush in a nearby bucket of water so that it wouldn't dry out and washed his hands, coming over to take the sandwich from me, and shaking his head slightly as I gave him a nod of encouragement to keep going, to keep eating.

He snorted. 'I didn't see it before,' he said, an amused glint in his dark eyes.

'What?' I asked, puzzled.

'Your Catalan side, you sound a bit like my mother. Eat… eat,' he joked.

I grinned.

I'd told him when we first met that my grandmother was from the island, but I hadn't gone into any great detail or explained about the house. Or the circumstances of how I'd got it.

'I think that's only because you don't eat enough.'

He sighed. 'I know – I forget. It's hard to remember when I'm busy. But you mustn't trouble yourself, Charlotte. I'm stronger than I look.'

There was something about the way he said my name that made me look away. It was so intimate. I couldn't help but take an involuntary step back.

I shrugged. 'I'm sorry, it's not my place to interfere. But it's just that I see you working so hard, often on an empty stomach, and I can't help feeling bad.' It couldn't be healthy to do that, I thought but stopped myself saying.

He stared at me, giving me a rare smile.

'It's a sign of a good mother. Thank you,' he said, then took another bite of his sandwich for my benefit.

After that, we began to speak a little more regularly.

I was putting on the coffee one morning when he came inside and answered the question I'd asked him a few days before, without ceremony.

'Barcelona,' he said, rinsing his plate in the sink.

I turned to him with a puzzled frown. 'Pardon?'

'That's where I grew up. You asked the other day, and I'm not sure I answered you.'

I nodded, slowly.

'Coffee?' I offered.

He nodded. 'Thanks.'

'Where in England did you grow up, London?' he asked.

I took down the mugs from the dresser and turned to him, trying to mask my surprise at his sudden loquaciousness.

'No. I grew up in the Surrey countryside. It's where I've lived all my life really.'

He considered this as he took his cup of coffee. His dark eyes contemplative. 'You never moved before?'

I shook my head. 'No, well, not very far. When I met James, we talked about moving to the city – London is about an hour away, not that far, really – but in the end, I didn't want to be away from my family.'

He stared at me, and I touched James's ring, twisting the metal in my fingers, feeling the zigzag pattern, the small gemstone. I was further from them now than I could ever have imagined. He saw the movement but didn't say anything.

'James is your husband?' he asked.

I nodded. 'He was. He died.'

To my horror, I found my eyes pooling with tears, which I dashed away.

'I'm sorry,' he said, his hand briefly touching mine, then letting go. I could see from his eyes that he meant it. I took a deep breath of air and told him a bit about it.

'It happened a few months ago. That's why I'm here, really.'

He nodded, his dark eyes boring into mine. 'I thought maybe it was something like that,' he said, his gaze falling on to James's ring. 'Well…' he paused, his eyes sad. 'I thought it was divorce—' He broke off.

I gave a small, short laugh. 'I wish.'

He nodded, then stared out of the window. His jaw tightened slightly. 'It's not the same, of course. I'm sorry. But it is a kind of death… well, that's how it feels for me.'

I looked at him in surprise. 'You're divorced?'

Somehow, I hadn't imagined that he might be married or that he ever had been. There was something so lost about him. Maybe that was why.

He nodded. 'It's been a year now. Some days it feels like it just happened, though.'

It was my turn to stare, and he looked away, perhaps regretting sharing a part of his story with me. Opening up.

He set his mug down and gave me a small smile. 'I must get back to work.'

As he left I thought of that famous quote about misery loving company. The thing was, more often than not, it didn't.

NINETEEN

Formentera, 1718

The man now known as Rafael Alvarez slipped outside once he was sure everyone had gone to sleep. His ribs hurt, even when he breathed, and it was hard to see out of his left eye, but it was nothing to the pain in his heart at the thought of his brother, Paulo, buried at sea.

He had failed him. Risked it all. He'd been careless. It's not like his family hadn't warned him. In Majorca, they tolerated 'new Christians', as they called people like them. People whose families had been forced to convert their faith. It was easy to turn a blind eye to these new Christians when they were deemed useful, but if someone with that type of background rose too high, suspicions could also rise, faster than you could blink. Paulo had warned him to be careful. Not to take that promotion in Palma. But Benito had thought that things were changing. What he hadn't realised was that they were changing for the worse. There had been another resurgence, a fresh new wave to get rid of these *conversos*, the ones they suspected of only pretending to have changed their faith, once and for all. And this time they were more bloodthirsty than ever. You had to be careful and he hadn't been careful enough.

They'd come for all of them. His brothers, and his cousins. What's worse is that the colleague who'd turned him in had come to his home just before to warn him, racked with guilt over what he'd done, an act that was inspired by jealousy but which quickly soured when he realised he couldn't take it back, couldn't call off the howling dogs he'd sent for their throats. Benito and his cousins had no choice but to run, to flee their homes. It was the only way. Very few *conversos* lived to tell the tale, and some said even Catholics would admit to being Jews when tortured, just to make them stop. Now Paulo was dead, his cousins had been separated from him and he was in a house full of strange women, who all seemed ready to risk their lives for him.

He couldn't allow it. He wasn't worth the risk. All he'd caused was misery and he refused to bring that here.

He waited until they were asleep so that he could step out into the starry night, the sound of the waves crashing, full in his ears. He would slip away, unheard and unseen.

Every step felt like lead, but he was determined, even if it meant death – at least then they would be safe; no one need ever know he had been here.

'I didn't take you for a fool,' said a voice from the dark, the tone casual, yet surprised.

He turned sharply, wincing as he did, the pain in his ribs making him clutch his side.

It was the other sister. The one with the dark waterfall of hair, Esperanza. She was sitting on a tree stump and next to her was a small dog, the size of a loaf of bread, whose fur was wiry and pale brown. It had only one eye, which it fixed on him, head cocked to the side, as if it, too, was waiting to hear his answer.

He sighed, ran a hand through his dark hair and decided to be honest. 'You don't want me here, so what's it to you if I just leave? Wouldn't that just make things easier?'

She'd made it clear enough that she didn't want him here. Not that he blamed her. To be honest, hers was the only reaction he'd understood.

Her face was bathed in moonlight, and she had been resting her head on her knees while she stared out to sea, deep in thought, till he'd arrived.

She didn't deny it. It wouldn't have occurred to her to try. 'That doesn't change anything. You can't *leave*.'

'Why?' he said, taking a seat on the stump next to her. She moved over to give him space. The dog made a soft growl, like a warning.

'Why not?'

'Because you can't do that to my aunt and uncle – they're pretending that their son, my cousin Rafael, is still alive, to save you. You can't make them go through all of that – not being able to mourn him properly – *for nothing.*'

His eyes widened. 'They would do that for me?'

She raised a shoulder, and then looked at him. 'Yes.'

He stared at her. Didn't know what to say to that.

She shrugged, turned back to look at the ocean. 'It's an excuse, one you need, and they know that it will protect you. People like to do their part, where they can.'

'But they don't even *know* me. I could be anyone. Maybe I'm not worth it.'

She sighed. 'Maybe not. But I suggest you go back inside, let my sister care for you and stop fighting it. I have. Cesca has made up her mind. You'd have more chance of changing Grunon's mind than hers,' she said pointing to the goat pen.

'Grunon?' he asked, with a snort at the name, which meant grump.

Her mouth twisted into a grin as she told him about the demon goat and he found himself laughing despite himself. It was the first time he'd laughed about anything in weeks, he realised. It was nice for once to talk about something other than his imminent discovery, illness or the people he'd lost.

'I'd like to meet this Grunon.'

'No, you wouldn't, she's the bane of my existence.'

His lips twitched. She didn't look like the type of girl who had a bane of existence. She seemed a little spoilt, and headstrong – but if the tall, hard-working woman, Cesca, who'd he'd half convinced himself in his delirious state was an angel, was the one who everyone in the family didn't dare cross, then looks could be deceiving.

'Maybe I can help with the goat.'

The girl turned to him. 'What, you didn't get enough injuries on your way here, you want a few more?'

TWENTY

Formentera, present day

'I've been thinking,' said Emmanuel a few days later after I'd made us both a quick sandwich while he prepped the kitchen for a fresh coat of paint.

'This table…'

'Yes?'

He was eating his sandwich over the sink, so as not to make a mess. I'd taken a break from writing, or in any case my attempts at writing. Unlike Emmanuel, I was easily distracted from any task at hand.

I looked at the kitchen table in question and sighed. It was hideously ugly.

'What about it?' I asked, wondering if he thought a touch of paint would make a difference, though I couldn't see how, or why one would bother painting Formica.

'I think it would look better somewhere else.'

'Like where?' I asked, confused.

'Like at a dump?' he said, and then laughed. It completely transformed his sombre face and I couldn't help joining in. Mostly due to shock.

'Every time I come inside I see it and think, you know, there's not enough Prozac in the world to make that all right.'

Which was when I really did laugh. 'You're right, it's horrible, but what can I do?'

He took a bite of his sandwich and his eye fell on the rest of the furniture in the room. He said, 'You like old stuff... old furniture. Like that wardrobe in your room?'

I nodded. 'I suppose so – I like furniture that has a story to tell.'

I'd always preferred a room to look like it had been assembled over time, and not as if it all came as part of some set from a catalogue. I called it eclectic. James called it flea market. It was a bit of both.

'Well, I know of a place where they sell good second-hand furniture. It's not too far from here. I could take you tomorrow if you like?'

I nodded, surprised. 'That would be great.'

It had been a few days since he'd told me that he was divorced, and I'd got the feeling that he'd regretted opening up to me, but perhaps this wasn't the case. Maybe he was the sort of person who just needed a bit of time to get used to change. Well, I could understand that. All I had now was time.

We left early the next morning, driving past the low walls that crossed the countryside. Emmanuel's old Range Rover had seen better days, clearly left to rust in the hot sun, but I supposed that it suited his needs as a local handyman. He told me as we were driving that he was going to get a sign painted on it soon as he had a few other clients on the island, and his small business was growing.

'How long have you been doing this?' I asked, meaning his business, and he shrugged.

'Just over a year.'

'What did you do before that?' I asked, curious. He was close to my own age, so I wondered what he used to do – especially living out here. It wasn't like there was that much opportunity, unless you worked in hospitality.

He shrugged. 'Oh, you know, this and that.'

I frowned, but let it go. Clearly he was only willing to open up when it suited him.

As we drove, I switched on the radio. 'Do you mind?' I asked as folksy indie music filled the car. It was a local station that I'd found a few days before, when I'd discovered an old transistor radio in the spare bedroom.

He shrugged. 'Fine by me.'

With the sun filtering through the window, and the views of the ocean flashing past us, we drove on in companionable silence.

The market, in a trendy part of the island, was full of a jumble of old furniture and there were many skimpily clad, tanned people walking about, chatting and laughing. Emmanuel and I trawled through rows of second-hand *brocantes* till I found the perfect table. It was in need of a paint and didn't have any chairs, but when I saw a set of four mismatching ones in a similar size, I thought that I could make them work with it. 'Eclectic,' he said, with a grin and a nod of approval. 'That could look very nice. You could paint them in similar colours maybe?'

I nodded. 'That's a nice idea.'

After I paid, he loaded the table into his Range Rover and I turned back for the chairs, only to find a strange woman waiting for me, an anxious look on her face. She had long ash-brown hair and honey-coloured skin, with trim, athletic limbs in a pair of impossibly short denims.

As soon as she saw me she started to speak in rapid Spanish, I frowned and apologised, saying that I didn't speak the language that well.

'English?' she guessed. I nodded.

'Are you with Emmanuel?'

'We came here together if that's what you mean?'

She looked away, her eyes nervous, watching out for him, I realised. 'Just be careful, okay?' she said, touching my shoulder.

I blinked. 'What?'

She chewed her bottom lip, as if she were deciding whether to say something more, then took a step back in fright when she saw Emmanuel walking towards us.

'What is it?' I asked, reaching out to stop her from leaving.

She looked at me, then blinked.

'He's not the kind of man you want to get involved with, is all I need to say – I just—' She broke off, shook her head and hurried away, and I was left staring after her retreating back and wondering what she meant.

As we drove home, there was none of the easy silence we'd shared on the way to the market. Though this time it was me who was being reticent. I couldn't help thinking about what that woman had said to me. The warning she had given me.

Of course, I wasn't at all ready or willing to enter into any kind of relationship so soon after my husband's death, but it got me worried nonetheless. Who was this man that I had welcomed into my home? Shared my meals with? Had I been wrong to put my trust in him? Was I so in need of a friend that I had looked for one in the wrong place? Was Emmanuel, with his quiet, sombre ways and his irreverent humour, someone I needed to worry about?

Because in a way that's what I had been hoping – that we'd be friends. That's what today had felt like. Besides, he was the first person I'd met here who seemed to really understand the kind of pain I was in.

He turned to me as we were driving. 'Is everything okay, Charlotte?'

It was always a surprise when he said my name, and I startled. Shook my head. The women's warning racing through my head. *He's not the kind of man you want to get involved with.*

What had she meant by that? Had she meant that he was some kind of adulterer? Or was it something else? There had been something in the woman's eyes that had seemed to imply that the warning ran deeper than that.

I cleared my throat. Forced a smile. 'Oh nothing. I'm just thinking of what to do with the kitchen,' I lied.

He nodded. 'It's going to look great,' he said.

'Yeah,' I said, twisting James's ring around my thumb, wondering whether I should just ask him about the woman I'd met, ask him who she was, but deciding at the last minute that that there was someone else I could turn to for answers. The person who'd put Emmanuel in my home in the first place.

TWENTY-ONE

Formentera, 1718

Benito's favourite time of day was just after he awoke, the sun filtering in through the small window in the kitchen and onto his pallet. In those first few days, he found that whenever he awoke, Cesca was there. Leaning over him, and caring for him. Her green eyes kind, thoughtful. She was an attentive nurse, and seemed to know exactly what he needed before he asked.

The illness that had struck down his brother was taking its time to leave his own body. It didn't help that he was so starved and thin. 'You have to give it time,' she said when he grew impatient, wanting to recover faster.

He felt useless, a burden. There was so much he could be helping with on their small farm, yet all he did was sleep, and it was driving him mad.

Cesca shook her head at his protestations that he needed to get out of bed. 'The best thing you can do for me is to rest, okay?'

He nodded. It was hard not to do what she wanted when she looked at him like that with those clear green eyes that seemed to see inside his soul.

Cesca was always the first to rise. It was she who brought in water from the well, swept the kitchen and lit the fire for breakfast. She had slim pale hands that were always busy, even as they were talking.

The only thing he enjoyed about being stuck in bed was those early hours just after dawn, the time he spent with her. Those hours felt hushed, and special somehow, because it was just the two of them speaking softly, and it felt like they had the house all to themselves. He had Cesca to himself. Before she was called away to her work with the doctor, or became busy on the farm with her sister.

Cesca liked to hear about his life in Majorca, and what it had been like. She'd sit on the edge of his bed and listen, her green eyes wide at all he told her, of his home, and the large island so very different from her own. At times Benito could feel himself staring, and would force himself to look away from those clear eyes that stared so intensely into his own.

As Benito slowly recovered, the Alvarez women became accustomed to having him in the house. Word soon spread that their cousin Rafael from the main island had come to stay, so that Cesca could look after him while he recovered.

He met the doctor, Señor Garcia, a thin, small man with an impressive moustache and dark, thoughtful eyes. He asked very few questions and seemed to take Benito's illness at face value, not enquiring about his injuries. Benito wondered how much Cesca had told him, or if he guessed the truth. It wasn't just the doctor, however: most of the islanders who came past in the next few days were oddly incurious. Most seemed to just accept the story that he was the girls' cousin, and that he was there to recover from an illness. Though there were one or two women who came over in the course of that week, bringing with them extra meat or cheese, to help ease some of the pressure of having another mouth to feed – the island way, he came to understand, sharing what they had – who seemed to look at him a little oddly when he spoke.

'It's your accent,' said Esperanza after she'd come in from collecting the eggs, when her friend and neighbour Riba had left. Flea was half sleeping in the doorway, willing Esperanza with his one eye to come outside, but she was doing her best to ignore him. 'The way you speak.'

He turned to her in surprise. 'The way I speak?'

'You don't sound like a sailor's son,' she explained.

'What does that mean?'

'It means…' She sighed as she gathered the breakfast dishes together, 'I don't know, maybe you need to stop sounding like you used to work in an office?'

He stared at her in confusion. 'But I did.'

'No, *you* didn't, remember, *Rafael*?'

He sighed. Closed his eyes. He was being stupid. 'Yes.'

She nodded and started to scrape cold, congealed cereal out of a wooden bowl, then swept it out of the door as she gave it some thought.

'You could try swearing.'

He looked shocked. 'What?'

She swallowed a giggle at his expression. 'Rafael was a sailor – don't they all swear?'

He shook his head. 'I think that's only in novels. And even then, certainly not around ladies.'

She shrugged, smirked. 'Well, maybe so, but maybe try to sound less, er, polished, I suppose – and another thing, you can stop reading that novel when people come over. Most men here can't write their name, let alone read.'

He looked down at the novel that he still held in his hands.

'But you can!' he protested. It was her book, after all. She'd lent it to him shortly after he'd first arrived, when he'd complained that he was bed-bound and useless. The novel was *Don Quixote* and it was nearly falling apart, it had been read so often. Esperanza could recite whole passages from it, not that anyone would have cared to listen to her rambles, not when there was work to do. There wasn't much time for reading on the island, where skills like Cesca's were far more prized. But Esperanza liked that Benito read; it wasn't often that she found something in common with the men on this island, who only ever spoke of salt or fishing and farming. She couldn't help noting, though, that this only made him stranger still. So he had to be made aware of it, for his own safety.

'Yes, well, try not to advertise it,' she said, then left, with Flea hot on her heels, before her mother could call her back with more chores for the day.

*

For a small island, a lot seemed to happen, Benito couldn't help noticing.

Most of the islanders seemed more preoccupied with the other stranger who'd arrived on Formentera than with him. The man from Barcelona. It seemed like everyone was on edge about him, and couldn't help speculating about what he was doing here – everyone, that was, apart from Cesca, who seemed just too busy to stop and consider the presence of another stranger.

As the island's only nurse she seemed to be in perpetual demand. The doctor, Señor Garcia, called for her most days shortly after breakfast, and there were many times that she only came back late at night, when everyone was already asleep. Benito found himself waiting up for her, listening out for her footsteps. Missing their easy chatter.

'Hurry, hurry,' said a small boy now, running inside without the courtesy of first knocking on the door. He raced to Cesca, pulling on her skirts. It was shortly after dawn early in his second week in their home, 'It's *Tia* Marianna, Señor Doctor is asking for you.'

Cesca nodded and fetched a small leather satchel from a peg on the wall in the kitchen. Seeing that Benito was watching, she stopped and explained. 'It's my friend Marianna's second child. She lost the last one. I must go, it will destroy her if she loses this one too.'

'Good luck,' he called as she raced after the boy, wondering at the sudden downturn in his spirits at her departure.

Later that morning, he heard Esperanza's curses from his pallet bed in the cellar. She'd been late for her chores as usual, and had to be kicked out of bed by her mother. He made his way outside slowly, still favouring his broken ribs. Walking wasn't easy, but he wanted to finally see the monster for himself.

Flea was barking madly as he neared. Benito stifled a laugh as he caught sight of the creature. Grunon, the goat, had soft, wiry hair and what almost looked like a beatific smile, which was belied by the rather fierce expression in its eyes, almost as if it were mocking Esperanza as it stood its ground, refusing to budge or let her come near. Every time she tried it made very loud honking noises.

'It's not like I'm happy about this either,' she told the goat. She tried again to step closer and the goat lowered its head, making her slap her legs in frustration.

'Let me try something,' he told her. He'd read about a trick for snakes and decided to try it on the goat... it was worth a try. He stared at the goat, who stared back, making more of the honking noises. Benito kept at it, not breaking eye contact, not blinking. Esperanza said something, but he raised a hand and she fell quiet. After five full minutes of this the honking stopped. Benito took a step forward and the goat took an involuntary step back, closer to Esperanza, whose eyes widened in shock. Benito carried on staring until the goat lowered its head, keeping an eye on Benito. Esperanza approached the goat cautiously, and then let out a small whoop when the animal allowed herself to be milked. When Esperanza finished the goat raised a leg, about to step it inside the pail, but stopped when Benito came forward again, seeming to decide against it.

Esperanza looked at him in awe. 'How did you do that?'

He shrugged. 'The trick is to not break eye contact. I read about it in one of those novels I'm not supposed to read.'

She grinned. It was hard *not* to like him after that.

When they went into the kitchen and she had put the goat's milk into a jug that she covered with muslin cloth, for the cheese she would make, he asked her about how Cesca had become the doctor's assistant.

'Señor Garcia was a friend of my father's. His wife passed away a few years ago. He and the señora didn't have any children, and as our closest neighbours over the years we became close with him. He taught us to read, and when Cesca took an interest in medicine he taught her. I think he enjoys having someone to discuss his cases with. When she becomes of age, they will marry,' she said.

He stared at her in shock. A part of him grew cold at the thought. She'd said it so matter-of-factly. Benito thought that the doctor seemed nice enough, but he was fifty if he was a day.

'But isn't he like an uncle to her?'

She shrugged. 'Yes. But that just means he will be kind. Maybe it's different in Majorca, but here he's one of the wealthier men on the island. He'll make a good husband. She is happy at the arrangement.'

He blinked at her. How could anyone be happy with that?

Privately, Esperanza felt the same horror as he did at the thought of her sister marrying Señor Garcia, but she was in the minority with her views. Not that he was particularly unattractive as far as older men went, but he had always been a father figure in their lives. She herself couldn't have contemplated sharing a marriage bed with him. But Cesca was resigned to her fate; she'd spoken a few times of the benefits of learning more from him once they were married, and taking on more responsibility. That was all there was to hope for really in an arranged marriage, and at least in her own way Cesca was looking forward to it. That was more than many of the women she knew. Though some did look forward to having children of their own – it was one of the consolations.

'Señor Garcia wants to announce their engagement soon, now that she will be coming of age in a few months,' she told him. As in mainland Spain, women on the island married a little older than many girls in Europe and were generally only wed when they'd reached the age of twenty. Cesca had just six months before she came of age.

Benito didn't say anything more. It wasn't his place to question the way they lived their lives here. It wasn't unusual to marry second or even first cousins, particularly in a secretive Jewish community where many feared what marriage with a stranger might do to them. They almost never married someone outside of their community; it was too much of a risk. So why was it that strange to think of Cesca marrying the doctor? Was it about the age gap? But that wasn't all that unusual either. So why did it make him feel sad? Why should he feel that way when Cesca didn't?

'Are you engaged?' he asked. He was simply curious, nothing more. She looked at him with a strange expression on her face that was gone so fast he thought he'd imagined it. 'No – well, not any more.'

'Why not any more? Was it cancelled?'

'No. Marriages don't get cancelled here, not unless something happens to one of the parties, generally. I was promised to my cousin at the age of six. It was to take place just after Cesca's wedding, actually. We are ten months apart, you see, so it was important that she went first.'

'What changed, then?'

She looked at him, raised an eyebrow. 'I thought you knew. He died. I was meant to marry my cousin, *Rafael*. You know, the man you're pretending to be.'

He stared at her and took a sip of water. His mouth had turned suddenly dry at the thought.

'You were meant to marry Rafael?'

She nodded. Then she looked at him and said, 'So as soon as you are well, we can discuss the wedding.'

His eyes bulged, and he started to choke.

She rolled her eyes, and then helped by pounding him on the back. 'Don't worry, you still have about six to eight months to get used to the idea,' she said, her dark eyes looking deeply into his.

He blinked, and Esperanza burst out laughing. 'I'm *joking*, of course. Rafael and I were engaged, yes, but my family doesn't expect you take on every part of his identity. Don't look so concerned.'

Though she wasn't quite sure how they were going to explain that to their neighbours. Most people knew she was meant to be marrying her cousin Rafael. She'd worry about that later.

As he breathed an audible sigh of relief, she narrowed her eyes, then tossed her dark hair over her shoulder, whistling for her dog Flea to join her, and quirked an eyebrow. 'Like I wanted to marry *you*.' He had the grace to look a little embarrassed, and started to apologise, but she didn't stay to hear it. She was aware of her own beauty – it was a simple fact of nature, and for the most part she didn't dwell on it (one of her few redeeming qualities, according to Cesca) – still, she thought, he needn't look *that* relieved. Surely there were worse things in this world than the idea of marriage to her? In fact, there were quite a few men in the village who could think of nothing better and would swap places in a blink of an eye if only they had half a chance… but she managed somehow to stop herself from telling him *that*.

TWENTY-TWO

Formentera, present day

I found Big Jim at the Blues Bar later that night. I'd found myself pacing the house, turning over the things that the woman in the market had said, wondering if I should be worried about having Emmanuel in my home. He didn't seem dangerous. But looks, I supposed, could be deceptive. I sighed. It could also be about something else... perhaps she had been simply warning me about a philandering husband. Well, that presented no harm to me. I was nowhere near thinking about getting involved in a relationship yet.

But I wanted an answer, or at least to put my mind at rest, about the man who was spending so much time in my home. Particularly if we were going to be friends. I'd had enough drama over the past year, and I didn't need to welcome someone into my life who would cause me harm.

Big Jim was sitting at the bar, his hands dipping into a bowl of salted nuts, his jaw working while his grey head bobbed along to the sound of Bob Marley. He paused his chewing and gave me his big, Texan grin when he saw me, opening his arms wide for a hug.

I stepped into it. I needed one.

'Well, hello kiddo, what brings you here this fine evening? Can I get you a drink?'

'That'll be great,' I said, taking a seat on a bar stool, 'Just a vodka and tonic for me.'

'Sure thing.'

'Sue not here tonight?' I asked.

He shook his head. 'Flying solo. Art group,' he explained.

I nodded, gave him a half grin and then took a sip of the drink the bartender handed me.

'Something on your mind?' he asked, watching me, his blue eyes locked on to mine and his long grey ponytail swung over his shoulder.

'Yes, actually. I was hoping I'd run into you tonight. There's something I need to ask you about the renovator you sent me, Emmanuel.'

'Oh yes,' he said, his face brightening. 'Good guy, ain't he? Your place coming along, I hope?'

I bit my lip. 'Yes, he's a great worker, and I'm happy you say that – that he's a good guy, but...'

He looked at me with a frown and I explained what had happened to me, about the woman who'd come over to warn me.

To my surprise, Big Jim waved a hand in dismissal. 'Oh that? Tall girl, long brown hair, kind of athletic-looking?'

If that was code for drop-dead-gorgeous body, then yes. Athletic. 'Yeah?'

He shook his head, dipped his hand into the bowl for more nuts and gave me a grin. 'Yeah, don't worry about that.'

'Why not?' I asked in surprise.

'Well,' he sighed, pausing his chewing as he considered his words. 'To tell you the truth, kiddo, it's just like some people won't let a man *be* the better man, you know? Won't see it when someone's trying... and well, Em's trying. No one who knows him and has seen him these past few years can deny that.'

'What do you mean?' I asked.

He sighed. 'Look, it's his story to tell. All you'll hear round here are rumours and not a lot of it is true. What I can say is that

I was there at the start and he's paid for what he did. A few times over. The fact of the matter is the only person he ever hurt was himself. That's all I'm saying.'

My mouth fell open. 'Jim, you can't leave it there! What do you mean, he was the only one who got hurt? Who else was there? *Should* I be worried?'

He sighed, then pinched the bridge of his nose, like he'd said too much. 'No, you shouldn't be worried. Okay, well. What I mean is that there was an accident, his kid was in the car and his wife, and well, he'd been drinking…'

I gasped. 'No!'

He shook his head. 'They're fine. They survived. Em was the one who got the worst damage, all these scars, man, pretty bad all down his chest. Anyway, that accident shook him straight. But it ended his marriage, I mean all things considered, I don't think he blames his wife for that, he understood why she left – though it was kind of cruel to make sure that he never saw the kid afterward, especially when he's done all that work to pull himself straight. He's sober now, has been for years, but I dunno, it's like some people – like his wife's sister Claudia, that's who you ran into by the way – it's like she just won't accept that he's not the same guy any more. I think that's what eats him alive, really.'

I went home that night thinking about what Big Jim had told me. It made so much sense now when I thought about how hard Emmanuel seemed to work himself. How sombre he was. It was like he was still punishing himself, and I couldn't help feeling a little sorry for him as a result. Also, a sense of relief that I wasn't welcoming someone dangerous into my home… but I still had so many questions.

I sat in the kitchen at my new table, the one Emmanuel had helped me to find when I'd seen the rare, almost fun side of this serious man, and touched the urn with James's ashes in.

'What would you do?' I asked. 'Would you try speaking to him about it? Do I tell him that I know? Will that make things awkward between us now?'

I wasn't surprised when, not long after, I could have sworn he said, 'I'd go to bed and stop worrying about it.'

So that's what I did.

In the morning, the sun came streaming in and I turned over and saw to my surprise that I hadn't brought James's ashes to bed with me. It was the first time I had done that since the funeral.

I twisted the ring on my thumb, and thought about what Maria had said when I'd told her about James, about what had happened.

At ninety-five she knew a lot about death, having outlived most of her own family.

'But you keep them here,' she'd said, pressing a fist into her chest as if it would enter her very heart. 'They never go far from there. Sometimes, little Ben will come into the kitchen, hearing me speaking, and ask me who am I talking to, and it's one of them. I'm speaking with my family. They never really leave you.'

I couldn't help but hope that was true.

TWENTY-THREE

Formentera, 1718

Cesca could hear the woman's screams before she entered the *finca*. An old woman, with a bent back, dressed in black, rushed out as soon as she saw her, relieved that she had arrived. 'Oh Señorita, please, she can't lose another one, it'll kill her!'

Cesca touched the old woman's lined face, nodded and ran inside. The doctor, Señor Garcia, was already there. 'It's a breech,' he said simply. She could see the fear in his brown eyes. She was the only one who could. It was important now for her to act calm. Chaos only led to fear and that led to panic and mistakes.

'Okay,' she said, putting her basket down. 'Señora,' she said to the old woman, 'We'll need a few more rags, and some warm water. Can you get that for us?'

The woman nodded, looking relieved to have some task to occupy herself with.

When the old woman was out of the room, Cesca knelt down next to the labouring woman's legs and waited for the doctor to give her an update.

He indicated that he was going to try to turn the baby with his fingers, encourage it to turn into the normal birth position.

'Marianna,' she said, getting up to clasp the pregnant woman's hand. 'We are going to try saving this baby, okay? But the doctor will have to do something that will feel a bit strange, perhaps painful.'

Cesca looked at the doctor. His eyes told her that painful was an understatement. She took a breath. 'You will need to be brave, and work harder than you ever have in your life. Can you do that?'

Marianna nodded, tears slipping down her cheeks. She looked ready to burst into proper crying.

'Save your tears, Señora,' Cesca said. 'You need the strength for the baby – use that for when you need to push but only when we tell you to, okay? It's very important.'

The woman nodded and Cesca returned to the doctor's side. She whispered to him, 'Have you done this before?'

'Just once,' he said.

'Did the baby survive?' He shook his head, and Cesca felt her heart clench. 'We have to try.'

He nodded. They had no choice.

The doctor's hands were too big, and he wasn't getting anywhere. All he was doing was making the mother cry out in pain. He looked at Cesca. 'You can reach further, your hands are smaller.'

'Me?' She was shocked. 'I don't know what to do!'

'I'll help you,' he said. 'Quickly now, before it's too late and we have no choice but to deliver this child as a breech.'

She inserted her fingers and turned the baby as gently as she could, the doctor describing to her all the while what she should be feeling for, while Marianna roared in pain. At last, she felt the baby move. 'It's turning! It's moving.'

They breathed a sigh of relief. Breech babies had a very low chance of survival, but with this one having turned, Marianna would have a normal birth, and the risk was much reduced.

At last they helped to bring a healthy baby boy into the world. Marianna fell back on the bed crying and gasping out of relief and sheer fatigue.

Cesca and the doctor dealt with the afterbirth while Marianna's mother helped to clean the baby, swaddling it in a blanket and placing it next to her. She stared at her son in amazement.

By the time Cesca got home it was early morning. She'd been on her feet for most of the night and it had taken its toll; all she wanted was a quick wash and to get in her bed and slip into a deep sleep.

She hadn't been that scared or that excited by medicine in the longest time. Working with the doctor always made her feel like they were part of a team. She hadn't spent much time wondering about their marriage. What it would mean to actually be his wife.

She tried to picture it. His kind, gentle brown eyes, the way that they always looked at her with such encouragement. It wouldn't be hard to be his wife, she thought. She'd learn so much.

She frowned as she turned over. Of course there was more to a marriage than that, she knew. She wasn't naive – she hadn't just spent the evening helping a woman to give birth without knowing a little about how it happened. And she'd grown up on a farm, after all. But she couldn't imagine that part of the marriage. She tried to imagine it, kissing him, but it felt odd to think of him that way. Did it matter, though, that she didn't desire him like that? Few wives felt that way. Her parents had grown to love each other despite their own arrangement, and she loved Señor Garcia in her own way. Before she knew it a pair of pale blue eyes swam before her eyes, followed by a soft smile, and she opened her eyes fast in the dark, her heart pounding, a faint flush beginning to creep up her neck as she realised just who she wouldn't mind kissing. She was picturing Benito's face. She lay awake for some time afterwards, despite her earlier fatigue, trying to put the thought out of her head, and when she did finally fall asleep it was with a frown on her face.

*

When she woke up she heard a moan from her mother. She went to check on her and was concerned to find her looking tired and unwell.

'Is it your stomach again, *Mare?*'

Her mother nodded. Her hair was in disarray and there was sweat beading on her forehead. She looked ashen. She'd long suffered from digestive complaints, but over the years it had been getting worse. Cesca would have to speak to Señor Garcia about giving her mother something stronger or seeing if they should be changing something in their diet. She hoped there was something he could suggest, something she hadn't thought of.

For now, she made her mother a tea with peppermint and calendula, something soothing to combat the pain.

When she saw that Benito was awake, his pale blue eyes looking at her in concern, she looked away, her face colouring at her thoughts from the night before.

'Is your mother all right?' he asked, his smile warm, concerned. She sat next to him, handing him the cup of tea she'd made.

'I'm not sure – she's had this stomach complaint before, but...' She looked away, and he touched her hand. 'What?'

She moved her arm back, her skin burning from his touch, and swallowed. 'It's just... it keeps happening. I hope the doctor will have something for her, something to help. I hate seeing her in pain.'

He nodded. 'I'm sure he will.'

Cesca stared at him, trying to will herself to go back to bed. She was still very tired. But talking with him first thing in the morning, when it was only the two of them awake in the house, had become the brightest part of her day, the part she looked forward to most. She bit her lip, knowing that she shouldn't think that way. Shouldn't want nothing more than to sit talking with this strange, handsome man just after dawn, as the sun began to shine through the small window, making his beautiful blue eyes look as if they were lit from within, when she was promised to another.

TWENTY-FOUR

Formentera, present day

I told Isla about James on a cool night as we walked along the harbour, sharing a bottle of wine she'd bought from the bar. I'd gone to hear her sing and afterwards we'd carried on talking well past closing time.

Her sandals dangled in her hand while we stared at the boats and the amber lights glinting off the water, and she looked at me and then grimaced.

'I didn't want to ask you about it – not until you were ready – but I'm here, if you want to talk.'

I took a sip from the bottle she offered and nodded. 'Thanks.'

I wondered if Big Jim had filled her in. I guessed he must have. I was relieved, in a way, not to have to rehash the whole sad tale.

As we walked I told her about how I was just trying to make sense of it all.

'What I'm finding hardest…' I sighed, hating to admit it, 'is being alone.'

I hadn't been alone since I was nineteen years old, and the truth was I was having a hard time with it.

Something told me that carrying my dead husband's ashes into every room I visited – apart from the bathroom – wasn't exactly the best form of coping with his death.

She nodded, took the bottle from me and took a swig, while she stared at the ships. 'Yeah, being alone isn't easy.'

I looked at her in surprise. 'But you make it look so *easy*.'

She did. She lived alone in a flat that she rented from the owner of the Blues Bar, and from what I could see lived a pretty amazing life on her own terms, selling her beautiful seascapes, playing in a band, living a kind of carefree, hippie life. She had the sort of effortless grace and cool I could only ever dream of achieving.

She laughed, and her shoulder-length hair swung behind her as she fixed me with a look of disbelief. 'Me? Okay with being alone? Well, I suppose *now*. But it took for ever. It almost killed me when Sebastian and I broke up. We were together since we were kids, you know. I thought we'd get married, have babies, all that jazz, you know... till one day he told me that he wasn't in love with me any more and that he wasn't sure if he ever had been. It was in the middle of a tour, when we were both feeling just so over the whole show-business thing, and I guess he decided to get honest about that as well.'

I stared at her. 'I'm so sorry.'

'Hey, it happens. I mean, it's not as bad as what you went through.'

'It still hurt.'

She nodded. 'Yeah. Anyway, I've never really minded my own company but being single was something I had to get used to, that feeling of being by yourself most of the time. You just got to push through it.'

'I'm working on that,' I admitted. 'It's a work in progress.'

'You'll get there. And I mean, look how far you've come.'

I nodded. That was true. Just a few weeks ago, just being in anyone's company had felt like torture. The only way I had felt I could survive was by keeping everything down to a minimum – interacting with people, life, the future. Perhaps that was slowly changing.

'Small wins,' she said, handing me the bottle as I made my way to my bicycle. 'That's what you've got to go for now – that's what adds up.'

It was a few days later when I got a call from Allan, as I was watching Emmanuel get to work on repairing the drainpipes.

'So are you up for some company?' my brother asked.

I stopped pacing the garden and sat down. 'What do you mean?'

'Yeah, well, I miss you, Twig, and God knows I could do with a break from the office…'

'You mean you're going to come and visit?'

'Yeah, if you're up for it?'

'Course I am! I'd love that. When were you thinking of coming?'

'In about a week, if that's all right?'

'That's perfect! Oh, Maria will be so happy!'

'Good, can't wait to meet her. Anyway, I just wanted to check before I booked my ticket.'

'Like I'd say no?'

'Well, you never know, I mean from what I hear you're leading this very exotic life…'

'Oh, and who are you hearing this from?'

'Mum,' he admitted. 'She keeps asking me how come you keep extending your holiday. Haven't you told her, Twig? About Marisal?'

I grimaced. 'Argh, no, not yet. I suppose I should.'

'Yeah. Probably. There's some things I want to ask her about it.'

'Yeah, like how come she never told us that Gran had a sister.'

'Yeah, like that.'

TWENTY-FIVE

Formentera, 1718

Don Santiago Martínez de Sánchez missed Barcelona. He missed the luxuries of home. The servants, his townhouse, the wide streets, the hustle and bustle of people and the urbane sense of living in a century that was going through an age of enlightenment. An age of discovery, of science and answers. And incredible advancements. It was exciting.

But he was first a businessman, and a researcher. He wasn't all that happy with his current role as the latter. A role he had found himself in against his will. There had been some trouble with the daughter of one of his colleagues and the administration had decided that it would be prudent for him to come and make a report on one of the crown's least profitable ventures – the salt flats in the Pitiusas – for the next few months. Officially he was told that the post was an important undertaking, one that required someone of his sensitivity, intelligence and knowledge. He would be going to ascertain how they could improve the production technologies of the salt flats to improve the profitability of the Spanish salt trade. He was told that it was vital, in fact, noble work, now that the establishment had been placed into the hands of the Crown where it belonged. As such, they would like it to be introduced to the latest technology and his instructions were to oversee the implementation of this technology, to make the venture the Crown had inherited a success.

But Don Santiago wasn't fooled. He knew what the move was really about – a ploy to get him out of the way. Don Hernando de Allandez's daughter had wanted him for a husband, and he hadn't been interested. So, this was his punishment – banishment to the least important island of the Crown.

Don Hernando de Allandez had powerful friends, and a long memory.

Don Santiago, however, was nothing if not a professional. And when the governors told him to start with Formentera, the tiniest slip of an island with perhaps the least productive of the salt flats, he agreed so that he could write his report and be done with it.

He hadn't needed to come to know that the process of extracting the salt was the same as it had been for the last four hundred years. They still used lead pans and wood, and most of the production was done by hand, as it always had been. He didn't need to be here to see that the work was back-breaking – literally: people carried the salt to the ships on their backs. But there was one positive of seeing the system with his own eyes. It was without question a system that could do with some innovation, some thought and guidance, and, despite his reservations in coming to visit these small, backward islands, a part of him was satisfied that at least by the end of his – hopefully brief – stay here he might leave some lasting legacy behind and be known as the person who helped transform its production.

Of course, he couldn't tell the islanders *that*. Officially he was introduced as a botanist. He was making a study of the minerals in the salt flats, the natural wildlife and its importance to the geography of the area.

He'd been warned that announcing what he was really doing on the island at first might just ensure that the islanders would be unhelpful in providing him with the information that he would need now that the salt flats were under the leadership of the Crown. He would need to gather information before he could start transforming the production. They were a taciturn community, he'd been told – one that had resisted the new regime. But seeing was something else. These islanders were so cautious in their conversations that they were bordering on being secretive.

He'd been staying at one of the official houses, not far from the salt pans, for over a week now, and he'd barely had more than a casual conversation with any of the locals. Even the servants were reluctant to say more than they had to; they were polite, but more wary than friendly. The female servants were attractive, as were many of the other island women, but none looked him in the eye, and a few times he found them whispering – but this wasn't the girlish chatter he was used to, followed by a blush; this was different, almost as if they had something to hide.

Don Santiago was walking to his *pension* after a hard day's work in the gruelling sun. The only way to truly understand the production of salt was to get stuck in, to talk to the men who spent the summer months working it. He was an office man, well used to sitting in a cool, ventilated room for the morning, followed by long siestas in the afternoon and lazy lunches that went well into the night as he discussed business and the finer things in life with his colleagues and friends. Just being out in the hot sun every day was proving enough to make him long to return home to the comforts of his normal life, where conversations were about other things: science, art, literature, music. Here they only ever spoke about salt, farming or fishing, and he was sick of hearing about all three.

For a poor community, though, they were interesting to observe, he had to concede. In some ways, a conundrum. Many of the women wore a lot of gold jewellery, sometimes up to a dozen ropes of gold chains across their shoulders. They wore gold earrings too. They were attractive but unusual, he couldn't help thinking as he passed them every day. Many of them had reddish hair and green eyes. An island trait, he presumed.

But it was a girl with long dark hair that fell down her back in a waterfall of deepest midnight who caught his attention.

Unlike most of the other women, who seemed to always walk in pairs, their hands full of fruit or loaves of bread, she walked empty-handed, and alone but for the small wiry dog that followed faithfully at her dusty heels.

He wasn't quite sure what possessed him to follow her when he saw her next. Perhaps it was the way she looked over her shoulder when she sensed that he was staring. The way that she didn't avert her dark eyes, or blush like any other young woman might. She didn't fuss her hair or straighten her dress; she simply gazed back at him with something almost like a challenge in her eyes, and didn't look away, not until he did.

As she turned to walk on, he thought it couldn't hurt to ask for her name. At least then he might have something to divert him from his present task, and the endless, mindless, talk of salt.

Lazy. Head-in-the-clouds. Spoilt. That's what the women in her family called her.

Maybe, thought Esperanza. But on a fine day, the last place she wanted to be was stuck inside the kitchen making more food. Why was it that Ibicenco women spent their lives cooking, cooking, cooking, she wondered with a sigh.

She liked eating just as much as anybody, but she didn't see the need to spend all your days locked up inside making food.

Besides, it was all very well for Cesca. Everything she made seemed to come easy to her. The bread she made always rose. Her paellas were always rich and tasty just the way their father had liked it. Her fish was *never* rubbery.

Even Grunon, the demon goat, thought better of stepping her hoof in *Cesca's* pail.

Aside from Esperanza's watercolours, which were excellent – but useless for life on a *finca* in the middle of nowhere – she wasn't particularly talented at anything useful. Not like her sister, anyway. When she'd wanted to learn how to be a nurse like her, her father had put his foot down. He hadn't seen the sense of having two of his daughters running around the island away from the house. Someone needed to stay and help their mother, and look after the household, he insisted. Of course, that wasn't the world's most well-thought-out plan – Esperanza simply wasn't that good at domestic chores. Things seemed to slip out of her hands and land on her feet, or scorch her wrists. The bread she tried to make was likely to burn or flop and everything she cooked always seemed to taste just a little burnt, because she got distracted too easily, often by the little dog she'd adopted, who wasn't allowed in the house.

Cesca would often get impatient with her. 'Just watch the food, Esperanza, when you cook it, don't do anything else. Don't worry about anything else. Why is that so hard?'

She couldn't explain. It just was. What she wanted deep in her heart was a life away from the chores of the farm, a life like the one her friend Riba described, with large airy homes, servants and time for art, for reading, dancing and music. Was she so very bad for wanting that? For wanting more?

She was silly, that she knew. Dreaming of the things her friend told her about, a life she could never have, only made things harder. But now that things had changed, with the man she was meant to marry – her betrothed, Rafael – dead, suddenly it felt as if the future was less decided than she'd first imagined. While she was sad that her cousin had passed away, albeit a cousin she'd only met a few times before, she couldn't help but feel something inside her come alive at the change, as if perhaps there was a chance for some of her dreams after all.

But now, as she hung the salted fish on their hooks outside to dry, a trickle of sweat ran down her spine and she puffed out her red cheeks, her mood growing darker, as she thought of the life that awaited. 'It'll hardly be a change,' she muttered as she faced the fact, which was that she was no doubt going to be married off to one of the boys she'd grown up with in the village, which meant just more of *this*.

It was hot, the wind had died down and she was feeling miserable. Cesca had left her the fish to do, after she'd run off with Señor Garcia on some or other medical emergency, and had given her strict instructions to finish it all this afternoon, but Esperanza was sure that the fish would dry whether she hung it on the wooden slats outside or not.

And a little swim would cool her down, restore her mood and let her work more easily, she told herself.

She slipped away while her mother was having a siesta, and whistled for Flea to join in her escape.

As they raced down to the cove, she sensed someone looking at her and turned to see, in the distance, a tall man staring at her. She blinked. He had light brown hair and he wasn't dressed like any of the men she knew. He was dressed like a gentleman, in a suit. It was that stranger, the one everyone had been talking about. She frowned in surprise. The one from Barcelona. No one had mentioned that he was handsome, though.

He kept staring at her, so she raised her chin and used the trick Rafael had taught her for Grunon. She was surprised and pleased to see that it worked on men just as much as on demon goats. Then she walked on with Flea until they reached her favourite, hidden cove.

She slipped off her dress and waded into the cool still water, sighing in pleasure. Flea raced and dived, following her, and she laughed at the little brown dog. Lying on her back in the cool sea, she looked up at the clear, azure-blue sky, her fingers tracing the water, Flea doing a paddle around her.

'So, this is where you ran off to? I did wonder,' said a refined, cultured Spanish voice, like fine brandy.

Esperanza choked on the water, and spun round to search for the source of the voice. On the rocks close by was the man she'd seen on the old salt road. The stranger.

She sat up in the water, coughing and spluttering. When she recovered, she remembered her modesty and threw an arm across her chest.

'It's a fine day for a swim,' was all he said, his voice mild. She stared at him, wishing he would go away. Searching for the courage to tell him to.

'I am Don Santiago Martínez de Sánchez. I don't believe we've met yet,' he said introducing himself as if they were not in a deeply compromising situation. He spoke in Eivissenc for her benefit.

She blinked at him, because of course they hadn't met yet. '*Buno tarda,*' she answered, to be polite. She didn't want to give her own name; swimming in her undergarments was not something she would like the entire island to know about, particularly in the presence of a strange, Spanish gentleman. One all the islanders were worried about.

He stared at her a moment longer, perhaps waiting for her to say who she was.

To stop him from asking, she said, inanely, 'I was hot', explaining the obvious. 'But I must get out now, my sister will be waiting for me.'

He smiled, showing white, even teeth. 'A swim seems lovely on a day like this. Stay a while. Perhaps I could join you?'

Her eyes widened as he made to take off his shirt. To her shock he actually did shrug it off and placed it on the rocks next to her own discarded dress. He stood half naked, revealing lightly tanned skin and golden body hair.

She felt herself blush. Her mother would be furious if she knew the situation she'd found herself in. Why was it that she somehow always managed to get herself in these predicaments?

'Señor – I think it best that I get out and leave you to swim, if you wouldn't mind turning round so I can get out?'

'Oh? Yes.' He sounded disappointed, but he remembered his manners. 'I suppose if that's what you'd prefer.' He turned round, then bent down to hold up her dress – which was when Cesca appeared in the cove, ready to berate her sister, her gaze fixed on Esperanza and the dog, who started to bark excitedly.

Incredibly, Cesca didn't see the man crouched on the rock, holding up her sister's dress, which he dropped quickly back onto the rocks.

'So, this is where you run off to? Do you even know the mess you left behind – there are hundreds of seagulls feasting on the bounty you left outside for them! They even went flying into the house. *Mare* had to scare them off with a broom! And you know she isn't feeling well. I can't believe you! I give you one simple instru—' She stopped abruptly, seeing movement out of the corner of her eye, and turned to finally see the half-naked man on the rocks. Her mouth fell open in utter shock. She blinked at him, at last speechless.

Esperanza wanted to sink below the water in mortification.

Don Santiago had the grace to look embarrassed, and quickly put on his shirt. '*Buno tarda*. I am Don Santiago Martínez de Sánchez,' he said, introducing himself politely and clearing his throat nervously. 'I'm afraid that I stumbled upon your sister and decided to have a swim myself. She was just about to get out, I assure you. I was turning round to protect her modesty.'

Cesca raised an eyebrow. 'I'm sure you were. Thank you, Señor, I believe that my sister getting out now is *best*,' she said, crossing her arms and staring at her sister meaningfully.

'Good – yes,' he said, awkwardly. Cesca could have that effect.

Esperanza waded out of the water while Flea padded to the shore and started barking at her to follow. Even he knew who was really in charge in their house, she thought, her shoulders slumped as she grabbed the dress from the rock and slipped it back over her wet skin, missing the admiring glance Don Santiago gave her.

'Good luck with your fish problem,' he called to her retreating back. He sounded amused.

Esperanza shot him a silencing look. Gentleman or not, because of him the fish were now the least of her worries.

As she followed after her sister's fast-disappearing, anger-stiffened back, she sighed. If she had imagined the moment she would meet someone like Don Santiago, this was not it: as a scolded child, running after her older sister.

Cesca was furious.

Why couldn't her sister just act like a sister for once? Why couldn't she think of them, ever?

She'd come home to find that most of the fish had to be thrown away, as the flies had made a meal over them, no doubt laying eggs. Esperanza hadn't salted them properly, as usual. She never did. And the birds had come for the rest. Cesca sighed, then took the remaining fish to a bucket and began scrubbing the flesh to see if it could be salvaged. Esperanza stayed away to let her vent for a few minutes, then came to help her. Flea lay asleep at her feet.

'That dog has to go.'

It caused Cesca no joy to see the pain in her sister's eyes. She didn't mean it, of course. Though she didn't see his charms the way her sister did.

The trouble was that it wasn't just the waste of the fish; it was the fact that she had drawn attention to the household at a time when they didn't need it. Esperanza had left Benito lying alone in the cellar and anyone could have found him there. He was still recovering, and he still had his habit of mumbling in his sleep, calling out his brother's name. If someone had come past and heard, what would have happened then? What if this new, strange visitor, Don Santiago Martinez de Sanchez, had followed Esperanza here? What if he started asking questions about their cousin? The news of the Moorish ship that had been captured and the Jewish prisoners taken had been spread far and wide, along with the names of the prisoners, the Nuñez brothers. One look at a man hidden in a cellar calling out for his brother Paulo could be enough to put them all in danger.

TWENTY-SIX

Formentera, present day

Maria's home always smelt like food, and the sea. There was warmth, made up of more than sunshine, in the old walls.

It wasn't just the past that I was learning about. It was about daily life, the rituals of old-fashioned practices that hadn't changed, for the most part, in hundreds of years.

Every week when I visited her, I discovered new things about my roots. I learned about the flavours and art of Jewish cooking, although it was a kind of cooking that had had to adapt greatly over the years. Like the history of the Jewish people themselves, who had no homeland for thousands of years and had to constantly flee hardship and persecution, their travels influencing what they cooked, ensuring that the Jewish cuisine was nothing if not varied.

There was a particular flavour to the Ibicenco Jewish table too – as Maria would tell me, a lot of the practices of keeping a kitchen kosher couldn't be strictly observed, particularly as certain things like not eating pork might act as a signal if anyone was watching. Also, times were tough; the people lived on an island with not much of an economy beyond farming and the salt trade, so limiting what they ate just wasn't practical, though behind closed doors things were sometimes a little different.

I learned what was kosher and what wasn't. In some ways, it was an eye-opener. There were practices that my father had followed – like the way he always used to move the yoghurt if it was on the shelf that stored cold meat. I had just thought this was a personal quirk, but now I realised that it was a habit derived from trying to keep kosher over the centuries that had been passed down without any of us realising.

Maria told me that the islanders used to have creative ways of getting round the practice of not working on the Sabbath. 'Even today most islanders will tell you that it is unlucky to work on a Saturday. In fact, many shops were manned on Saturdays by children.'

There were other things too, like the fact that we only ate fish with scales when I was growing up, never shellfish – though I had since rebelled – or that we hardly, if ever, ate pork or game. I hadn't questioned those things. Or the fact that every Friday night, without fail, my father used to light candles, and that it was the one time of the week that he always made sure we sat down to eat as a family, even though it used to drive me crazy because I wanted to go out with friends on a Friday night and not sit at home. I hadn't realised that this whole time we'd really been practising *shabbat.*

My legs were getting stronger from riding the bicycle every day. The longest excursion I took was to the Cap de Barbaria lighthouse. Isla was right; it was thirsty work and an arduous ride: a stretch of scratchy brown earth through narrow paths and desolate golden fields until I found the lighthouse at the end. As I rode, my thoughts cast back over time and I realised that, in the time of Maria's stories, there hadn't been a lighthouse. I couldn't help but wonder how much else had changed, like our family, when people like me didn't even know about who we once were. At least that was shifting now, I thought as I pedalled home, towards Marisal.

*

A few days later Emmanuel came into the kitchen, his sombre face dark, almost forbidding. 'Did someone, a woman, come to speak to you about me?' he asked.

I swallowed. 'Yes.'

A muscle went in his jaw. 'I see.'

I chewed my lip. 'Look, it's none of my business, obviously…'

He nodded. 'No, it isn't.'

I sucked in a breath.

He sighed. 'Except that she made it your business – so why didn't you come and speak to me about it?'

I closed the notebook I'd been attempting to do some writing in. 'Would you like a coffee?'

He frowned. So I stood up and shrugged. 'Well, I'm going to make myself one, so…'

'Okay.'

I went past him and switched the kettle on. 'Honestly, I didn't know what to think – so I asked Big Jim about it. Sorry.'

'Instead of asking me?'

'Well, yes. I didn't know if it was something I had to worry about – you're in my house…'

His jaw tensed again but he nodded.

'And Big Jim, he…'

'Told me I had nothing to worry about.'

He stared. 'Is that all?'

'Yes – well, that was the gist.'

He nodded. 'Okay.'

'Okay?'

'Sure.'

Then he got back to work.

But after that, we were friends, real friends. It started slowly – an extra cup of coffee before he left, then a sandwich that led to lunch or dinner.

When I told Isla about it she raised an eyebrow. 'Do you think it's going to be something more?'

I shook my head. 'No – well not for a long while, not for either of us.'

I wouldn't be able to cope with anything more right now. And I didn't know if it was wrong or right, I liked the fact that there was someone male in the house, someone made of flesh and blood, who occasionally spoke back.' To: I wouldn't be able to cope with anything more right now. And I didn't know if it was wrong or right, I liked the fact that there was someone male in the house, someone made of flesh and blood, who occasionally spoke back.

I didn't need it to be anything more than that.

TWENTY-SEVEN

Formentera, 1718

Cesca was teaching Benito about herbal medicine, an important part of island life, he discovered, particularly when it came to survival. There were times, she said, during bad weather, when Formentera was cut off from the main island, and these herbs had kept them alive. Most islanders, she said, had learned to use what grew wild. Though Cesca was fortunate in that her brother Antoni brought back many medicines, including exotic herbs and spices that could be used for healing. Benito marvelled at what she knew, what she'd learned as the doctor's apprentice and at how her face lit up when she spoke of it.

He discovered that aniseed was used to help cool high temperatures – she'd used that on him when he'd had a fever. Calendula helped with swelling in the mouth and stomach, and it could be used on the body to help wound recovery. He listened as she went through the jars, naming each one.

It was a pity, he thought, that she couldn't train the way that a man could. He had a feeling that she would do better than he had at university. He smiled at the thought. She was explaining how ordinary vegetables also had healing properties, such as garlic, which could be used to help someone recover faster from a cold. What?' she asked, noting his smile, her face colouring.

'I was just thinking that there were a few men I've known who have long argued about the dangers of teaching women – perhaps they feared that many of the women they knew would become cleverer than them.'

Cesca looked down, vaguely embarrassed. She knew it was meant as a compliment, but she had, in fact, been accused many times of being 'something like a man' by those who saw her passion for medicine as an oddity. Those who didn't mean it as a compliment.

She was resilient, and hard-working. Her father had encouraged it. There was no place for weakness on an island like this. Life could be tough and they had all learned to be tougher. And those who struggled, like her sister at times, had to be forced to be strong for their own good.

'How is it that you and your sister are so different?' he asked, as if he were reading her thoughts.

Cesca tried hard not to bristle at the question. Esperanza was beautiful, and feminine to her core. She was wild, and spirited, and said what she thought. Whereas Cesca was careful and hard-working and slow to temper. The boys they'd grown up with had been falling in love with her beautiful, wild sister for most of their lives.

'I don't know.'

'She's so lazy,' he said, laughing. 'And she's always got an excuse. She'll let anyone else do the work if you give her half a chance.' Which had happened to him a lot over the past few weeks, he'd noticed. It was he who now milked the goat and made the cheese. 'I've never met anyone who can waste time the way she does. She's always talking, it takes her hours to finish things.' He said it fondly though, and Cesca couldn't help laughing.

'My father always used to say if you want time to go slowly have Esperanza make your breakfast,' she said.

Benito grinned. 'Exactly.'

Cesca looked away, her heart starting to pound. Not many men saw the laziness, or saw beyond the dark eyes and beautiful visage.

'She has a kind heart though,' he said, thinking of Esperanza's affection for the dog.

She looked back at him and raised an eyebrow. He grinned, adding, 'Deep down.' She laughed.

Then she sighed. She did love Esperanza, for all her exasperation with her. 'Sometimes I feel like I'm more her mother than her sister, and it makes me angry, I often just don't understand her. Then I feel bad because I'm snapping at her. It's a horrible cycle.'

She knew that Esperanza tried to be better, but she didn't understand why she made her life harder – if she just concentrated on what she was doing then she wouldn't have to be reprimanded, and she could go out and enjoy her free time once she'd earned it.

She sighed, then admitted, 'My sister would have perhaps thrived more in a home where she would have been praised for the things she's good at. She enjoys drawing, reading, and she has a fine ear for music. She's really talented. Here there just isn't time for such things. We all have to work hard just to survive.'

'She would have enjoyed Majorca,' Benito said, thinking of some of the women he'd known there, who came from wealthy homes and lived more affluent lives. Women who were called accomplished because of their skills in conversation and art and music.

Cesca nodded. 'Maybe. I don't know, though – because she is wild too. I sometimes think she would sleep outside if we let her just to be with that dog of hers.'

He laughed, and she sighed. 'The truth is my sister just needs to grow up – and fast.'

Benito shook his head. 'I've met some people who grew up too quickly – friends, cousins, people who were forced to. People who were treated like something under a shoe because of what they believed in. Don't wish that on Esperanza.'

TWENTY-EIGHT

Formentera, present day

'So, I've got a serious question for you,' said Isla, one afternoon while we were sitting beneath the orange tree in my garden, watching the gentle lap of the water in the distance. I had my feet up on my table, crossed at the ankles, and I'd been idly scribbling notes on my novel when she spoke. Her sketchpad lay abandoned, and she took a sip of Sue's home-made sangria.

Big Jim was leaning against the trunk of a nearby tree, his eyes closed as he lazily strummed a melody on the guitar.

The sun was still warm, just beginning to go down, and already I could hear the cicadas starting to stir in the dry grass. It was an impromptu, lazy Saturday afternoon. I turned to her in surprise.

'Okay?' Wondering if she was going to ask me something about James.

'Well, you've got rhythm, right?'

I stared at her, then burst out laughing. 'Um, I'm not sure… why?'

'Well, I think you do – I mean you're always tapping your fingers along to the music.'

'Okay,' I hedged, not really seeing where she was going with this.

Sue came out of the kitchen, with a grin and a tambourine.

'Well, we brought you this,' she said.

I frowned, and took it. 'A tambourine?'

'We thought, you know, maybe you could be the fourth member of the band,' said Big Jim, opening up one lazy blue eye.

I laughed. 'With the tambourine?'

Isla grinned. 'Easy to learn.'

I gave it a little shake. Big Jim put on a very bad English accent and said, 'By George, I think she's got it!' Then he roared with laughter.

I looked at them all, then grinned. 'You're all bonkers.'

They were all waiting, staring at me, so I grinned too. 'Okay,' I said with a chuckle.

'Cool,' said Isla, winking. 'We practise on Tuesdays. And perform two nights a week.'

I started at her. Then I had a thought. I sat up straight. 'Oh, maybe I could also sing backup?' I said, a big grin spreading across my face.

Isla raised an eyebrow. 'Ah…'

'Tone deaf, darlin',' said Big Jim. 'But the girl's sure got rhythm.'

I grinned. Took a sip of sangria. I'd take it.

Which is how, somehow, at age forty-five, I became a member of a *band*.

'You're what?' asked Sage, barely suppressing a giggle, when I told her about it a few days later.

'Part of a band,' I said, laughing myself, and then I explained, which made her laugh so much that I got hysterics, too.

'The tambourine,' she cried, after a full minute of howling laughter. 'Oh God, Mum, I needed that. I can't freaking *wait* to come and see you.'

'Me too, darling, you have no idea how much I miss you.'

'Is it about *five*-texts-a-day worth?'

'What makes you say that?' I asked, affecting a casual, nonchalant air.

'Because I get on average five texts a day from you,' she said, deadpan.

'Ah – *yes*. That. Sorry.'

'Nah, I'm just teasing. They've helped, thanks, Mum.'

I breathed a sigh of relief.

Then she said, 'I cannot wait to tell Uncle Allan that you've joined a band.'

I giggled. 'Ah God, no don't, he already thinks I've lost it a bit.'

Which was sort of true.

But for once I didn't mind.

That night after they'd left, I couldn't sleep. I sat up in bed, twisting James's ring over and over on my thumb, listening to the sound of the waves outside.

I got up, put on my robe, padded through to the kitchen and put the kettle on, then went back to my room. I was too tired to try to work, and too wired to go back to sleep. Tired but wired. It seemed to be a recent new state of events.

I prowled around the room, casually opening up drawers, avoiding looking at James's ashes – I knew what he'd tell me to do: go back to sleep. But instead I went about idly looking through cupboards. This is why I needed a TV, I thought, as I opened the old wardrobe in my bedroom more out of boredom than anything else.

It was as I slowly opened one of the empty drawers that I saw it, the sharp edge of what looked like an old photograph wedged in far at the back. I knelt down and prised it loose with my fingers. After a full minute it came free, bent and slightly jagged from where I'd pulled it out. It was a faded photograph of two young girls standing with their backs to the house. Much of it was blurry but I could just make out a familiar smile.

It was Maria, and she had her arm across the shoulders of another younger girl, who I realised must be my grandmother, Alba. She had her eyes closed and was laughing uproariously at whatever Maria was whispering in her ear.

I touched the photograph, and felt my eyes smart. They had been close once. I couldn't help wondering, as Maria told me Cesca and Esperanza's story, what had happened between these other sisters. Why hadn't my gran ever mentioned Maria to me? How could you forget to mention your own sister? Why had their relationship fallen so drastically apart?

TWENTY-NINE

Formentera, 1718

'It seems you have made quite an impression,' said Riba to Esperanza a few days later.

'What do you mean?' asked Esperanza, who was loading the bread into the communal oven.

'On Don Santiago, of course. You were all he could talk about the other night, when he came for dinner.'

Esperanza closed her eyes in shame, recollecting their encounter on the beach. She had been afraid of that. Her sister would be *furious*.

'It seems that at first he didn't even know your name... but then he started to describe you and of course, they knew it had to be you.'

'How?' asked Esperanza. She was hardly the only woman with dark hair on the island. Couldn't she be spared the shame, just for once?'

'Well, there was Flea too – he's quite a distinctive dog.'

Esperanza rolled her eyes.

Riba nudged her in her ribs. 'Well, according to him you are the most beautiful woman on the island. I half believed he was going to go straight over there and propose, the way he was speaking.'

Esperanza sighed. Ordinarily she would have enjoyed the compliment. She was aware of her good fortune in being attractive – she couldn't help but be aware of it considering how some of the men had stared at her when she was growing up.

'Apparently, you went swimming and that's how he found you. He likened you to a mermaid.'

Esperanza blushed, pushing her hair out of her eyes and looking away. 'Hardly. I was hot and tired, and in a bad mood because Cesca had left me all the fish to do while she ran off with Señor Garcia, as usual, so I took a little break and went for a swim. I had no idea he was there.'

Riba shrugged. 'Well, anyway. I think he was trying to get me to invite you for dinner the next time he comes.'

Esperanza stared at her friend. 'Best to tell him that I am betrothed to someone else.'

'I will. I mean, your marriage should be taking place soon after Cesca's, yes? But why wait if Rafael is already living in your house? We need something to celebrate here after all, and a marriage feast would be perfect.'

Esperanza stared at her friend, then swallowed. Riba didn't know that Rafael was dead, and that the man in their home was actually a stranger. She hadn't told her – she'd been sworn to secrecy. It was best to come up with some or other excuse for why she couldn't marry the man she had been promised to since the age of six. She just couldn't think of the reason just yet. 'Um, well, my mother wants us to focus on Cesca's wedding first… and with my cousin unwell it is best not to overtax him, I think.'

Riba nodded. 'Of course, yes. How is he doing?' she asked. There was real concern in her friend's eyes, and Esperanza felt a stab of guilt at lying to her, but she had no choice.

'He's starting to recover. It is slow though.' They had told their friends and neighbours that Rafael had come to their home to be treated by Señor Garcia and her sister for an illness that had struck him down. Riba squeezed her shoulder. 'I am glad to hear it, my friend.'

Esperanza walked home with Riba's words flying around in her head. Of course people would start asking questions about 'Rafael' and their intended marriage. They would need to come up with a reason that the wedding couldn't go ahead as planned. Perhaps when Benito had recovered and returned to his own family they could tell the islanders that Rafael had died. Till then she was trapped, she realised, promised to a ghost. And worse, people's attention was being drawn to it because of Don Santiago. She didn't need him nosing about, asking questions about her. Her family would not be pleased that out of all the men on the island, she'd managed to capture *his* attention. A stranger who people were wary of – whose story about being a botanist was not quite believed, who, people suspected, might actually have been sent from the Holy Office to uncover their secret and report it.

Over the past few weeks Benito had recovered well. He was helpful around the house, and easy to be around. He and Esperanza often got to talking when her mother was having a siesta or her sister was out with Señor Garcia.

It was Rafael who taught her how to make crumbly goat's cheese. He'd told her, 'Camila used to make the cheese at home, and when I was a boy she used to let me help. My mother thought it was funny.' Camila was a servant, so she discovered.

She liked to hear about his life in Majorca, and before that in Bayonne, though she knew that she shouldn't. Cesca had warned her that they should be careful, that if Esperanza repeated the wrong thing it could raise suspicions, so it was best to stick to the facts, especially now with Don Santiago in their midst, who might report what he heard to the authorities.

That night after dinner they all sat in the garden, where the air smelt of oranges and lemons, and Benito played a lute that used to belong to their father. Cesca and her mother sang a song to the melody, an old island lullaby about the changing tides.

Esperanza found herself staring at Benito as he played, Riba's words swimming in her head. He was handsome, even more so than Don Santiago. Benito's blue eyes and dark curls were wilder, and somehow more alive, than the gentleman's clean blond lines. She bit her lip when Benito looked at her and smiled. The truth was she wouldn't mind being married to him that much.

The invitation to have dinner at Riba's house was extended a week later. It seemed that Riba's husband had befriended Don Santiago, in order to discover more of the reasons that he was on the island.

'Apparently, he's actually making a study about the salt pans. Francisco managed to ply him with some brandy and the truth came out,' said Riba, who looked relieved. Francisco was Riba's husband, and one of the key overseers of the salt trade.

'He admitted that he's here on orders from the Crown to see how they can best improve the production process,' she went on. 'He wanted to keep it quiet so that there wasn't a rebellion.' The islanders were tough and proud and such things had been known to occur.

This news would be welcomed by the small secret Jewish population, but not by everyone. The islanders, who valued freedom over everything, would not be overjoyed at the thought of more interference in the salt trade; it had long been their only means of survival. With the recent War of Succession, one of their worst fears had already come to pass – the loss of the salt pans to the Crown.

'What does that mean for us?' asked Esperanza.

'Well,' explained Riba, 'apparently, for now, it means that the only real threat Don Santiago presents is to business, not our community – though of course, we must remain vigilant and ensure that he leaves none the wiser about our secret. Which is why Francisco has befriended him. He's discovered that the man was sent here against his will to make this report.'

Esperanza knew that many of the islanders were hoping Don Santiago would leave soon, though they worried about what he would say. They'd been careful though. They always were. Don Santiago was not the only stranger who'd come asking questions.

Dinner in Riba's home was always a delight. Cesca had instructed her to send their excuses, that both Rafael and their mother were unwell and Cesca would be caring for them. For Esperanza this meant a rare treat – to be in her friend's home, in the presence of a gentleman, without her sister's dark scowls. She couldn't help feeling a small spurt of excitement at the thought.

Riba used all her best silver and her table was beautifully presented. She was one of the few islanders who occasionally had a servant come in to help her.

Over dinner Riba turned to Esperanza and asked her how Rafael was doing. It was a moment before she remembered that to them *Benito* was Rafael. 'He's recovering, well, thank you,' she said briefly, hoping to change the subject.

'It's incredible how he's changed,' said Riba. 'I went past there not long after he'd first come to stay with you to give Cesca some of our home-made wine, and I saw how he'd grown. I met him when he was a boy, you know? But I don't remember him having such beautiful eyes, so blue – they're quite unusual. I also remember him being quite pale as a boy, with fair hair, yet now it's so dark. It's strange.'

Esperanza shrugged. 'I hadn't noticed any change – I suppose I'd only met him once, when we were children.'

Riba nodded. 'You were so young, that's true.' Don Santiago turned to them, listening to their conversation.

'That happens,' he said, interrupting. 'My sister had blonde hair when she was born but now her hair is much darker, it's almost brown.'

'That must explain it,' said Esperanza in relief, giving him a big smile that, to her surprise, he returned at full volume. She would have done anything right then to steer the conversation away from the man in her kitchen and the fact that he didn't look like he should.

As the evening progressed, Esperanza enjoyed herself more than she'd thought she would, despite her initial reservations about Don Santiago. He was the perfect gentleman, and when he discovered her talent for drawing and painting, and Riba pointed out one of her watercolours that she had hung in the dining room, he exclaimed that he too had a passion for art. They soon got caught up in speaking of their favourite artists, such as Velázquez. Her brother Antoni had brought her books over the years from his travels, in which she had seen reproductions, but she longed to see them in real life. It turned out Don Santiago had seen many of them himself. 'They are every bit as wondrous as you can imagine,' he said.

Esperanza clasped her hands together, imagining it. The last person she had spoken to about art was her father, and she hadn't realised how much she missed talking about it. All Cesca and her mother spoke of was medicine, food and the neighbours.

When Don Santiago discovered that she could read too he was incredibly impressed, offering to bring her some of his most favoured novels, which he said he always travelled with.

Esperanza had only two cherished novels in her bedroom at home. The idea of travelling with a small library filled her with awe, and she said as much.

When she was leaving that night, Riba looked amused. 'I fear that you have surpassed his expectations. You may find him harder to get rid of now than ever.'

Esperanza sighed. It was true; she should have just kept quiet – but it had been wonderful, for just one night, to feel special. To be praised for her artistic side instead of having her family lament at how impractical it was, and tell her that Antoni only had room to bring them a small number of things from his voyages and that they were best served by herbs and medicines, clothing and other important supplies, not books or paper and art materials. How she should be more practical, like her sister.

She sighed, feeling her cheeks warm in that first flush of remorse. She couldn't help it; she'd enjoyed the attention, the spotlight that had been on her in a positive way for once. But Riba was right – she shouldn't have encouraged him. She should not have expressed excitement at the idea of borrowing his books! She was meant to be portraying herself as a betrothed woman, not as someone who could be courted. If he came to her house, she would just have to remind him that she was promised to someone else. Perhaps then, if he saw nothing more for him here, he'd leave the island quicker and everyone could breathe easier at night.

THIRTY

Formentera, present day

I finally got up the courage to tell my mother about where I was really staying after I'd been living on the island for a month. Emmanuel had finished painting the interior of the house and had helped to repair some of the old furniture from the bedrooms, so now I had two spare bedrooms and a lounge with a sofa I'd got from Big Jim. My kitchen was also coming along nicely since Maria had taken me under her wing; I now had a full collection of beautiful artisanal cutlery and crockery, pots, pans and my own set of kitchen herbs in pots on the windowsill.

It was high time I told my mother about what I'd done. So one afternoon, before my courage could evaporate, I phoned her. Explaining everything, but wanting answers too. Answers that only she could provide.

I listened to her silence for a moment, picturing her in that Queen Anne chair in the hallway, the one with the forest green twill, as she tried to take in all that I was telling her.

'You're on Formentera?' she repeated. 'In Alba's old house? Marisal?'

Even she knew the name well.

'Yes.'

'Did you know?' I asked her. 'About Maria de Palma?' I was sitting in the only spot that got reception, at the bottom of the garden where the old tyre lay. My foot absently kicked a stray orange as I stared out to sea.

'Alba's sister?'

So that was a *yes*. I couldn't believe it.

'Why didn't you tell me about her – why didn't she?'

I heard an intake of breath. 'I don't know, Twig, I'm sure it wasn't deliberate… I think there was just so much heartbreak there for her, heartbreak that she didn't want to revisit, that's what your father said.'

'But did you know about us though, about it?'

There was an impatient sigh. 'Know what? You aren't making much sense.'

'Did you know that we were… we're Jewish?'

'Jewish?' Her voice crackled across the line and I could picture her twisting her slim gold watch like she always did when she was puzzled, her shoulder-length hair straight and sleek and dark as she stared out of the window at the Surrey countryside.

'What do you mean, Jewish?'

'I mean that Dad came from a family of Sephardi Jews.'

'What Jews?'

'Sephardi – it means Spanish. Gran was one too – in fact, apparently, there were a few families living on Ibiza and Formentera who escaped one of the uprisings in Majorca during the Inquisition and lived here – in secret.'

There was an intake of breath. 'I had no idea. So that's what you've been doing – finding out about Gran and about that side of the family?'

'Yes. Mostly. I've been getting the house liveable too. Sage is coming soon, you should come, too, Mum,' I said, realising as I said it that it was something I *did* want – it wasn't just some impulse. It's funny – you can have a difficult relationship with your mother but still want to see her, still need to, in fact.

Love was hardly if ever straightforward, and it was love, at the heart of it.

There was a pause. 'You want that?'

It was so eager and vulnerable that it made my heart skip. 'Of course, Mum. I love you.'

'I love you, too.'

Next thing there was the excited babble of her talking about what she'd need to get. Shopping trips. Swimming costumes. 'I suppose they all wear bikinis over there, or go topless.' I could sense her mentally shuddering at the very thought.

'Not all of them – Mum, just wear what you like. Don't overthink it.'

'Okay. But…' She hesitated.

'What?' I asked.

'Well, I'm just proud of you, darling, for doing this, for going there and making a new start.'

'Is that what I'm doing?'

'Sounds like it, love.'

I nodded, though of course she couldn't see. 'The thing is,' I said, tears welling in my eyes, 'I didn't want to, not at first.'

To my surprise, she said. 'Of course you didn't. God, when your father died all I wanted to do was go to bed for the rest of my life.'

I blinked. How had I not considered that there was someone who knew exactly what I was going through, who would understand, someone who had also lost her husband too early – my own mother? I wiped away a tear. 'Me too.'

I could hear her suck in her breath. 'Oh love, it does get easier though, I promise – and I think what you're doing, well, it's wonderful.'

'Thanks Mum.'

THIRTY-ONE

Formentera, 1718

For a while Cesca tried to tell herself she'd got it wrong. Her mother wasn't seriously ill, it was just her old complaint, something that flared up every now and again, particularly when she was feeling stressed.

Until she saw the blood.

Her mother clutched at her hand. 'It's worse, I know,' she said, reading her daughter's stricken face. She'd suspected herself; perhaps somewhere deep inside she'd known that this time things were worse.

Cesca swallowed and fat tears fell from her green eyes, landing on the bed.

How had this happened? She should have spent more time at home, less time running around caring for everyone else! Her mother was sick, and she hadn't been here as much as she should.

'Oh, *Mare*,' she cried, falling into her mother's lap, sobs racking her thin shoulders. Her mother stroked her hair. 'Shush child, stop it. Everybody has to go some time. I'm luckier than most.'

This only made her cry harder.

'Come on now, it's not over just yet, let's wait to hear from the doctor first. We'll still have some time, I'm sure.'

Cesca choked on her sobs at the way her mother spoke. It was like she knew that there was no recovering from this.

'But I will be sad to miss your wedding...'

'Oh *Mare*,' she sobbed. 'You will still be here for it, we can move it. Don't worry about that now, please... and maybe' – she wiped her eyes – 'maybe it's not as bad as we fear.'

They feared that she had the same disease that had taken Cesca's grandmother from them, stomach cancer. In the beginning when they'd worried that it could be the same thing the doctor had seemed sure it wasn't.

But later that day, Señor Garcia confirmed Cesca's worst fears. 'It is cancer, I am afraid.'

'But you were so sure it wasn't before. Could it not be an ulcer of some kind?'

He shook his head and touched her hand, his brown eyes gentle. 'No, unfortunately not. I'm so sorry, Cesca. The signs are very clear. She's in the last stages. I wish we had thought to examine her again.'

Cesca looked up at the ceiling. She was to blame, assuming that it was the same digestive complaint her mother had suffered with for years. It had been this all along, hadn't it? She'd been slowly losing her mother – she, a nurse – and she hadn't even known it. The thought almost stopped her heart cold.

Tears slipped unchecked down her cheeks.

Señor Garcia looked wretched, his gaze full of pain for her.

She couldn't look at him now. 'Thank you for telling me. I must get on with my chores,' she said, then went to the well to fill a pail with water.

Señor Garcia watched her go, helplessly. Then he made his way home with a heavy heart, deciding to leave her alone with her grief.

Benito had kept out of the house while the doctor had been there, but when Cesca motored past him, only to stand frozen by the well, her shoulders heaving as if she were about to be sick, he rushed towards her.

'Are you all right?'

'I'm fine,' she said jumping as he came near, dashing away the tears and making to leave.

'You're not.'

She looked at him and nodded. 'No.' And he saw the raw pain in her eyes. It made him start. He sucked in air and came forward to touch her arm.

'It's my mother, she's sick… she's dying,' she breathed, her face crumpling. She made to hurry past him, but he held out an arm to stop her, then pulled her into a tight hug.

As his arms closed around her, the last of her strength left her and she dissolved into sobs that racked through her body, making her gasp for breath.

Benito held her close, his strong hands calming her as she wailed all her grief, all her shame at not noticing how ill her mother had become and not being able to nurse her better.

When her sobs died down at last, he looked at her, wiping the tears from under her eyes, his fingers tracing her jaw.

'Benito,' she said, her gaze taking in the rest of the *finca*, noting that they were alone, knowing that she should stop the inevitable, but she didn't pull away as he stepped closer and stared into her eyes before he kissed her. His lips were warm, and she sank into them like a person drowning, even though a part of her knew it was wrong, that he didn't belong to her, that this could never be – right then, nothing had ever felt more right.

THIRTY-TWO

Formentera, present day

Allan came off the ferry with a fresh wave of tourists, looking pale and thin and as nervous as ever, and dressed in a suit. So out of place with all the relaxed holidaymakers leaving the ferry in a throng of suntan cream, multicoloured shorts, sandals and toothpaste grins.

'Twig,' he said, sounding relieved, when he spotted me. We embraced.

'You're wearing a suit,' I said.

He looked down, then grinned. 'I had a meeting, and then...' He rolled his eyes, 'God, I need this, don't I?'

I grinned. 'You do,' I said, throwing an arm round his shoulders and leading him away from the crowds.

He grinned, readjusted the strap of his satchel and followed, his eyes taking in everything. 'It's incredible.'

'Yeah,' I said, looking at the span of turquoise waters and, in the distance, the hazy tip of Ibiza.

'You hungry?' I asked.

'Yeah – I...'

'You didn't eat on the plane.'

I grinned as he gave me a kind of nodding shrug. Allan had a weird thing about food. He didn't eat at places he felt he couldn't trust. That included anywhere with a drive-through – this earned extra bonus points if it was spelt 'thru' – food that sat under heat lamps, like in canteens; and, apparently, budget airlines. You wouldn't believe that he worked in London, and caught the Tube every day of his life.

He had once admitted after a few too many tequilas, the scary amount of money he spent on hand sanitiser every month. It was then that I suggested it might be cheaper to see a therapist.

'Okay, so I'm going to take you to a local restaurant. They have amazing food, and I have it on good authority that the hygiene is impeccable.'

Only with Allan would this be my opening premise – with anyone else I would sell the place on the fresh seafood, the incredible sauces…

'Oh really?' he said, brightening considerably. I hid a grin.

We ate fresh seafood pasta and drank wine, and stared at the boats in the port. I played with James's ring on my thumb as I told Allan all about what I'd seen and done while I'd been here. He stared at me, somewhat awed. He was most interested, of course, in Maria, and was looking forward to meeting my gran's long-lost sister.

As we sat and ordered our second glass of rosé, I saw Isla walking across the street from her stall. I waved and she came over.

My brother looked at me in surprise. 'You know that girl?'

I nodded.

'Of course – that's Isla.'

'That's Isla?' Something about the way he said that meant perhaps I hadn't done my pretty young friend justice; or perhaps when I'd described the somewhat hippie girl who sometimes went barefoot on the street he'd pictured someone, well, a little less lovely. Perhaps he hadn't been able to stop picturing the sand on her feet.

Isla came to our table and gave me a hug, and I introduced Allan, who had actually turned, of all things, shy.

I couldn't help stifling a laugh.

She put both of her hands on top of Allan's. The type of gesture that Allan, ordinarily, would have found a bit too airy fairy but seemed to find rather charming now.

I raised an eyebrow at him, and he had the grace to flush.

'How long are you staying for?' she asked him.

'About a week.'

She grinned at me. 'That's great – maybe you can drag your sister down to the beach. Can you believe she hasn't swum in the sea yet?'

Allan, despite the fact that he was wearing a suit, looked at me in surprise.

'You haven't?'

I shrugged. I'd bought a costume, but that was as far as I'd got. I'd been far too busy with the house, and with getting to know Maria.

'She has not,' said Isla, touching my shoulder affectionately. 'Though I've invited her a few times now.'

I wrinkled my nose. The idea of being on a beach in a bikini with Isla and some of her younger friends hadn't appealed as much as listening to her sing or having the band over for dinner.

'You should go, Twig.'

I raised an eyebrow. 'Et tu, Brute?'

He grinned. 'It's an island – you can't tell people you came here and never swam in the sea!'

I nodded. It did sound crazy, I had to admit.

'Exactly, you tell her, Allan,' she said, giving him a megawatt smile that made him blink.

I grinned. I knew that soppy look on his face.

'Anyway, I better get back,' she said, pointing to her stall, where we could see someone idling, perhaps hoping to buy some of her seascapes.

'You're coming tonight, right?' she asked him. 'To the Blues Bar. To hear us play?'

'Yeah,' he said, eyes shining. 'Wouldn't miss it – heard so much about the band.'

'Great,' she said, then when he wasn't looking she looked at me and mouthed, 'Wow, he's hot.'

Allan? Hot? I had to hide a grin, even as I looked from her to him and thought, oh hell, here comes trouble.

After she left, I managed to restrain myself from teasing my brother when he asked casually if she were single.

'Yeah, she is.'

'Ah.'

I hid another grin, and took a sip of wine.

He pointed at the second bag he'd brought, which was by his feet. 'Got those things you asked me for, including this,' he said, opening the case and handing me my laptop. I whooped in glee at the sight of it.

'You're a saint. Thank you for going by the house and getting it. I can start transcribing my book now – there's only so much I can write in my notebook before my fingers start cramping. The pace has been glacial.'

He raised an eyebrow. 'And, how's that different from the last decade?'

I gave him a look. 'Touché.'

He took a sip of wine and loosened his tie.

'So, it *is* a book?'

I nodded. 'Yeah, I think so.'

'That's pretty great, Twig.'

'Thanks.'

'Mum's looking after the plants and stuff, she helped me pack some other things – there's dresses and a few bits that she wanted you to have,' he said, indicating the bag.

'Oh, great, thanks.'

'I was glad to hear you finally told her by the way – about this – about Marisal.'

I nodded. 'Yeah, me too. You know, she's been great actually.'

He raised an eyebrow again, and I shrugged. It was true. It was almost like it was before James died, when I could tell my mother anything. I knew we still had some way to go, but ever since I'd opened up to her the other day, it had been like a dam had burst, and I'd been finding it easier to speak to her. We were texting each other a lot, and I was keeping her updated on everything, sending her pictures of the island, the house and even the Blues Bar, and though we were separated now by an ocean, I felt closer to her than I had in years.

'Well, I'm glad.'

I grinned. 'So, have you got anything besides a suit in that satchel of yours?'

I could see the beads of sweat on his forehead. He looked uncomfortably hot.

He made a face and answered honestly. 'Yeah, got some chinos, and golf shirts.'

I laughed.

'Tell you what, let's go past the market and get you some shorts.'

'Shorts?' he said, aghast. I could see him picturing his own lily-white knees and grinned.

'Yeah, it *is* an island, Al,' I said as he had pointed out to me and Isla earlier. 'Plus it gets bloody hot here, and it's not like there's air con at the villa.'

'Oh, good point.'

After lunch, I steered him towards a small stall that sold men's clothing, and together we picked out a few funky tees and a couple of pairs of shorts. I couldn't help but notice how his eyes kept wandering to Isla and her art stall.

We got into a taxi afterwards and he sat in silence, staring out at the open window, taking it all in. The sweeping view of turquoise ocean, the scent of wild rosemary and the stretches of white sandy beaches winking in the sun.

He looked at me as the taxi turned into the drive and stopped. He squeezed my hand as I pointed at the villa, and its blush of bougainvillea spilling over the whitewashed walls, and the impossibly blue ocean behind it. 'Marisal,' he breathed. 'I can't believe I'm seeing it at last.'

'I know, that's exactly how I felt.'

I showed Allan the house, watched as he tried to take it all in, shaking his head. 'It's really come along. Pretty amazing what you have done in a few weeks.'

I nodded. 'It's all thanks to Emmanuel.'

I'd told him a little about the renovator, but not everything.

Allan put his bags in his room, and decided to get changed into the shorts that he'd insisted earlier he wouldn't need. 'It's boiling…'

I nodded. 'If you like we can talk a walk to a nearby cove.'

'There's a cove nearby? That's great.'

I nodded. At least I hoped it was still around – it used to exist about two hundred years ago… and after hearing Maria's stories I was dying to see it for myself.

For all that I teased my brother, we were a pair, I thought, as I slipped back inside and put on the swimming costume I'd bought at the market. It was a stripy navy one-piece, but weeks of wearing shorts had given me an advantage over him – I had an impressive knee tan, which wasn't all that attractive on reflection, considering my pale thighs.

We walked with colourful towels round our necks and Allan told me all the latest happenings in his office. Who was sleeping with whom. Who had quit spontaneously, and who had been fired for stealing. I liked to hear about things like that even though the closest I'd ever got to working in an office was helping man the phones at home occasionally for James's design business.

We found the cove, along a narrow road not too far from the house. We traipsed over rocks that ended in a clear stretch of lagoon, filled with dazzlingly still turquoise water, then both yelped and ran to jump in, flinging towels and sandals on to the nearby rocks.

The water was warm, the sun high up in the sky and the sky a periwinkle blue as we lay on our backs, idly floating, our hair spread out behind us.

As we drifted, Allan picked up my hand and ran a finger over James's ring, but said nothing. Just winked at me, before he let it go.

But I answered his unspoken question. 'I'm not sure if I should keep wearing it… I don't really know what "should" is any more. It's like in some ways I've moved so far past what I thought I should be doing, I don't even recognise what's normal any more.'

'Twig, I think the only thing you *should* be doing right now is this – trying to put yourself back together. That's what he wanted.'

I nodded. He was right, I supposed.

'But, look, if you're wondering about what to do with the ring, well, I heard about a woman from work who took her husband's ring to a jeweller and got it remodelled into a bracelet, so that she could wear it – that might be an idea?'

I bit my lip. I wasn't sure if I was ready to let go of the ring, even just by having it made into a different form – but it did give me an idea for when I might be.

THIRTY-THREE

Genoa, 1718

Antoni stood on the deck of the ship, surveying the horizon through the brass spyglass in his hands. It telescoped neatly into itself as he squared his shoulders. It looked like a Crown ship approaching.

They would have some explaining to do.

He ran a hand through his hair, and thought of his mother and sisters, and the man he'd brought into their care. He clenched his jaw.

As the crew rushed about, dropping anchor to welcome their visitors on board, he looked around, saw the determined looks from all the men. They were all Ibicencos. They came from families he'd known most of his life, since he was a boy. Not everyone was like them. They weren't all *marranos*, but it didn't matter; they may as well have been, they'd been neighbours and friends for years. He gave the nod to welcome their visitor on board. They would protect his secret. Of that he had no doubt.

Two men came aboard. The one who was no doubt in charge greeted them with a kind of warm look that didn't quite meet his eyes. Antoni recognised that look. It was the kind of wariness that all mainlanders shared for the Ibicencos. It was based on years of careful rumours. Rumours the islanders had encouraged. About them all being thieves in league with barbarians and bloodthirsty pirates.

Antoni wondered if the men had drawn the short straws to be the ones to come aboard, and his lips twitched in amusement.

The first man introduced himself as Don Matías Fernandez, introducing the other as Señor Alfonso Deltorres. 'I've come to ask you if you've heard anything about the capture of the Moorish vessel in these waters a few weeks ago,' he said. 'It seems a pair of brothers, suspected *chuetas* by the name of Paulo and Benito Nuñez, were taken from aboard the vessel. We recovered one of the bodies, but it is feared that the other is still alive and has escaped, and we wondered if you knew anything about it.'

Antoni kept his expression neutral, though his heart started to pound. 'We have heard rumours, of course, Señor, but no one mentioned that a body had been found.'

The man didn't answer him, just looked around, pacing up and down the ship. 'Do you know, Captain, that the Moors who lost their cargo of *chuetas* described a ship just like this one?'

Antoni laughed. 'What are you suggesting, Señor? That the *Invictus*, one of the trade's most recognisable vessels, masquerades as a pirate ship? I admit of course that we have the authority to act as corsairs – to act against enemy ships – but that is all, as you no doubt are aware.'

It was a serious accusation – one that he knew couldn't be taken lightly.

The other man, Señor Deltorres, had the grace to laugh, which eased Antoni's fears.

'I wouldn't dare to make such an accusation, Señor Capitan,' said Don Fernandez. 'But a body washed up not far from where you were last in port, the body of Paulo Nuñez, so of course questions must be asked, do you not agree?'

He nodded. 'I suppose questions must be asked, but I wonder, Don Fernandez, at how well you are doing your job, if you are stopping a salt vessel to ask about *chueta* prisoners – surely you don't mean to imply that we are in the habit of taking aboard prisoners while we are doing the Crown's work?'

The man bristled. 'Of course not. Though you won't mind if we have a look around.'

Antoni raised an eyebrow. 'Of course,' he said, and as the man stepped forward, past the crew, who were all eyeing them with dark glints in their eyes, Antoni called, 'You are welcome to sift through the salt too – perhaps you could help us offload it when we arrive in port – do something useful with your time?'

The crew erupted into loud guffaws.

The man's spine straightened. He called to Señor Deltorres, and after a cursory glance around, the two made to leave the ship, bidding them good day.

Antoni only breathed out when he saw the two men return to their ship, and maintained his air of amused nonchalance until they were well out of sight.

He turned to the men, the fear in his eyes echoing theirs. 'It'll be fine,' said Hernandez, his first mate. 'They went away feeling like fools.'

'Yes,' muttered several of the crew.

Antoni nodded. They'd got rid of them, yes, but for how long? He sighed. He'd have to go back home, warn them – how long would it be before they started searching there, before they thought of looking on the small island where the captain of the *Invictus* lived?

THIRTY-FOUR

Formentera, present day

Isla was singing Bill Withers' 'Lovely Day' in her haunting voice when Allan and I arrived at the Blues Bar. The beach bar was full of laughing couples, all sitting beneath the string lights, sipping on beers and closing their eyes to better listen to the music.

We got a drink, and then I said. 'You'll be all right here, by yourself?'

He looked at me oddly. 'Yeah, why?'

I took a sip of my drink. 'Well, I've got to go – I'm in the next song.'

'What?' he said, his mouth falling open.

I laughed, then made my way onstage where I picked up the tambourine from next to Big Jim's feet, laughing at Allan's shocked face as I took a seat, and I shook it the way they had shown me to.

After the set we all took a seat next to Allan, who, every time he looked at me, started laughing again. 'I've taken pics for Sage and Mum.'

I grinned, took a sip of my drink – Pineapple Lady – and shrugged. 'Okay. That's fine.'

And it was. Being onstage with Big Jim, Isla and Sue was pure fun. I got caught up in the music and though a part of me knew that I probably looked a bit silly, a forty-five-year-old woman shaking a tambourine, I honestly didn't care.

'You should try it,' said Isla, looking at Allan, who stopped laughing immediately. 'Um – no thanks.'

Big Jim looked at him. 'You play anything?'

Allan shook his head.

I grinned. 'He used to sing in the school choir – he went to one of those all-boys' ones, posh, you know? He even won an award – before his, er, man bits came in. Remember Al, Mum actually cried. What did she say again: "I'm going to miss my little voice of an angel!"?'

Allan went pink, closing his eyes in mortification as we all erupted into guffaws. 'Thanks for that,' he said as Big Jim started choking on his beer as he howled, Isla pounding his back.

Allan looked at me and shook his head. 'You couldn't give me one day?'

I bit my lip, trying hard not to laugh. 'Sorry.'

Big Jim was still sniggering while he muttered, 'man bits'.

'Sibling love, eh?' said Isla, turning to Allan and offering to buy him a drink.

'Yup.'

She grinned. 'Well, I think that's pretty cool anyway – that you used to sing. Maybe we can tempt you on stage one day.'

He snorted. 'No, I think, um, that, ah, died when my, er, bits came in,' he said, and she giggled. 'But I'd come listen to you guys any time – you're amazing, honestly.'

'Thanks,' she said, smiling. 'I'd like that.'

I sat watching the two of them as they talked, moving closer together, their heads bent over a low, flickering lantern, as soft reggae music filled the air.

Big Jim elbowed me in the ribs, then raised his beer in their direction. 'Looks like his week has got off to a pretty decent start.'

I nodded. 'Yep.' I took a sip of my Pineapple Lady and grinned. I couldn't remember the last time my brother had had a crush – he wasn't the kind who had casual holiday flings. I sighed. I hoped I wouldn't have to warn Isla not to hurt him.

THIRTY-FIVE

Formentera, 1718

The rumour about the missing brother who had been captured by a pirate vessel had reached Formentera. Officials were searching all the surrounding islands, and Riba's husband brought the unwelcome news that it was likely they would start looking on Formentera soon.

Further rumours of an artist's sketch, and a note about the missing man's bright blue eyes, caused Cesca to toss and turn in her sheets at night.

Since Señor Garcia had confirmed her mother's condition, she seemed to have deteriorated even further. She was weak and easily tired, and found walking difficult, but she was determined not to lie in bed, spending as long as she could sitting at the kitchen table, hand-sewing the lace for Cesca's trousseau.

Señor Garcia had suggested that it was time to begin preparations for the wedding, and Cesca had agreed, with a pang, her guilt over her kiss with Benito twisting her inside.

They hadn't spoken of it and she'd been avoiding him as much as she could, but he had to know that it couldn't go any further than a kiss between them.

She didn't want to worry her mother about the pirate capture and the missing man, so she and Esperanza kept it from her, privately panicking at what would happen if people here started asking questions.

At first they kept it from Benito too; he had only just recovered from his long illness and they didn't want to cause him to regress – but it wasn't long before news reached him too, when Riba came one afternoon all abuzz with the news that officials had begun searching Ibiza, and many thought they might start looking on this island as well.

After she left, she saw that his face had gone ashen. 'I'll leave,' he said, standing up, 'now, before it's too late.' And he moved to get his coat. 'I can't have them looking here.'

'No you won't,' said their mother. She stood up from her chair with difficulty, sweat blooming on her forehead, her green eyes fierce despite the pain she was in.

Cesca and Esperanza looked at their mother in surprise. She was fierce, despite her frailty.

Benito looked at her, his eyes full of sympathy. 'I can't let you do this for me any longer, don't you see? I can't tell you how grateful I am but I have put you in danger. We can't go on like this, especially now. It's just not fair.'

She closed her eyes. 'Fair?' She gave a short laugh. 'Nothing about our history has ever been fair, Benito. But you must think properly. You can't leave – if you do then they will know what we have done, they will ask questions about the man who lived here, Rafael. They will wonder what happened to him. Perhaps they would uncover the real Rafael's body buried at his parents' home in Ibiza, and discover what we have done – if you leave you will just make it worse. This way no one will ask or question it.'

They all stared at her in shock. She was right. They were stuck. Cesca looked at him. 'We're in it together now, for better or worse.'

He nodded, sat down. 'Yes.'

He watched, knowing that his presence had caused nothing but danger. Cesca's mother picked up the lace again for the wedding he was powerless to prevent, and felt even more wretched.

*

Later that afternoon, oblivious to the tense atmosphere that had lingered since the morning, Esperanza sat peeling the same potato for a quarter of an hour while she talked non-stop about dinner at Riba's house the night before. At this rate, they'd only have their dinner at midnight.

'Pass the potatoes,' Cesca said with a sigh, which Esperanza promptly did.

Benito was outside, feeding the animals and talking to Señor Garcia. He'd been avoiding them ever since her mother had told him that he had no choice but to stay, risking all their lives.

Cesca listened to her sister with half an ear as the other listened in to Benito and Señor Garcia's conversation. Like the other islanders, the doctor had accepted the presence of their 'cousin' without much fuss, though she had seen that the doctor made a point now of coming every day, sometimes twice a day. At first she'd put this down to his care for her mother, but it had slowly become clear that he was always there whenever she and Benito were alone. It made her uncomfortable, and a little guilty, wondering if he sensed that something was changing between them, something Cesca felt powerless against.

'He's always here,' complained Esperanza, echoing Cesca's thoughts. 'Señor Garcia, I mean.'

Cesca nodded. She herself wasn't too thrilled about it either, but how could she complain about it when she was going to be married to the man shortly? 'When we are married, you'll see even more of him, most likely, best to get used to it. I thought you liked Señor Garcia anyway?'

She couldn't move out with her mother being so ill, and with Esperanza unmarried. She hadn't discussed it with Señor Garcia but perhaps it would be best if they lived here after they were wed.

Esperanza blushed slightly. 'I don't mind him – I just… never mind.' The real reason was that with Señor Garcia always being here, they were both always home now. She used to get a lot of time with Benito, just the two of them as they tended to the chores and looked after Grunon. She missed how they used to speak about books and Barcelona, art and music, but she knew it was silly to be jealous that she didn't have him to herself. She'd hadn't considered though that Senor Garcia would move in here after he and Cesca were married.

'You think you will live here?'

Cesca nodded. 'It makes sense with *Mare*, we must be practical.'

Tears flooded Esperanza's eyes. 'Don't talk like that.'

''Spranza, I'm sorry, but I've explained to you that she's not doing well. I'm not sure she will even make it to the wedding, even though we're trying to make it happen as quickly as possible.'

Esperanza's chair shot out.

'*Mare* will get better!'

Cesca shook her head, tears welling up in her eyes. She had explained this to Esperanza, but her sister wouldn't accept it, even now.

'There must be something you can do… you haven't tried *everything*. Can't you take her to the mainland, or Majorca?'

Cesca touched her sister's hand. 'She wouldn't make it – she's too weak to travel, and even if she could, you know how she feels about that – she wouldn't want to say anything that could point suspicion at our community.' Such was the fear of their community, one that had been stressed enough times at their secret synagogue. They'd all heard stories of people who had died beneath a loved one's pillow to ensure that they didn't confess anything incriminating to a priest. Here there would be little danger of that, as Father Samuel was also the secret local rabbi. But still. ''Spranza, it's too late. We must face it together, and be strong for one another. There is nothing to do. We can only spend our time with her and pray.'

Esperanza shook her head, angry tears falling fast. She'd seen her sister and the doctor cure people all the time. Seen them do the impossible. How could Cesca, who spent her days healing people, give up on their own mother? She stared at her, trying to take it in, trying to understand, but she couldn't. She could only turn on her heel and run sobbing from the *finca*. She didn't turn even when she heard Benito calling her name. Flea ran to be by her side, and together they fled towards their little cove.

She stripped off her dress and left it in a tangle on the rocks, not caring if it got wet, as she dived into the cool, turquoise water and swam furiously. Flea dived in after her, but she soon outpaced him, swimming as hard and as fast as she could. Part of her wanted to swim all the way to Ibiza, and further, towards a world where her mother wasn't dying and her heart wasn't breaking in two.

She stopped only when her foot started to cramp. She cried out in pain and from twenty metres back she heard a voice call out to her to wait.

She was in too much pain to do anything more than that. Don Santiago.

'What's wrong?' he asked.

'My foot,' she cried, clutching it, her face twisted in pain.

'Give it here,' he said, taking her foot from out of her hands. 'Hold on to me.' His blond hair was slicked back and there were water droplets on his long eyelashes. She blinked. His face was handsome, his features even.

He took her foot and flexed it back and forth while she cried out. 'You must be careful. You're a strong swimmer, but cramps are an easy way to drown,' he admonished and she winced as his hands forced her foot out of the cramp, the tendons pulling tightly so that it felt as if she'd stepped on glass. It would be painful even to walk on.

'Did you follow me?' she asked.

He stared at her for some time, until she realised how bold her question was. How presumptuous.

'Yes,' he answered.

Then before she could stop him he was kissing her. His body was warm against her own, and his touch gentle. She felt a small furl of excitement at being so desired that someone would follow her miles out to sea. She felt reckless too. She blamed Cesca and Señor Garcia, even Benito – if Benito hadn't been there then maybe they would have noticed how serious her mother's illness really was sooner. She was angry with her sister most of all. She'd believed that Cesca could do anything... but she couldn't keep alive the one person she loved the most. It hardly seemed fair.

She sank into his kiss, though she knew she shouldn't. She could hear her sister's admonishments even now, and it was that perhaps that made her kiss him all the harder. She'd kissed a few of the boys in the village when she was younger, on a dare at the village festivals, but nothing this passionate before. As she closed her eyes she pictured Benito's face, and kissed Don Santiago even harder, wrapping her arms tightly round his neck.

They stopped only when they heard barking. Poor Flea was exhausted. He'd paddled after her but his tiny little body was now close to giving up. She broke away from Don Santiago and went to fetch her little dog, and in that moment she felt herself come to her senses, like a fog had lifted. She felt terrible, and showered the creature with love. She was utterly embarrassed, and when Don Santiago followed after her, an odd look on his face, she felt a twist of shame at what she'd done. What he must think of her.

'I'm sorry,' she said, but he caught her. 'Don't be – that was wonderful.'

She closed her eyes. 'Please, just forget it.'

'How can I?'

She looked at him. 'I am sorry,' she said again, then picked up her dress and ran, Flea barking madly at her heels.

THIRTY-SIX

Formentera, present day

I took Allan to meet Maria on his second day at Marisal.

We walked to her house through the dry, scrubbed farmland, breathing in the scent of wild herbs and taking in the welcome sight of daisies and poppies, a wild carpet that had seemingly been laid out for us overnight.

'I can understand how you came here for a week and stayed a month,' he said as we stopped in at a bakery and exited with fresh croissants.

'Yeah – though perhaps there are other charms to this island for you,' I said, waggling my eyebrows at him. He laughed. 'Yeah, a certain brown-haired singer who happens to live a thousand miles away from me, and is probably my polar opposite, you mean?'

I shrugged. 'Yup. It's okay to have fun, you know?'

'Yeah – I've never been good at that – at just keeping things light.'

I nodded. We had that in common.

Maria hugged Allan as soon as I introduced them, and I could see in his face how much she reminded him of our grandmother.

The two hit it off immediately and we filled him in on the story that she had been telling me of our distant great-grandmother,

Cesca, while I helped to peel the potatoes and she put him to work dicing vegetables.

She stirred a pot filled with a rich tomato stew, and we listened companionably as she told us the story of the two women who had helped shape the family into what it was today – whose stories could so easily have been lost if it hadn't been for James.

Allan looked at me as he cut a cucumber into tiny chunks. 'After all this time, Twig, to finally be here, this, it's incredible, isn't it?'

I couldn't help but agree as we were swept back on a cloud of steam, into the past.

THIRTY-SEVEN

Formentera, 1718

The books had been left on the table. Every one that he'd mentioned to Esperanza. They were tied up in a ribbon, along with one long, wild Spanish rose.

There was a card with his name written in fine script: Don Santiago Marquez de Sanchez. 'Like you,' was all it said.

Esperanza felt her cheeks flush when she saw it. It was one of the real disadvantages of being a late riser.

'It looks like you have an admirer,' said Benito archly, with a grin.

Cesca didn't look impressed. She paused, tying up a bunch of herbs to dry, and nodded. 'I was afraid of that,' she said, her green eyes troubled.

Esperanza looked at her. For one awful moment she thought that her sister was talking about the kiss between her and Don Santiago, but then she said, 'I've been worried since that dinner. I wasn't thinking. I should have just said that you were needed at home. Riba said that he seemed so taken with you…' She shook her head. 'Now he'll be impossible to get rid of.'

'It's hardly Esperanza's fault though,' said Benito. 'She couldn't help it.'

Cesca raised an eyebrow. 'Riba said that it was hard to get a word in while they kept chattering on about their favourite books and artists.'

Esperanza closed her eyes and sank into a chair. Usually she would have hotly denied it, but she knew her sister was right, that she had encouraged him. She felt a little ill at what she'd done, at the kiss she'd let happen. It wasn't what she wanted – what she'd realised as she kissed him was how much she had wanted that kiss to be with Benito, how much she had begun to fall for him.

Benito touched her shoulder. 'Don't worry about it. It'll be okay.'

She looked at him. Her fingers shook as she touched his hand. He was always so kind to her, so understanding. He would make a wonderful husband, she realised, then blushed.

He gave her shoulder a squeeze, then got up to go and deal with the goat.

She watched him leave, tuning out Cesca's tirade.

She didn't need her sister's admonishments to know that she hadn't behaved the way she should have. But the more she sat there, listening to Benito as he whistled while tending to the goat, the more she began to think that the solution to her problem was right under their noses. She was amazed that she hadn't thought of it until now.

She turned to her sister and said, 'It's hard to imagine the *finca* without him now, don't you think?'

Cesca stared at her, then looked away, almost as if she were sad, and Esperanza frowned. She couldn't see why that thought seemed to make her upset, unless it was because of the danger he presented?

Esperanza touched the books. It would be wrong to accept the gift, she knew, but she ached to read them. It had been years since she'd had something new to read.

Cesca left soon after, saying something about checking on Marianna and the new baby.

Esperanza sat at the table alone, thinking of Benito and how he'd stood up for her. It was rare in this house for someone to take her side. If she were honest, it was rare that she deserved it too. But still, he was a kind man. Handsome, and fair. For the first time in her life when she thought of marriage, she thought of how nice it would be to be with someone like him. She'd have to tell Don Santiago that what had happened between them was a mistake, that was all.

Perhaps – who knows – after Cesca was married, Benito really could take Rafael's place… it wouldn't be the worst idea in the world… in fact, she wouldn't mind it at all.

*

Benito grabbed Cesca's hand as she was about to leave the *finca*.

'I'm going to make bread,' she mumbled, trying to release herself from his grip.

He looked at her, oddly. 'With what?'

She had nothing in her arms.

She bit her lip. 'I mean, I'm going to help the new mother, Marianna, to check on her and the baby.'

She was referring to the woman who had almost lost her baby a few weeks before, but Benito knew Cesca had been to check on Marianna earlier that week. He couldn't help feeling like she was using the visit as an excuse to get away from the *finca*, away from him.

He touched her face. 'Is something wrong?'

She jumped at his touch, looking quickly towards the house in case anyone had seen, and moved away towards the street.

'I have to go, excuse me,' she said and hurried past, not meeting his eyes.

He caught up with her on the long dirt road, grabbing her arm and staring at her with those eyes that always seemed to look inside her soul.

'Tell me, what is it?'

Cesca looked down, bit her lip. 'Benito, don't…'

He touched her face. 'Why?

'Because it's *wrong*. We shouldn't, you know that. I am promised to someone else.'

'An old man? It was never your decision. How can this be wrong? What we feel?'

She leant her head on his shoulder for a second, breathing in his clean, soapy scent. It would be so easy to slip back into those arms.

Too easy.

But she'd made a promise to someone else. How could she think of breaking that now – what would people say? What would *he* say?

She broke away. 'I think it will be better for us both if we stay away from each other. This can't happen, we can never be. I'm sorry.'

He stared at her, shook his head. His eyes were stricken. She couldn't look at the pain she was causing.

'Don't say that. What's it all for if we can't be together?'

'What do you mean?' she asked.

'Living when you should have died? Finding this island where people like us can live free? What's it for if we can't even choose each other?'

'Sometimes you aren't free to choose – sometimes you just have to do what is right.'

'And this is *right*? You promised to someone else? How is that right?'

'It's not,' she said, tears welling in her eyes. The way she felt about Benito was the best thing that had ever happened to her. It was also the worst because the cost was everything she held dear – her love of medicine, her life, her reputation. He was asking too much.

'Exactly,' he said, kissing her.

She pulled away. 'You don't understand. We can't do this – I can't do this to him. Not after everything he has done for my family. It would be too cruel.'

Benito blinked. 'More cruel than having him stand between *us*?'

She shook her head. 'It's you standing in the way, between him and me.'

He looked as if he'd been kicked. 'Is that how you feel? Truly? You love him, is that it?'

She blinked, 'Of course I do, in my own way.'

'That's not what I mean.'

He kissed her again, and she shook her head, pushed him back and hurried away. This time he didn't follow. Didn't notice either that someone had seen them. Someone who felt a piece of himself break as he watched.

THIRTY-EIGHT

Formentera, present day

'Argh, I'm so jealous,' said Sage, when I told her all that Allan and I had been doing that week. 'I cannot wait for my turn.'

'Me too, love,' I said, with a pang. I was concerned about how tired she was, and how hard she was working.

'One more month, then I'll get a break.'

'One more month,' I repeated. 'I can't wait for you to meet Maria – and to hear what she's been telling me about our family. There's this one woman – Cesca – she was one of the island's first trained nurses – she learned everything from a local doctor. Maybe it runs in the family.'

'You're kidding? When was that?'

'The early eighteenth century, I believe. She was pretty amazing – helped to deliver babies, helped to keep alive a Jewish prisoner the family had helped escape. They fell in love.'

'Wow. That's amazing, Mum, what happened to them?'

'I'm not sure – we haven't got that far yet. Maybe you can hear about it when you get here.'

'Yeah – I'd like that.'

'Me too,' I said as I rolled a ripe orange beneath my feet. I was standing in the garden. Emmanuel was hard at work on the roof while Allan chatted to him, holding the ladder.

Isla was sitting at the table, an abandoned sketchbook in her hands, eyes closed while she soaked up the sun, and Big Jim was in his customary spot by the orange tree, his big Texan hat shading his eyes.

Allan had fitted in as easily as I had. He and Isla had been spending some time together, going for walks and trips to the beach, but, aside from catching a few longing looks between the two of them, I wasn't sure if they had taken anything further. Perhaps, as they'd both been burned in the past, they weren't willing to risk it again.

THIRTY-NINE

Formentera, 1718

Esperanza tied up the books Don Santiago had left for her with a pang, leaving them outside the door to his house where one of the servants would find them in the morning. She'd written him a note, politely thanking him for his gifts but stating that unfortunately she couldn't accept them in good conscience as she was promised to someone else.

She just hoped he would let it go.

The rumours of the escaped prisoner were weighing heavily on Esperanza's mind and, combined with her worries for her mother, and what would happen to her once Cesca was married, meant that she couldn't sleep. She slipped out of the *finca* and went to the cove with Flea, where she could breathe beneath the stars.

Don Santiago found her there, bathed in the moonlight, skimming rocks off the water the way her brother Antoni had shown her when she was a little girl, a habit that Cesca had said only served to make her seem wilder still.

When she heard his footfall, she started. Her face coloured in the dark when she saw who it was. He was always there, whenever she turned. It made her feel guilty, and ashamed when she thought of what had happened between them the other night.

She sat up, making to leave.

'Please – don't rush off, just talk to me,' he pleaded, taking a seat next to her.

She bit her lip, undecided, but when he picked up a flat rock and skimmed it over the surface of the water, she sat back down.

'I was thinking,' he said, clearing his throat. 'That I owe you an apology.'

'Don San—'she started, but he shook his head.

'No look, I took advantage of you the other day. I shouldn't have kissed you like that – you were clearly upset. Why was that? Tell me about it, maybe I can help?'

'It's my mother,' she said, then took a deep breath and told him about what had happened. As she tried to make sense of a future without her mother in it, she began, to her horror, to sob. He gathered her in his arms and held her. Esperanza knew she should have just walked away, that she shouldn't let him comfort her, knew that it was selfish when she had to tell him once again that they could never be.

When she was made weak by crying, she got up and let him walk her home. She pulled away when he tried to kiss her again, but he only looked at her tenderly, squeezing her hand as he took his leave. He shook his head. 'I could wonder if you'd put a spell on me.'

She bit her lip. 'I'm sorry.'

'Don't be.'

Don Santiago was waiting for her on the old salt road a few days afterwards. She closed her eyes in mortification, shame flooding through her, when she saw him. She had to end this thing that had blossomed between them – she had to be strong, not let the fact that she found comfort in his presence get in the way of doing what she knew she had to do.

She bit her lip, then turned to go the opposite way, but of course he ran towards her.

'Wait, Esperanza, please.'

She blinked. 'D-Don Santiago, I can't be here, you must understand… the other day, well…'

He touched her arm. 'It was my fault – I shouldn't have followed after you… kissed you the other day.'

She closed her eyes again in shame. 'Please – just forget it ever happened.'

His hazel eyes widened. 'Forget? I cannot, you're all I think about. I have never known a woman like you before.'

Her cheeks burned. She didn't want to hear that. Right now that felt like the opposite of a compliment.

'Don—'

'Please just call me Santiago.'

'Don Santiago,' she said pointedly. Please, we cannot. I am not the sort of woman you might think I am… the other day was a mistake, that's all.'

His hand gripped her arm. 'What do you mean?'

'I am not the kind of woman who kisses strange men, or meets them after midnight. I'm sorry – my whole world has turned on its head since my mother got sick, and I'm afraid that I haven't been behaving as I should. I should never have kissed you, for a start.'

'Don't say that.'

'I must! Now please, if you don't mind…'

He shook his blond head. 'The only way I think of you is as a man who is falling for a beautiful woman. Please believe that – my intentions towards you are only honourable. I've never met anyone like you – you're all I think of. I'd like to court you properly, and to make you my wife one day if you'll have me.'

She stared at him. Her mouth fell open. He couldn't be serious. 'Your wife?'

'Yes.'

She shook her head. 'I can't. Please don't ask me. I am promised to someone else.'

He blinked. 'Your cousin – the one who was ill?'

She nodded. 'Yes.'

'Perhaps there is a way we can get out of it, I could speak to your family, speak to your father or your mother. I'd make you a good husband. You – they – would never want for anything, I promise you that.'

'My father is dead.'

'Your mother then. I'll speak with her.'

'No, we can't – please just understand,' she said, then hurried away.

'Wait,' he called, but she ignored him, trying to put as much distance between them as she could. She was so ashamed of herself. Why had she let it get so out of hand? What was she going to do now? How was she going to get rid of Don Santiago, convince him that there was no hope for them? She closed her eyes. Cesca was going to be furious. For the first time, she felt that her sister had every right to be.

FORTY

Formentera, present day

'So Emmanuel?' said Allan one morning while we were sitting outside, the cool breeze from the ocean riffling our hair.

'What about him?' I asked as I poured myself some more coffee from the cafetière, and paused from transcribing the start of my novel onto my laptop.

He sighed. 'Well, it's just …' He hesitated and watched Emmanuel working in the garden. 'He's nice, Twig.'

I nodded. 'Yeah, he's a friend, Al, that's it.'

He shrugged. 'Yeah, look, I didn't mean to pry but I saw it, you know.'

'Saw what?'

'James's ashes.'

I bit my lip. I'd thought I'd been more careful with that.

'I mean, I helped pick out the urn, Twig. You brought him *with* you?'

I sighed. Closed my eyes. 'Yeah.'

Then I laughed. 'I talk to him, sometimes.'

'You talk to him?'

'Not like in a crazy way.'

He raised an eyebrow.

'Okay, yeah, pretty crazy, but it was helping. I just felt like I couldn't leave him behind, you know?'

He nodded. 'Yeah, I suppose so. Did he say what he wanted to be done with them? Anywhere specific he wanted you to scatter them?'

I shook my head. 'He just said I'd know when the time was right.'

'And do you?'

I shook my head. 'No. Not yet anyway.' Though over the past few weeks, I'd felt less need to take James along to every room I visited. I supposed that was progress.

'So you and Em aren't like secretly…'

I gave him a look. 'No. Unlike some people.'

He had the courtesy to blush. 'It's nothing.'

'Really? I love Isla but since you met, it's like she's living here. I mean, you've been here a week and you've only met Maria once… I've had to make your excuses while you run off with Isla.'

He shrugged. 'I know. The thing is, she's kind of great. It's pretty awful, actually.'

I looked at him in surprise. 'Awful, why?'

'Because she lives here.'

I sighed. 'Yeah, well, we do have a house here now. And I know you work in London, but there are jobs here too – just an idea.'

'Jobs? Here?'

'Okay, well in Ibiza probably.'

'As an investment banker?'

'Possibly – maybe they do those offshore account things here.'

He gave me a look. 'You're thinking of the Cayman Islands.'

'Ah,' I said with a laugh. 'But still, look I hate to call this card but it's true – the love of my life is gone, and I can tell you from where I'm standing that a little thing like the ocean isn't that big of a problem. Not really.'

FORTY-ONE

Formentera, 1718

Cesca was miserable. Every time she sensed Benito's gaze on her, she felt something in her twist in pain. It would be so easy to just give in to this thing between them, but what then? Would she have to turn her back on everything else?

She made sure that nothing could happen by ensuring they were never alone, by keeping busy at her mother's bedside.

To make matters worse, Señor Garcia was behaving oddly. Finding excuses for her not to come on any of his visits to his patients, even when her mother slept.

'Spend your time with your mother,' he told her, not looking her in the eye. It was as if something had changed between them and it made her uncomfortable, particularly as the wedding was drawing nearer. Why was he behaving so strangely?

It felt like everything had changed since her mother had got ill. Things with Benito were stilted and strange – gone was their easy camaraderie, their slow mornings together as they greeted the dawn while the rest of the household slept. She missed that more than she could say. It would be so easy – too easy – to just give in to what she was feeling, but at what cost?

*

Esperanza puzzled at the change in her sister, the way she seemed to always be on edge. How she would snap at the slightest provocation.

She figured that it had to do with their mother. She couldn't face it herself. The idea of life without her left her reeling. She spent as much time as she could with her, and didn't complain when Cesca asked her to do the chores. For the first time in her life she welcomed the distraction from what was happening inside her head.

What she couldn't understand was the change between Cesca and Benito, how short Cesca was being with him. She didn't like it. He didn't deserve it. He was kind and thoughtful, always helping out where he could. He hadn't asked to come into their home – the least Cesca could do was be civil to the man, she thought.

As the days passed it was Benito who got up early, fetched the water from the well and started on breakfast. She couldn't imagine what they would have done without him during this time. His solid presence was a comfort and a balm, while she struggled to deal with the prospect of saying goodbye to her mother.

'What are you doing?' Benito asked one evening as he paused from playing the lute.

Esperanza was sitting next to her mother by the orange tree, sketching.

She shrugged, though her face coloured slightly.

The evening was mild. Her mother had wanted to sit out by the stars, so they'd made a picnic in the garden, but nobody could bring themselves to eat.

Señor Garcia had warned them that there wouldn't be long now, which had made Esperanza so sad she'd walked from one end of the island to the other all through the night. She didn't know how she was going to face life without her. Didn't want to contemplate it.

To take her mind off things she had taken out her sketchbook and started to draw Benito as he played one of her mother's favourite songs. Sketching Benito had become something of a habit, one she was finding difficult to break.

There were tracks of tears coursing down Cesca's cheeks, and she was holding their mother's hand to her chest.

'Antoni has sent word that he is coming home soon,' she said. 'I hope he makes it in time.'

Which was when Esperanza started to cry too.

FORTY-TWO

Formentera, present day

When the taxi came to take Allan to the ferry, I was reluctant to let him go. The house had been so much fuller for having him in it, and I'd enjoyed, as a spectator, watching his and Isla's budding romance. It felt too soon for him to leave now, to return to his life in London.

'Do you have to go back?' I asked for perhaps the third time that morning.

He sighed as he zipped up his bag, and gave me a look. 'Twig, you're going to be fine without me. I mean, God, you've made more friends in the past few weeks than you have in a lifetime. You're part of a band!' He laughed and I joined in. 'You're going to be okay.'

I sighed, then repeated his words. 'I'm going to be okay.'

'Besides, Sage will be coming soon – just three more weeks.'

I nodded. That was true.

'But what about you and Isla?'

'Well, we're going to keep in touch, we're going to take it super slow. I'll be back in a couple of weeks for a longer break – if you'll have me – and we'll see from there.'

I grinned. 'Course I'll have you.'

After he left, I had a shower and then made my way to Maria's house, cycling through the dry scrubland, past pine trees and the glittering ocean. Emmanuel's work on Marisal was coming to an end, and I was running out of tasks for him to do, so soon it would just be me and the house again. And then what? A return home to Surrey? As I cycled I considered my options. Right now, this felt right. I was doing what James had asked; I'd started writing again and had made new friends, discovered a family I never knew existed and was starting to live again. Going back to Surrey would be a step in the wrong direction. And perhaps without Emmanuel or Allan around I would be forced to stand more securely on my own two feet. But I'd learned that, despite what I'd initially thought, I wasn't ever truly alone, not any more.

'I was sad to see him go,' said Maria as we got started on making a lemon cake for her grandchild's birthday.

'I know, but he'll be back soon.'

'That's good, I want to get to know him better.'

I nodded. 'He wants that, too.'

I was showing her how to make a classic lemon drizzle.

'Now this is something the English can brag about – much better than those muffins with jam and cream.'

I laughed. 'It's scones.'

'*Ai carai*. Those things. Like little balls of bread with jam.'

I snorted. 'Hardly! Have you had them before?'

'*Ai*, no,' she admitted.

I looked at her. 'Then don't knock it.'

She grinned. 'Okay.'

'Maria,' I asked, as the windows steamed up and I stepped over the sleeping cat, who was always lodged in front of the warming drawer, 'what was my gran like when she was little?'

'Alba?' she said, wiping her hands on an apron. 'She was a big joker. She was always pulling practical jokes on us.'

'Gran? Really? Like what?'

'Well,' she said, then started to laugh as she remembered. 'There was this one time when she came home and she told my father that she'd spent all her money on a rare, purebred dog, a border collie. He was really cross, as it was all the money she'd saved. But she said it didn't matter – she had to have this prize beast and we had to come and see him for ourselves to understand. So we came outside, only see that she'd put a wig on one of the pigs!'

I laughed. 'Really?'

'Yes. She was always doing things like that.'

I liked to think of that, this younger, more carefree version of the serious woman I'd known.

As if she was reading my thoughts, Maria sobered and said, 'Nothing changes a person more than tragedy and she faced a lot of it with the war.'

I thought of the tragedies in my own life – losing her, my father and James. I couldn't deny how true that was.

FORTY-THREE

Formentera, 1718

'I think that Benito and I should marry,' Esperanza told Cesca when the two of them were sitting on their mother's bed a few days later. Cesca had been brushing her mother's hair, but at Esperanza's words the brush fell from her grasp to clatter on the floor. She shared a startled look with her mother.

'What?'

Esperanza nodded. Her eyes were shining and she couldn't contain the burst of happiness that the idea brought her – or how much she cared for him. She bit her lip. 'It makes sense. I mean he *is* living here, people will ask questions... Riba has already started asking if we will marry soon after you and Señor Garcia as planned, and well, with things the way they are... with Don Santiago, well, maybe it would be for the best. Besides, he's a wonderful man, so good and kind. I'd be happy to be his wife, truly, and well, I think that it would be good for us both.'

Cesca blinked. *Esperanza marry Benito?*

She felt her heart stop completely at the thought.

'I- I'm not sure that's the best idea,' she stammered.

'Why not? I know you don't like him. I'm not sure what changed between you – I mean you two used to get on so well, always chatting in the mornings, and laughing, and now since *Mare* got sick it's like you blame him for it or something—'

Cesca's face blanched. 'I don't blame him!'

Esperanza sighed. 'Well, maybe you think he's made it harder being here – with people looking for him, creating more stress – but he can't help that. He's even offered to leave. We're the ones who took him in, it was our choice, and besides, he's a good man, a kind man.'

'I know *that* – it's not that, Esperanza, it's not that at all.' She opened her mouth, trying to find the right words. But she couldn't find any. She stared at her sister in anguish, not wanting to shout out the truth: Esperanza couldn't marry Benito because *she* was in love with him.

Her mother touched Esperanza's hand. 'I don't know, my love… I'm not sure it is a good idea.'

'Why not? I was meant to marry Rafael – it makes sense for us.'

'Things don't have to always make sense for it to work.'

'You don't want me to marry him?'

'I just want you to be happy.'

Esperanza kissed her mother's cheek. 'This would make me happy, *Mare*. I know we would be poor, I know I've always said that I wanted a different kind of life, but now I understand what you meant when you said with the right person it wouldn't matter, and it doesn't, not at all. I mean he doesn't have any money or a career, but I don't care. I want to be with him.'

Cesca blanched at her sister's words.

'And Benito – does he feel the same way?' asked their mother, looking at Cesca, noting her stricken expression.

'I don't know. He has only ever been a gentleman. But *Mare*, when you're gone people will wonder at him living here with us… It wouldn't be right. Maybe this would be the best solution all round.'

Her mother looked at her, then squeezed her hand. 'I see, but I think there might be another solution,' she said, giving Cesca a meaningful look.

When Esperanza left, her mother looked at her, 'My child. There's something you should know.'

Cesca frowned. 'What is it?'

'You know your father never had a formal agreement with Señor Garcia about the marriage, don't you? It was just a general conversation between them – your father didn't actually *agree*.'

'What do you mean?' Cesca asked with a frown.

'Your father told the doctor when he asked for your hand in marriage that he would *think* about it. He told him that it was a good match and that it was an honour, but he had his reservations, he thought it wouldn't be fair to wish an old man on a young bride. Your father loved you very much, and the two men were great friends, so this didn't offend Señor Garcia, of course. He agreed to give your father time to think it over.'

Cesca was confused. She thought, the way everyone else had always spoken about it, that it was a matter that had long been decided. 'Well, he must have gone back to him and told him that he agreed,' she said with a frown. 'Because we've been betrothed ever since.'

Her mother shook her head. 'No, he didn't. He never got the chance. He died that week.'

Cesca gasped. 'What does that mean? Why are you telling me this now?'

'Because you deserve to know that if, for whatever reason, you break your engagement, no one would be able to hold it against you as you were not officially promised. Señor Garcia knows this, and he can be reminded if need be.'

Cesca blinked at her mother. 'What are you saying, *Mare*? You don't want us to get married?'

Her mother clutched her hand. 'No, Cesca, I want you to be happy, is all I am saying, and if for some other reason you choose not to marry the doctor, know that it is a choice you can make, in clear conscience.'

Cesca squeezed her mother's hands. 'Thank you for telling me, but I have become accustomed to the idea of marrying him. I'm not sure that I could' – she swallowed – 'that I could step aside now. So much has already been promised. It wouldn't be right. Even if – even if I wanted to step away,' she admitted.

Her mother touched her cheek. 'My daughter, always so good, but happiness is not always about being "good". Take your sister for example.'

Cesca stared at her mother in confusion. She'd never been told to look to her sister for guidance before.

'What do you mean?'

'Well, let's just say that there is something to be admired about following your own heart sometimes. Don't be afraid to do the same – before it's too late.'

Tears filled Cesca's eyes, but she nodded, then kissed her mother's cheek.

Cesca would have to tell Benito that he would have to leave. It was the only real solution – she couldn't face the idea of him being betrothed to her sister, and Esperanza was right; everyone would begin to ask questions about why she wasn't getting married to him when he was living there.

But when she found him in the garden, sitting on a tree stump and staring out to sea, she couldn't find the right words.

'My sister has fallen for you – I believe that she wants to marry you,' she blurted out.

He turned to look at her. Even under the cover of darkness she could see the blue of his eyes.

He said nothing and she felt herself growing angry. 'Did you hear what I said?'

'I heard you.'

His voice was soft, and despite herself she stepped closer.

'She wants to marry you.'

He gave a small sigh.

'So you'd give me to your sister, rather than face what was inside your own heart?'

Cesca blinked. 'No – that's not what I'm trying to tell you.'

'What then?' he said, standing up and clutching her shoulder. 'What do you want to tell me? Just say it.'

'Forget it,' she said, making to leave.

He made an angry noise. 'Fine, go then… run away, as usual.'

She turned on her heel. 'What does that mean?'

'It means that at least your sister knows when to stand up for what she wants.'

She bristled at that. It was so like what her mother had told her. 'Oh, so you admire her then?'

'Yes.'

'Well, then maybe you *should* marry her!'

'I can't do that.'

'Why not – if you admire her so?'

'Because I'm in love with *her* sister, and call me old-fashioned but I think that would just make things much harder than they already are.'

She sucked in air, felt her heart soar at his words. 'You love me?'

'Yes,' he said, coming closer to her. 'I think I've been falling for you since the first day we met.'

She swallowed, looked up into his eyes. She was tired of fighting it, tired of feeling miserable. 'Me too.'

She sank into his kiss. If the sky fell, at least they'd be together.

*

Esperanza stared at the couple clasped together in the moonlight, and felt something inside her break.

Benito was the first man she'd ever fallen for, the first person who'd seemed to like her for who she was, and now he was wrapped up in the arms of her *sister*. Was there nothing Cesca didn't take from her? She'd never felt more betrayed in her life.

She left the *finca* and walked all night, till finally the tears came, and with them a decision that she would later regret.

FORTY-FOUR

Formentera, 1718

The storm had come in from the sea and the windows were rattling violently when Don Santiago opened the door to find Esperanza outside, shivering with cold, a fierce expression in her dark eyes.

She looked frozen through, her hair in wet tendrils down her back, her dress plastered to her body.

'You're frozen!' he cried, stepping forward to touch her ice-cold skin. 'What are you doing here – is everything all right?'

She shook her head.

'Come with me,' he said, taking her by her arm and leading her inside, where she stood dripping onto the cool tile of the hallway.

He went to fetch her a towel, shouting for one of the servants, a young girl, who came running and then stared at them with large eyes till he barked at her to make some tea and to find something for the señorita to wear. 'Go now,' he snapped and she ran to do his bidding.

He wrapped the towel round Esperanza's shoulders, rubbing it against her skin, noting that her lips were blue. Her teeth chattered as she stared at him.

'I will marry you,' she said.

He blinked. 'What?'

She nodded. 'If you still want to.'

He stared at her, hardly daring to believe it was true. 'I do.'

FORTY-FIVE

Formentera, present day

The name Marisal, I learned, came from the Catalan for sea and salt. The two forces that had shaped the lives of the Alvarez family on this tiny slip of an island for so many years.

I'd been thinking of it a lot since Maria had told me about the two sisters, Cesca and Esperanza. I thought of them often, especially now.

'So Cesca was my great-great-grandmother,' I said. 'It was because of her that we are here now, because she and her family took in Benito, no?'

She looked at me, then frowned. 'Cesca? No.'

'What?'

'No, well, your great-great-grandmother wasn't Cesca… it was Esperanza. I thought you knew that?'

I looked at her and gasped. 'But I thought…'

'No, you come from the other one – the one who almost ruined it all.'

I blinked.

Maria touched my arm. 'The key word here is almost – she learned from what she did. She learned how to put her life back together again.'

*

Later that day, she told me that on the island it was tradition to have the coastal land pass to the youngest child, then divide up the rest of the land between the other children. 'So this house would have gone to your grandmother, not our brother, Stefan, but with the war I left, and went to mainland Spain for a few years,' she said. 'So I didn't know what happened to it, till it was too late.'

'You left?' I was surprised. Somehow, I'd got the impression that she had stayed.

'Only until the end of the Second World War.'

'When I came back my brother was gone. He'd sold the house to pay off some gambling debts, then he died – there was an accident, at the salt pans where he was working.

'I married my husband Bernabè, who was also from the island, and we moved back to his family home. It was sad to see my house in the hands of strangers and I tried to fight the sale – but we couldn't prove the ownership, there hadn't been a deed, so for many years I avoided the house, even looking at it, because of what it reminded me of – all that we had lost. But you know how it is – every so often I couldn't help walking past… trying to look for ghosts, I suppose.' She sighed.

I'd told her about why James had bought it for me, and the story had touched her deeply. 'He sounds like a man I would have been honoured to have met.'

There were tears in both of our eyes when she said that.

I think James would have liked her, too.

'I'm happy your husband bought it for you, and that it is where it belongs,' she said, touching my shoulder. 'Glad I got a chance to meet you.'

'Would you like to come and see it?' I asked.

Her eyes grew dark and sad. She didn't say anything for a while and then she nodded. 'Yes, I'd like that, very much.'

*

She was a tiny figure in her brown house dress, hugging her arms to herself, her grey-dark hair wispy around her face, when she stepped inside the kitchen in Marisal. There was an old brown kerchief over her hair; a few of the island's older women still wore their hair that way.

Despite her size, she felt like a big presence in the small room.

Her dark eyes seemed to drink everything in. I hung back. I knew enough about leaving people alone with their ghosts.

A mottled brown hand ran around the whitewashed stone. 'There used to be a painting here.' She laughed softly as she remembered. 'A silly thing someone painted of a little goat.'

She walked further into the kitchen, and said, 'There used to be a big table here, in the centre', and when I looked, trying to picture it, I could see the scuff marks on the floors from the chairs.

'And here,' she said, lifting up one of the loose flagstone tiles. 'We kept our treasures.'

My eyes widened. 'Treasures?'

'Simple things. Things we put there as children.'

She put the flagstone back. 'Empty now, of course.'

I didn't say anything, just let her lead me through the rest of the house. It was strange after having stayed here to have her tell me about it. Or perhaps not that strange, really. Houses are often mysteries, and old houses have many stories to tell.

'My parents slept in here,' she said, going into the room I'd made for myself, the old bed fitted with the new sheets I'd bought from the market, the day I met my new friend Isla. 'They had one of those big four-poster beds, and this hard mattress that made even sitting on it a trial – but no matter what my mother said, my father wouldn't be persuaded to change it. He said it helped him to start the day early – and there was no rest on *fincas* like ours.' She smiled at the memory. 'He was a hard-worker, my *pare*.'

'What was it like here when you were a child?' I asked.

'Oh, it was a simple, but happy time,' she said readily. 'We had no idea about the threat that was looming ahead, I suppose, so maybe I look back at it fondly, more honey-coloured than I should.' She shrugged.

That was normal, I guessed, and I knew having a happy childhood was something to cherish.

'We kept chickens, cows, a few goats. They gave us cheese and milk. We lived a lot off the land. I'm not sure I knew that we were poor, it's just how it was, you know? My father was one of the last of the Alvarez men who worked for the salt trade – by then it had really started to flounder. The Bourbons never took much of an interest in the salt trade after they took it over during the War of Succession in the eighteenth century, and the demand for salt, as you know, had died down a lot by the end of the century with the invention of tinned food.'

I hadn't known that, to be honest, but I nodded anyway. 'After he died, that's when we knew what poor was. At one time Formentera was called Woman Island – there were no men left. The ones who survived the wars left to find work elsewhere. Some never returned home and some came home only every few months or even just once a year. They got work in America or elsewhere, wherever they could. But… back when my parents lived here, this was home, and we were happy here.'

'And Alba – my grandmother?'

'Oh yes. She was very happy. Of course, she was always ambitious, though; she wanted more of an adventurous life. She was a fine artist, did you know that?'

I nodded. I did. I still had some of her paintings. It was only now that I knew it had run in the family.

'Why did she not come back? Did you have a fallout? Was that what it was?'

'The short answer is yes. The long one is that life was hard during the Franco regime. People like us were persecuted. It was a very difficult time. The Inquisition was long over, yes, but when the war broke out in 1936, there was an almost complete breakdown of the secret Jewish community that had lived here and on Ibiza for many years. Many who fought died, and the socialists found themselves in concentration camps. Shortly after the war ended, the Second World War began and German soldiers flooded the shores, taking note of Jewish residents. It became prudent once again for families to convert to Catholicism.

'Alba had a particularly tough time as an unmarried woman. She was harassed by Nazi soldiers—'

I gasped. 'Nazis! But that must mean that she was here during the Second World War!'

Maria nodded. 'She was, yes.'

'But she told me that she left during the civil war, to escape.'

Maria looked grave. 'Yes, that is what she told you, I suppose to protect her secret, her past. She left here in 1944, when she was twenty-four years old. Beautiful but damaged, perhaps beyond repair. I am not sure what they did to her, if they raped her or not. I can only hope that they did not. Though you can rape someone without ever harming their body.

'What I do know is that she was interrogated at length, that she was kept inside a cell and half-starved and beaten, while they attempted to get her to confess.

'You see, we had been secret Jews for so long that when the Nazis discovered this, they took special satisfaction in trying to get us to admit it. She didn't confess. I think because by the time they were finished with her, she had decided in her heart that she wasn't Jewish any more.

'When she was finally released, she discovered that she was now on a list. There were rumours reaching us from afar of what was happening to people who were on lists like this. It was a small island after all, and they'd started to build a concentration camp here.'

I gasped. 'Here, on Formentera?'

Maria nodded. 'Yes.'

'She left in the night, taken to safety through the old Ibicenco pirate network – they helped rescue quite a lot of Jewish people, I believe. It was on this ship that she met your grandfather. I don't know the details of why he was on board or what part he played. I do know that he wasn't Jewish though.'

I took a seat on the bed. Rocked to my core. 'But you said that the two of you had a fallout? Why?'

'When she got to England, she decided that she never wanted to be reminded of her past ever again. The only trouble was that I was a living, breathing reminder.' She started to cry then. 'And I'd failed her. Failed to protect my little sister, because at the time they'd taken her for questioning I wasn't here.'

I held the old woman in my arms. I didn't know what to say. My heart felt broken for her, for my grandmother too. I could understand, now more than ever, why she never wanted to speak about her past, about what had had happened to her. I could perhaps even understand why she'd given up her faith: in the end it had seemed to ask so much of her and her family.

But I knew one thing, and that was that Maria couldn't blame herself for what had happened to her. 'It's not your fault. If you'd been here, they would have just taken you too. You couldn't have prevented it.'

She looked at me, her eyes so haunted and sad. 'But maybe I could have.'

FORTY-SIX

Formentera, 1718

Esperanza entered the *finca* with the intention of getting her things and leaving. She was planning to stay at Riba's until she was married. But one look at her mother stopped her in her tracks.

Cesca got up fast, and came to her side. There were tears in her eyes. 'Señor Garcia thinks it will be soon,' she whispered, her lips wobbling.

Tears pooled in Esperanza's eyes, but she stepped away when her sister made to take her hand.

Cesca blinked. ''Spranza, what is it?'

Esperanza shook her head, then went and sat with her mother. They'd made a bed for her in the corner, as she could no longer sit at the table. Her face was pale, and she was so frail. Esperanza felt a stab of guilt that she'd been gone all night when her mother was like this.

'I'm so sorry, *Mare*,' she cried, clutching her hand.

Her mother gave her a weak smile. 'Don't cry, my pet. And don't fight with your sister. Not now. You need each other.'

Esperanza kissed her check, but she didn't respond. She would never forgive Cesca, not after what she had done – not after she had come to her with her heart laid bare, telling her of how she felt about Benito, only to watch her sister throw herself at him a few short hours later. She could never forgive her that.

*

Their mother died just before dawn, with Esperanza asleep at her side. She woke up to the sound of her sister's sobs.

She looked at her mother's dear face, and kissed her. She had never felt more alone in all her life.

The week passed slowly, with Esperanza barely saying a word to Cesca. The day after the burial she moved into Riba's house, and shortly afterwards she told Don Santiago that she wanted to get married as soon as he could arrange it. She didn't want to wait until her brother arrived, when he would be able to prevent it.

Don Santiago was happy to oblige. He arranged for a local fisherman to row them to Ibiza and, hearing that her brother was still at sea – the one person who could potentially object the most – he decided that it would be a good idea to get married straight away too, mostly because he was afraid she would change her mind.

By that afternoon, they were husband and wife.

Esperanza told him that she would join him later at the governor's house, where they would be staying until he could make other arrangements, but that she would face her sister alone, to tell her the news. He had wanted to come, too. 'I can't let you do this alone,' he'd said, touching her face, and she'd given him a thin smile. 'You must – she won't understand. We can speak to them later about it, properly. But for now I think this way would be best.'

'If you think so – I will be waiting for you.'

She nodded, forced a smile and made for her home, realising with a pang that it would no longer be *her* home.

But the news had travelled fast and by the time she got to the *finca*, intending to fetch Flea and pack her things, her sister had heard.

'What have you done?' she asked as soon as Esperanza stepped inside. Her voice cold, her face furious. She was sitting in the kitchen with Señor Garcia and Benito, whose face also couldn't hide its shock. Esperanza couldn't look at him. It hurt too much.

Cesca snapped. 'Is it true?' she said, standing up so fast the kitchen chair toppled over, hitting the flagstone floor with a crash. '*Mare*'s body is not even cold and you betray all of us like this by marrying a stranger – someone who will ask questions about all of us, our secret community?'

Esperanza's eyebrows shot up into her hair. 'I betrayed *you*? It wasn't the other way round? Because the way I saw it, I came home the other night to find my sister wrapped up in the arms of *my* betrothed!'

Cesca gasped and looked swiftly from Benito to Señor Garcia, her face colouring.

Señor Garcia's face flushed. He looked at Cesca. 'Is that true?'

'I—'

'It is,' said Esperanza. 'She has been going behind both our backs, the filthy little—'

'Esperanza,' said Benito, stopping her.

'Oh yes, heaven forbid I say anything against my perfect sister,' she said, then turned to go and fetch her things from her room.

Cesca followed after her, with Benito at her heels. 'So that's what this was about – revenge?'

Esperanza stared at her as she shoved her things into a basket. There wasn't much.

'No.'

Cesca shook her head. 'I hope not, for your sake.'

'Why – why do you care if it was?'

'Because the only one you'll end up hurting is yourself.'

Esperanza shook her head. 'Don't pretend that you care about me now.'

Cesca crossed her arms. 'After you put us all at risk by marrying Don Santiago – no, I won't pretend to care about you.'

'Well, at least you're being honest. I know after keeping your little affair a secret for so long, the truth is a strange concept to you, so thank you for that at least,' she said, then she turned and left.

When she got to Don Santiago's house that night he welcomed her in, kissing her as she came inside, Flea at her side. He eyed the dog in some surprise. 'You brought this fellow, did you?'

She nodded. 'I hope that's all right?'

He smiled at her, touched her cheek. 'Of course it is.'

He called for his servant, the same young girl as before. 'Daniella, please take this dog into the kitchen, make a bed for him – he is the señora's special pet.'

Daniella blinked, then looked at Esperanza. The two had often seen each other on the island, had grown up not far from each other, and Esperanza was shocked when she curtsied.

'Oh, and Daniella, please draw a bath, and bring our dinner to the chamber. My bride and I will be dining in tonight.'

Daniella nodded and hurried away. Esperanza watched her leave, feeling her cheeks flush. She looked at Don Santiago, who put an arm round her and led her to the bedroom, and Cesca's words raced through her head: 'I hope that you haven't done this out of revenge.'

She bit her lip, and tears filled her eyes. There was no turning back now.

FORTY-SEVEN

Formentera, present day

'One more sleep,' texted Sage, and I grinned as I lay in bed and stared at the phone. I couldn't wait to see her. She wasn't the only one counting the days.

'I can't wait for her to see it,' I told James's ashes as I started cleaning the kitchen, making a list of all the things I would need before she arrived.

The spare room had fresh bed linen, and a vase of wildflowers, and I'd hung one of Isla's beautiful seascapes on the wall.

Sage would be coming for two whole weeks, a proper break after a very long year.

I couldn't wait.

That afternoon, I took a trip to a local jeweller to fetch something I'd had made. Something for Sage. My finger came up to touch my bare thumb.

On the way back I cut through the dry scrubland and went to visit Maria, where we sat outside in the sunshine and she told me more about Esperanza. I still couldn't believe that it was her that we were descended from – I couldn't help it, a small part of me had been a little disappointed to hear that. Maria had laughed when I told her that. 'Things always seem darkest before the dawn, you know that – and for Esperanza there was a very long night before the dawn.'

FORTY-EIGHT

Formentera, 1718

Esperanza had everything she'd once wished for. A grand home, servants and a husband who was part of a world she'd only ever dreamt about. The only trouble was that she was more miserable than she'd ever been in the whole of her life.

Don Santiago was eager for them to make a new start in Barcelona, for him to present his new wife to his family.

The house that he was staying in wasn't a home and he thought that now they were married it was time for him to return to his old life.

With her mother gone, and things between her and Cesca so strained, there seemed no reason for her to want to stay on the island.

Except that for the first time in her life she understood the danger she was in. Especially when he started to ask questions – questions he hadn't asked her before.

'Your family – are they originally from Ibiza?' he'd asked one morning.

'I… yes.'

'From where?'

She named the village where her cousin had lived.

He looked at her strangely. 'Really?'

'Yes, why?'

'It's just that area was one of the old Jewish settlements.'

She blinked in shock. He smiled. 'It was a long time ago – I mean, they're all gone now.'

She nodded. 'Yes, of course. My family came from the capital too – and then came here to help with the salt trade.'

There were other things too – things she didn't think of. Like her habit of lighting a candle on a Friday night.

'You know you do that every week?' he asked. 'On the same night.'

She turned to find him in the doorway. 'I… um.'

'Why is that?' He looked curious.

'For my mother. I light it for her.'

'Every Friday? Why not on a Sunday?'

'I'm not sure. I can do it on a Sunday if you prefer?'

He shook his head. 'No, it's fine, it's just – never mind. It's your home. If that's what you want to do then that's fine with me.'

She bit her lip as he left the room. It was a habit, passed down for centuries, and she hadn't thought of why she was doing it till he had asked her – it was only then that she realised it was something that marked her as different, and could lead him to question her background, question her faith.

How many other of her cultural practices were from their secret faith? Things that could mark her as different without her even realising it? This was why they married their own – these things that announced who they were without them even being aware of it.

Don Santiago took his wife's feelings into account when she asked him to delay their departure to Barcelona, even though he was eager to leave the island. He loved his wife and if she wanted to stay for now, he would.

She'd told him that she wanted some time just for the two of them to get to know each other, while he finished up his report on the salt trade, and he'd agreed. 'Of course, once we are in Barcelona I'll have to share you with all the other wives, it's true,' he'd said.

'Perhaps we could see this time as a honeymoon…' she suggested. He seemed charmed by the idea, and she'd breathed a sigh of relief.

'You were promised to Rafael Alvarez?' demanded Don Santiago a week after they were married.

She looked up from the wildflowers she was arranging in the dining room and felt her stomach clench in sudden fear. There was something in his eyes, something dark and forbidding.

'Yes.' She attempted a casual tone. 'I thought you knew that.'

He frowned. 'I didn't realise it was the man staying in your house. But you decided to break your engagement – why?' he demanded, taking hold of her arm.

She swallowed. 'Because of you.'

He blinked. She could see the small flare of hope her words caused, and felt bad.

'Because of me,' he repeated.

She nodded. 'What we had.'

'So you broke it off with him.'

His hands were biting into her flesh now, twisting her arm. There would be a bruise there later. There was rage just beneath the surface of his eyes.

She bit her lip, realising then that she would need to lie. 'It was a mutual decision.'

He stared at her, then suddenly his face seemed to relax. It was the answer he was looking for, she realised. 'Good,' he said simply. His eyes warmed. She felt her knees give out.

She should have known that news of 'Rafael' and her sister would have spread – especially after she'd confronted them in front of Señor Garcia. She hadn't thought though of the consequences it would have brought for her – that Don Santiago would want to know why their engagement had fallen through and that he would wonder if she had fled to him because Rafael had fallen in love with her sister.

But he seemed satisfied with her answer – pleased even. 'It worked out quite well actually, them falling for each other,' he said that night as he handed her a glass of wine while they sat outside in the garden. She was rolling a ball to Flea, who was returning it to her with his nose. 'If not, we'd never have been able to wed. We should have them over for dinner, celebrate their union, don't you think?'

Esperanza shook her head. 'I'd prefer not to, if you don't mind. My sister and I had a falling-out.'

'Why?'

'We haven't always got on, and after my mother died it seemed there was no point in keeping up the pretence.'

He frowned as he took a sip of wine, but left it at that.

*

Antoni came home in the autumn, tired, with his hair grown long, and devastated to hear the news of his mother's passing. 'I should have been here,' he said, hugging Cesca close.

'There was nothing you could have done.'

He took a seat at the table, across from Benito. He'd seen the way the man lingered near his sister, the way they looked at each other. The news of their union had greeted him as soon as he'd got off the boat. 'A lot has changed in my absence,' he said.

Benito nodded. 'I am sorry about that – you invited me into your home, I should have asked for your permission.'

'Yes,' said Antoni, who was a man of strong convictions and principles; he hadn't been made one of the salt trade's youngest captains for nothing. 'But it is done now.'

'And Señor Garcia – what did he have to say about this?'

Cesca sighed. 'It wasn't easy – at first he would not speak to us, but the truth is that we were never actually promised to one another.'

'What?' asked Antoni, shocked. 'Of course you were – since you were young!'

'No – *Mare* told me Señor Garcia had asked *Pare* but he never actually agreed, he died before he gave the doctor his word, and after that we all just accepted that he had.'

Antoni looked amazed. 'And so you told him that you and Ben— Rafael were to wed?'

She nodded. 'He said that he was disappointed but that he wouldn't stand in our way.'

Antoni shook his head.

'It is the least of your worries though, brother,' said Cesca.

'What do you mean?' he asked, looking surprised at that.

'It is your other sister we need to worry about.'

He blinked. 'Esperanza? Why?'

Cesca looked at Benito. How was it possible that he hadn't heard? 'She is married.'

Antoni shot out of his chair. 'What do you mean, married?'

'She married Don Santiago – a week ago.'

'Don Santiago?' he said in confusion. Cesca nodded and explained, 'The stranger – the one from Barcelona, who everyone was worried might be here for other reasons than what he said – to study the flora of the salt flats.'

He blanched. 'The one people think may be working for the Holy Office? She married him? How is that even possible?'

'They had the ceremony in Ibiza, one week ago – apparently he paid a priest.'

It was inconceivable. 'Why – why the hurry? And why would she marry him, are they in love?'

Cesca and Benito shared a look. 'I think he is.'

'And Esperanza?' Antoni ran an anguished hand through his hair. 'No, don't tell me – this is our little sister – she was swayed by the promise of a grand life, the promises of a wealthy husband. No wonder she agreed to get married straight away – she knew I was coming and wanted to make sure I didn't stop it. Can we get it annulled?'

'I don't think so. They have been living together as man and wife.'

Antoni went pale.

Benito nodded. 'Riba's husband, Francisco, told us that Don Santiago confessed that he's a researcher – paid by the Crown to make observations. He's here to help modernise the salt trade – but – a man like that…'

Cesca nodded. 'Would notice when things didn't add up.'

'Wasn't there anything you could have said? She listened to you,' he said to Cesca.

Cesca's eyes filled with tears. 'Not any more – not after what we did.'

'What do you mean?'

So Cesca told him, about how Esperanza had fallen for Benito, how she had come to her and their mother to tell her that she thought she and Benito should marry. How it would solve all their problems.

'But I – we…' began Cesca.

'You'd already fallen in love,' he guessed. 'I see. And as a result, she did the one thing that could hurt us all.'

She nodded, tears slipping down her cheeks. 'Yes.'

*

Don Santiago read aloud to his new wife the letter from his sister, Florentina, in Barcelona. 'She says that she cannot believe that I am married – she thought of me as a committed bachelor.'

Esperanza took a sip of tea and smiled at him indulgently.

'But she has other news – apparently two Majorcan prisoners were kidnapped by pirates not far from these shores – two brothers by the name of Nuñez – she asks if we knew anything about it?'

Esperanza choked on her tea as he continued to read from the letter. 'She says that they are circulating a likeness of one of the brothers – a man with blue eyes, Benito – apparently, the other one turned up dead.'

He looked at her. 'You know, I heard something about this a while ago from your friend Riba's husband, Francisco – I can't believe this story has got to Barcelona already. It must be the pirate angle, big news,' he said. 'Well, Francisco said that the officers even went so far as to question your bother, as captain of the *Invictus*, to see if he knew anything. Apparently, the ship that was described was similar, can you imagine?'

Esperanza sat mute, thunderstruck. When he looked at her, his expression turned soft. 'I wouldn't worry. From what I heard he made them all look like fools…'

Don Santiago found the sketches hidden in a dresser drawer by accident, on a cold night when he went looking for a shawl for her while she sat in the garden, staring out to sea, Flea at her heels.

'You look cold. I'll get you a shawl. Sit, relax,'

'Thank you,' she said, and he went to the bedroom to fetch it for her, opening the drawers, looking for her wrap, his fingers pausing when they came across something hard. It was a leather-bound case filled with sketches.

He opened it in surprise and paused, a smile on his face. She'd mentioned her art before, but he'd never seen it. He flipped through the pages. There were sketches of Flea, her old house, ordinary things – then suddenly he stopped, and frowned. Sketch after sketch showed the same face over and over again. There were dozens of the man. Of her former betrothed, Rafael. Don Santiago's fist clenched when he saw that one of them was dated recently – she had drawn it since she was married to him! At the bottom of each sketch along with the date were the initials B.N. The truth hit him like a thunderbolt. She had been in love with him.

He shoved the sketches back inside the drawer, then left the house without a word.

As he walked through the night he thought back to when he'd first fallen in love with Esperanza, when they'd spoken so passionately about their mutual love for art and books. He remembered how Riba had remarked upon the oddly changed appearance of her cousin. And that Rafael had been brought here to recover from an illness. For the first time, he stopped to think about how strange that was.

Why was he brought here when there were far more doctors in Ibiza? Why make a journey like that when you were ill, close to death, why rely on the care of a young nurse? He hadn't thought to question it before, but with the suspicions racing through his mind, and the rumours he had heard about a ship that looked a lot like the *Invictus* being part of the capture – the ship captained by Esperanza's brother – he couldn't help but wonder.

He reread the letter from his sister. The names of the men who had fled. The Nuñez brothers. Paulo and Benito Nuñez… Paulo had turned up dead.

When he got home, Esperanza was asleep. He slowly opened the dresser to look through his wife's sketchbooks again, at the small B.N. on each of the drawings she'd made of him. Could it be?

*

Esperanza woke up to find her sketches lined up all over the bedroom floor, a dozen or more images of Benito's face staring back at her. She sat up fast, her heart jackhammering in her chest.

'Do you love him?'

She closed her eyes.

He sucked in a deep breath. She couldn't deny it. 'Say it!'

She nodded her head slightly, and he let out a deep cry.

'Does he love you?'

She shook her head.

He sighed, then slumped against the wall. 'So that's why you married me – because he didn't want you?' Realisation was hitting him hard.

She bit her lip. 'It's not the only reason.'

His face twisted at that. 'Don't pretend you ached for me.'

'I did – I do.'

'Not like for him though,' he said, and felt like he'd been punched when she nodded.

'He's not your cousin, is he?'

She looked up in sudden fear. 'Of course he is.'

His lips went thin. 'Riba said it that night at dinner at their house... she mentioned his eyes.'

He unfolded a poster. 'You know they are circulating this around all the Balearics – it's a likeness of a man who looks just like him. I went out this morning to go and get one from the docks. It says it here. Vivid blue eyes. Dark hair. Benito Nuñez. In fact they say that he was taken by a ship that looked just like your brother's... I think it must have been *exactly* like his ship, come to think of it.'

Esperanza blanched. 'That's not true.'

'Oh, but I think it is. I think you've been lying to me this whole time. You all have, and I'm not taking it any more.'

There was something about the way he said that. Something final. Something that chilled her blood. 'What did you do?' she asked.

He shrugged. 'What was right.'

Esperanza got up. He looked at her coldly. 'Where do you think you're going?'

She sucked in a breath. 'Away – you're not thinking calmly.'

His eyes flashed fire. 'Running off to warn your lover, is that it? I don't think so,' he said, teeth bared as he shoved her painfully back onto the bed.

'No, I think you will stay here until the letter has been delivered to the governor – until he comes here and arrests your family for what they've done…'

'No!' she cried, running to the door. He grabbed her arm and jerked her back so that she fell over, but she got up again, fighting and pulling at him to try to get out. He slapped her hard across the face and she went flying, hitting her head against the wall. She gasped, sliding down, doubling over in pain.

'I don't want to hurt you,' he said, 'so I suggest you stop fighting me.'

Esperanza tried to breathe, but all she saw was stars. She sank to the floor, where she spied the pistol he always kept beneath the bed. She made to grab for it but he saw what she was doing and grabbed her by the ankle. Her hands scrabbled, and she kicked out and kept reaching for the pistol until she had it in her hands at last.

'You won't shoot me,' he said.

'You're threatening my family, Santiago, you don't know what I'd do.'

'I thought you said that you didn't care about them.'

'Yes, well, I lied.'

There was the sound of loud barking. Flea had heard her screams and was trying to get in. Don Santiago opened the door and the dog went straight for his leg. Don Santiago roared in pain and threw Flea against the wall and he yelped. Esperanza flew at him, and he tried to fight her off, but then suddenly the pistol went off with a deafening bang.

Esperanza fell backwards with a thud, pain bludgeoning her skull. Distantly as if from a tunnel she heard the sound of barking, and there was a heavy weight on her chest. She couldn't breathe and blood like wine was oozing all around her. Don Santiago was on top of her, his hazel eyes unseeing. She gasped.

He was dead, killed by his own pistol.

She struggled to get him off of her. He was heavy, cumbersome, but at last she rolled his body off and sat up feeling her head. Flea rushed over to help. Tears coursed down her face, but as she sat up, gasping for breath, she had one thought in her mind, and one only – she had to get back that letter.

Cesca opened the door in shock. Esperanza was standing outside, her hair dishevelled, a wild look in her eyes, her arms covered in blood.

''Spranza! What happened?'

She blinked, trying and failing to find the words as she stared into her sister's eyes.

'Come inside, take a seat.'

Esperanza nodded and sat down shakily at the table. 'There was an accident.'

'Are you hurt?' It was Antoni's voice. He came in from the bedroom. It was the first time they'd seen each other since he came back. Esperanza's eyes filled, seeing him. 'Santiago was.'

Cesca blinked, then took a seat next to her, picking up her sister's hand. 'What happened?'

Esperanza stared at her. 'I killed him.'

They all started to speak at once. Esperanza shook her head. They didn't understand. 'There's no time, we have to stop it.'

'Stop what?' asked Benito.

'The letter.'

'The letter?'

She explained about the letter Don Santiago had written to the governor. How he knew everything, how he'd worked it all out about what they'd done. 'We have to get it back.'

Antoni tried to stop her, but she shook her head. She'd run to the port if she had to – perhaps there was time, maybe she could say that Don Santiago had asked her to recall the letter? Or that he'd sent the wrong one… yes, that's what she'd do.

Antoni stood in front of the door, blocking her exit. 'You can't do that.'

She looked at him, her eyes raw. 'I have to try, I have to get them to give it back.'

He didn't let her go, but his face was set.

'It's too late.'

'No, it's not,' she protested.' I can convince them, they will give it back. If not I'll steal it, rip it up… they can't read it then and I'll deal with whatever happens to me.'

Antoni shook his head. 'It's too late – that's what I'm trying to tell you. The mail ship went this morning. I'm sorry.'

Her knees buckled and she sank to the floor. At last the sobs came. 'It's my fault,' she said gasping through her tears.

'It's not your fault,' said Cesca, bringing her a cup of tea for the shock. 'We'll face it together, we can get out of this…'

They all shared the same defeated glance. No one was sure how.

The storm rolled in, as if it knew what was coming. Formentera was cut off from Ibiza for the better part of a week. There would be no one coming to the island till it passed, and no chance of any mail coming through either, or investigators.

They sat uneasy, not able to leave until it cleared. 'Where can we go, France?' asked Cesca.

Benito shook his head. 'Not now. It's one of the first places they will look – they will look at our last address in Bayonne.'

'There's a friend from Genoa who might be able to take us to safety,' said Antoni.

Esperanza sat numbly, Flea in her lap, not saying a word. She didn't feel as if she deserved to think of her own freedom – not after what she'd done to cost everyone theirs.

She couldn't help thinking about the greater consequences of the letter. What about the rest of the island? Their neighbours – how long before the officials started looking more closely at them? How long before they realised that they didn't belong here either?

FORTY-NINE

Formentera, 1718

When the storm finally cleared, they made their plans to leave and packed up all they could carry. They would row first to Ibiza, then catch a ship bound to Genoa. That was the plan.

'We will need to be fast. It won't be long before they will start asking questions about Don Santiago's death,' said Antoni.

They had called Señor Garcia, explaining to him what had happened with the accident, but it didn't look good. Esperanza could hang if they found her, especially after they read that letter. Who would think that it was really an accident?

They were getting ready to leave when the strangers arrived, a band of them walking straight for their *finca*.

Cesca ran inside and bolted the door.

'It's them – they have come already,' she cried. Esperanza came forward to stare out of the window, then closed her eyes in panic, her hand reaching out to grasp her sister's.

Antoni and Benito rushed into the kitchen, and Antoni threw a pistol to him.

'We die fighting,' he said. They nodded as the men on the other side began to pound the door.

Esperanza clutched her sister's hand tighter. Whatever their differences, they were in this together now. They'd face it like a family.

Antoni opened the door.

'Can I help you?'

'Yes, good day, *buno tarda*, my name is Salvador de Rimbaud. I came because my father received this letter written by Don Santiago.'

Esperanza felt herself go weak as the man took out the letter written in her husband's hand.

He put it on the table, open. 'I thought, under the circumstances, it was best to come here. I've since heard that Don Santiago passed away from a fever, correct?'

Careful not to let the man see, they all shared looks of surprise. Wherever had the man got that idea?

'Yes, I'm sorry for your loss – I saw the doctor, Señor Garcia earlier, who confirmed it,' he went on. 'Perhaps it explains the contents of this letter?'

They had never expected or imagined that the doctor would lie for them.

'Which, as you can imagine, is also a relief. We wouldn't want this to have got into the wrong hands – I'm sure you can understand.'

Esperanza blinked in shock.

'Pardon?'

Salvador de Rimbaud continued. 'Not many people are aware of this but my grandfather was on that first boat that came here, half a century ago now, when they left Majorca to come to live on this island. He settled in Ibiza instead and later rose to the rank of governor. You see,' he said, touching the letter, 'this is all our secret to keep. I came in person because I must stress that this cannot go any further – we cannot let anyone know about us. I hope you can agree.'

FIFTY

Formentera, present day

Sage arrived when the sun was high in the sky and the air was that hazy, still blue that transformed the ocean into a clear turquoise pool. She looked thinner, her face pale and her hair lank, though her eyes brightened when she saw me. It caused me a pang to see the strain on her young face, the toll it had taken on her to lose her father and to try somehow to put her life back together again. I was glad though that she was here now, and I hoped that the break would chase away some of those shadows beneath her eyes.

'Mum, you've got a tan!' she said in surprise.

I laughed. 'There's a first time for everything. You know, it feels like a year of firsts for me.'

'I know what you mean,' she said.

I touched her face. 'I know you do, kiddo,' I said, then I took her bag and wheeled it towards the waiting taxi.

On the drive to Marisal, she exclaimed at all that she saw, her eyes taking in the sweep of the ocean, the low walls that threaded across the terrain, the grassy farmland, till we entered the area of Can Morraig, and she saw the villa close to the sea, through the taxi window.

'This is amazing, Mum,' she gasped as we got out of the taxi and she stood in front of the low garden gate, looking up at the villa as I had done when I arrived.

'Geez, what an improvement on the pictures you sent.'

'It's just a bit of paint and a tidy-up – but I'm glad it's looking better,' I said, opening the door to show her round and take her suitcase into her room.

It was still sparsely furnished but clean and neat, with its vase of wildflowers on top of the old dresser and its small window offering a dazzling view of the ocean.

Sage had a shower while I went into the kitchen to make sure everything was all right. I'd bought candles, and soon Big Jim, Sue and Isla would be coming over for dinner – and my first official *shabbat*. And then, tomorrow, I'd take Sage to meet Maria.

After her shower we caught up, and Sage watched in bemusement as I got dinner started. I was making a new fish dish that Maria had taught me, and the kitchen was full of the scent of turmeric, tomatoes and lemon butter.

'I can't believe this is you, Mum,' said Sage, staring at me. 'Cooking!'

I laughed. 'Well, I've been learning, you see, and I've had some practice.'

'Wow, Mum. Dad would be proud.'

I swallowed, my eyes smarting. Did that ever stop? Did you ever hear his name and not want to fall apart? After a pause, when I had put myself back together, I said, 'I think you're right.' I went on, 'You don't mind that my friends are coming – the band, and my friend, Emmanuel, you're sure? They're pretty easy-going and I'm sure they won't mind if I cancel—'

'No! I want to meet them, they sound amazing. And tell me, this Emmanuel – is he going to be someone special?'

I shook my head. 'He's a friend. That's all.'

She raised an eyebrow. I sighed. 'Maybe some day.'

She smiled. 'As long as there's a some day.'

I looked at her. 'You're incredible, you know that?' I didn't know how I'd been so lucky as to have a daughter like her. Most other children would be furious at the prospect. I would be if I were in her shoes. 'Wouldn't you hate it if I moved on?'

'You're forty-five, Mum, it's not like what happened to you was fair. And I wouldn't see it as moving on – Dad was the love of your life. I'd see it as you trying to hang on.'

I bit my lip, then wiped away a tear. 'When did you start speaking in bloody Hallmark cards?'

She laughed. 'I know, right?'

After dinner, the band treated my daughter to a private show and I realised something as I looked around me: when Maria had taken me under her wing, she had told me about the family that had been left behind. She said that traditions were the things that linked you to them, and without these things you could lose the sense of where you'd come from. Maybe it wasn't too late to introduce them to a new generation, I thought. Perhaps that's how they lived on.

FIFTY-ONE

I took Sage to meet Maria the next morning. We walked into the aromatic kitchen where the old woman was busy cooking, and as soon as she saw Sage she gasped. 'This must be Sage – the doctor – or soon to be!'

Sage grinned. 'That's the plan – it's lovely to meet you at last. I have heard so much about you.'

'As have I about you. Sit, sit,' she said, inviting Sage to take a seat on one of the chairs not occupied by the cat, who was as usual basking in the scents of the kitchen.

We spoke for hours, about Cesca and Esperanza, filling Sage in on their story.

'But what happened to her – to Esperanza?' I asked. 'Was she pregnant that night when Don Santiago died?'

'No – she married again. She married another one of Benito's cousins – another escapee. Together, she, Cesca and Esperanza and Salvador de Rimbaud set up a network that helped other *chuetas* to flee to safety, providing a safe haven for them to stay.

'It was she who wrote down her story – and passed it on to all of us, as a lesson, I think,' she said, getting up and coming back with an old, leather-bound journal and handing it to me.

'It is how her story survived, that and because we kept it alive by telling it. Maybe now it can keep going, with you two.'

Sage looked at me, then squeezed my hand. 'She was the first writer in the family.'

I touched the journal in awe, seeing her words, in her beautiful script, and felt my eyes grow moist.

'I want you to keep it.'

'Me?' I said looking at it in shock. Maria nodded. 'It belongs with you – the next generation; it belongs with Marisal. So we never forget again who we are.'

I nodded and thanked her, touched beyond belief.

When the sky was painted gold and we were sitting outside, the scent of oranges and lemons perfuming the ocean air, I showed Sage what I'd got from the jewellers.

'Open it.'

Inside were two necklaces, each with a heart-shaped pendant, a tiny gemstone in their centres.

'What's this, Mum?'

'It's made from Dad's ring.'

Her fingers shook as she touched it. 'I wanted you to have a part of it,' I said. 'A piece of him for us to carry in our hearts.'

Her dark eyes filled with tears. 'That's beautiful, Mum.'

'I think your dad would have wanted that too.'

She swallowed, dashed away the tears. Then I took out something else from the bag at my feet. 'Okay, now the next one is going to be tough.'

She looked up, and then her face crumpled as she saw the urn, recognised what it was.

'It's time for this, I think.'

She closed her eyes, then nodded.

'Are you sure about this, Mum?'

'Yes, I think so – I knew it had to be us, when we were together.'

I touched the necklace, my half of James's ring, and thought of what he'd told me – that I'd know when to do it. I hadn't thought

I'd ever be able to do this, but I was ready now because I'd realised something over these last few months – thanks to Maria – that the people you love never truly leave you.

I opened up the urn and scattered the ashes to the wind, where he became a part of Marisal, like me and Sage, a part of the wind and sky; though a part of him would always be, as Maria had said, here, beating inside my own heart.

AUTHOR'S NOTE

The idea of a secret Jewish community on the island of Formentera was popularised by researcher Gloria Mound, who believed that one existed from around the fifteenth century, after the Spanish expulsion order of the Jews during the Inquisition, up until the Spanish Civil War.

Over the years some convincing evidence for this appeared to come to light, including what seemed to be the presence of a secret synagogue in a building in the Can Morraig area, where certain Hebrew documents were discovered. It remained for many years a powerful, positive story of Jewish survival.

Alas, according to historian Martin Davies, the origins of the building have been dated to the nineteenth century, and modern historians now believe that the Hebrew scrolls were brought over from Majorca during the 1930s, when the island can conclusively be linked to helping Jewish exiles during the Second World War.

It cannot however be said that there was *no* Jewish presence on the island before then, or that there definitely wasn't a secret community that existed there as for a long period it lay mostly abandoned. In this tale, I have blended fiction with fact – there were persecuted *chuetas* (secret Jews) who had been forced to convert, who fled the uprisings in Majorca as well as a Moorish sloop vessel containing two Nuñez cousins who were said to have been captured by Ibicenco corsairs. While Jewish pirates existed, it is believed that they would not have operated within the Mediterranean, however, according to historian Martin Davies.

Whether or not it is based on myth, more than fact, the idea that a secret community existed, one that protected its inhabitants from the Inquisitors, as was previously claimed, deserved to be shared.

A LETTER FROM LILY

Thank you so much for reading *The Island Villa*. I really hope you enjoyed it. Formentera is a special place, and the research conducted by people like Gloria Mound into the history of a supposed secret Jewish community there is a fascinating one.

If you enjoyed this story, I'd so appreciate it if you could leave a review; it really helps to spread the word! If you're wondering what's next, I'm busy working on my next novel, set in Paris, featuring an old bookshop and a secret that goes back to the Second World War.

If you'd like to find out more please join my newsletter *www.bookouture.com/lily-graham*, or follow me on Facebook and Twitter and my website *www.lilygraham.net*.

f : LilyRoseGrahamAuthor

🐦 : @lilygrahambooks

🖥 : www.lilygraham.net

ACKNOWLEDGEMENTS

I couldn't have written this novel without my incredible editor, Lydia Vassar-Smith, who held my hand and patiently guided me through to the other side as I got lost in the rabbit warren of research and self-doubt – thank you so much for all your support and help with this, pulling the threads together and coaxing it into existence, and as ever for your belief and support for my stories!

Thanks as ever to my husband and family. When books are being written in our household, I have a tendency to retreat into the writing cave and nothing much else gets done, so thank you for keeping the home fires burning, and making sure everything still stood.

To the team at Bookouture – I couldn't do it without you.

I spent a lot of time researching this novel; to be honest the rabbit warren of the past was a tangle that I couldn't get out of for months. As soon as I went to write a single word I discovered how much more I had to learn and would just freeze.

For placing the novel in time, as well as life during the Inquisition, the fears regarding torture and rubber wheeled carriages that came in the night, as well as marriage practices etc. I read *Spain in The Later Seventeenth Century, 1665-1700*, by Henry Kamen.

Thank you to everyone who helped me to finally put words on the page – to Adina Morysofe from the Netanya Academic College in Jerusalem for supplying material from the late Gloria Mound, who'd first discovered the 'presence' of a secret Jewish community on the island, one that was later, sadly, disputed. Still, it was due to Gloria's research – including the supposed rescue of a group of *marrano* prisoners by Ibicenco pirates, pirates who later hid these Majorcan Jews, the young Nuñez brothers and cousins from the Inquisition – that inspired this story. She also provided the description of the Jewish population of reddish hair and beards and green eyes, and the women who wore kerchiefs and many strands of golden necklaces, called gonellas.

Thank you especially to historian Martin Davies for helping me to place the novel in time – and for giving me a plausible explanation for my fictional community by introducing the Majorcan angle of refugees from that time period, to offer some 'credibility' to the story. I fear I may have still failed in making any of this credible – but the fault will be entirely my own! Thank you, Martin as well for all your help in trying to unpack the myth of a Jewish presence on the islands.

Thank you as well to Ibiza historian Emily Kaufman for your insight into the history of the salt trade in Formentera and Ibiza, and for providing the missing piece of the puzzle regarding the Bourbons and their involvement. Please note however that this my own interpretation of the salt trade and the governorship of Formentera; they would not necessarily have been run this way, and I had to bend a few facts – for instance, to most people's knowledge it is unlikely that anyone from the Crown conducted any real investigation into the salt trade on the islands once it fell into the hands of the Bourbons, which is perhaps one of the reasons that it declined so much in later years.

Also thank you to my dear readers, particularly the gorgeous Kathy Schaffer, who sent messages of encouragement throughout the writing of this book. It meant the world.

All mistakes are of course my own.

GLOSSARY

Chuetas: (literally, pork-eaters), as the local descendants of *marranos* are called.

Marrano: A Spanish or Portuguese Jew who converted to Christianity during the late Middle Ages, usually under threat of death or persecution, especially one who continued to adhere to Judaism in secret. The term translates as swine, though it has lost much of its derogatory connotation.

Shabbat: The seventh day of the week – the day God rested. It's a day of rest, God and family.

Sephardi: Jews from Spain, Portugal, North Africa and the Middle East as well as their descendants. It is the Hebrew word for Spain.

Kosher: Hebrew word for dietary laws. It can also be used as a term for other things that are Jewish law.

Magen David: Six-pointed star.